JUST A MOTHER

ROY JACOBSEN

JUST A MOTHER

Translated from the Norwegian by
Don Bartlett and Don Shaw

MACLEHOSE PRESS
QUERCUS · LONDON

First published in the Norwegian language as *Bare en mor*
by Cappelen Damm AS, Oslo, in 2020

First published in Great Britain in 2022 by

MacLehose Press
an imprint of Quercus Editions Ltd
Carmelite House
50 Victoria Embankment
London EC4Y 0DZ

An Hachette UK Company

This translation has been published with the financial support of NORLA

A CIP catalogue record for this book is available from the British Library

ISBN (HB) 978 1 52941 742 5
ISBN (Ebook) 978 1 52941 743 2

2 4 6 8 10 9 7 5 3 1

Designed and typeset by Libanus Press Ltd in Adobe Caslon
Printed and bound in Great Britain by Clays Ltd, Elcograf S.p.A.

Papers used by Quercus Books are from well-managed forests and other responsible sources.

TRANSLATORS' NOTE

Just a Mother is the fourth novel in Jacobsen's Ingrid Barrøy series. The first, *The Unseen*, opens with Ingrid as a small child before the First World War. When she comes of age, she leaves the island to work for a rich family on the coast, but returns to inherit it after her parents' death.

The second, *White Shadow*, is set during the German occupation of Norway in World War Two. Ingrid falls in love with Alexander, a Russian P.O.W. washed up from a bombed prisoner ship, but is subsequently raped by Henriksen, a collaborator, and ends up in hospital with amnesia. When she returns to the island, she welcomes a number of refugees from the war, who settle on Barrøy.

In the third, *Eyes of the Rigel*, Ingrid goes in search of Alexander, with whom she now has a child, Kaja. Her long journey merely turns up the unwelcome news that she was not the only woman he sought comfort in, though she does strike up a lasting friendship with Mariann, her "rival".

I

1

On a sparsely populated island any arrival at the quay, even a wretched milk boat, triggers some kind of activity. Today, the skipper leaned over the gunwale of the old fishing cutter and handed Ingrid the newspaper, as if it were a receipt for the milk churns he was hoisting aboard, slowly and painstakingly. This is what Johannes Hartvigsen will be remembered for, his laborious, ponderous manner.

But on this occasion a letter fell out of the newspaper, from Trondheim, bearing postage stamps Ingrid had never seen before, and the sender's name and address on the back. Ingrid flushed, let the newspaper drop onto the quay and slowly set off south across the island.

She walked past the Swedes' boathouse and the iron peg hammered into solid rock, heading towards the Lundeskjære skerries, agitated and barefoot, over boulders and warm, sea-smoothed rocks, through the parched heather and yellowing grass, holding a letter that would have to be read in solitude, there was no doubt about that, a letter from the unpredictable Mariann Vollheim, whom Ingrid had not heard from for years, and whom she had done her best to forget – to no avail, she realised with tremulous clarity.

She walked on past Love Spinney and over the rocks to Bosom Acre, for some reason still with the image of the milk-run skipper on her retinas, the sun-tanned, calloused hand of Johannes passing her the newspaper, together with a letter today, a mystery in itself, as Barrøy didn't receive post at any time of the year apart from during the Lofoten season, and even then, only very few brief messages from the men of the island, to confirm they were still alive.

In her mind's eye, behind the skipper she saw the oily deck in the sparkling sunlight, the port gunwale with its knife-holders and whetstones and coils of rope, beyond them the tranquil sea and the skerries and the islets where the motionless gulls made less and less noise as every new day moved the land further into autumn.

But most of all she saw the skipper's four- or five-year-old son, Mattis, who once again was sitting on the hold hatch, the poor slavering wretch, in far too tight, ragged clothes, vomit all down his chest, three fingers in his mouth, a clumsy, shoe-less boy to whom Ingrid was in the habit of addressing a few kindly words:

Hvur's it goen, Mattis? Has tha bin sick?

In the hope of injecting some life into this apathetic creature who had been a regular fixture on the boat ever since his mother went missing one day in the early summer, for reasons no-one believed. The end of the war was too recent for there not to be some connection between the two. At any rate, no-one had taken the missing woman's whining about the hardship and tedium in Johannes Hartvigsen's house seriously, there had never been less hardship, and tedium was no more than a modern term for sloth. There was definitely no plausible reason for turning one's back on husband and child and allowing oneself to be swallowed up in a city's seething mass of humanity, and then not even to send some sign of life, there was no other possible explanation, of course it had something to do with the war.

Mattis' mother was Olavia Hartvigsen, her maiden name was Storm, from a very "good" family on the landed estate in the north of the main island, an attractive girl who had manoeuvred her way confidently and graciously through her childhood and adolescent years before, in the final phase of the war, breaking with all the privileges accorded by Providence and going off to live with Johannes Hartvigsen, who was twice her age and whom not a single woman up to that time had dignified with a glance. The question was whether she had done this of her own free will. Hardly. Out of love? Not a chance. With suspicious intentions? Without a doubt.

At least that meant the flight from Johannes was not forced upon her?

With the consequence, however, that from then on the

archipelago's daily lifeline was run not only by an abandoned husband but also by his even more abandoned son, who, day in, day out, sat on the swaying deck of the cutter with three fingers in his mouth, waiting for the boat to put in at some quay or other, such as Barrøy, so that his insides could settle for a moment and one of the islanders might take pity on him with a kind word, which of course he never reciprocated, but acknowledged nonetheless, that was Ingrid's impression, with a slight flinch, which she could see now as she trudged south carrying the puzzling letter that had nothing to do with the poor lad.

Occasionally two separate things happen concurrently and merge into one and the same wound, in one's memory, except that you don't realise this until it is too late. So why didn't Ingrid pull herself together and tear open the envelope and read what Mariann had on her mind and get it over and done with?

Ingrid wasn't ready, she carried on walking to Barrøy's southernmost point, to the Bench, as they called it, the mighty Russian larch a storm had cast ashore at one time in her childhood, where she used to go to process her innermost thoughts, where she sat when the island threatened to become too small for her, when life threatened to come to a halt. And today, holding the letter from Mariann Vollheim, she was petrified.

2

Mattis was on the face of it an ordinary lad, who had played on the beach and his father's smallholding, in the fields and forest and snowdrifts, and had thrown his legs and arms about and laughed and cried like all other children, in no way different from them except that by and large only his parents were able to recognise him from a distance. Until he suddenly changed, from one day to the next, at a speed that only a child is capable of, towards the end of May.

The first signs of this became apparent as Johannes Hartvigsen was sitting at the boy's bedside, when he opened his eyes and saw his father's furrowed and bearded face, the morose expression of a man who neither knew, nor cared, what he looked like, to the sound of the rain hammering down on the rusty tin roof. Mattis used to call it thunder and did so now.

His father corrected him, once again, and repeated that the boy had never heard thunder, that it was rare in this part of the country.

That's rain you can hear, it's pissen down.

Mattis had to get up and put on his clothes now and board

the boat with him, there would be no playing with Ole and Slutter today, that Mamma of yours has gone.

My Mamma?

Yes, your Mamma.

Where is she, Mamma?

Johannes was in no position to answer that question, and neither did he have the energy to speculate too deeply on the reasons for his wife, Olavia, leaving them. True, she had complained about Johannes being full of "gloomy thoughts", a man with a "gloomy disposition", which rubbed off on those around him, in other words, on her, a trait she had known nothing of before they had got married, she maintained. Johannes didn't seem to be happy in his own home, but preferred to be as free as a bird on the open sea, she also maintained.

Johannes himself regarded this as absolute nonsense. The milk-run was no more than a mind-numbing source of income he had inherited from his father. If truth be told, Johannes thought of nothing else but Olavia and the lad, as he bustled around in that idiotic wheelhouse of his, musing on how good it would be at the end of another pointless day to dock and walk the hundred and thirty metres up to the farm, take off his gumboots and work clothes and scrub the oil from his fingers and sit down at the dining table with Olavia and Mattis, the joys of his life, there was nothing more precious to Johannes than them.

These words of course were far too grand for him, Johannes

enjoyed his wife in the privacy of silence, relishing the luxurious fragrances of soap and unattainable middle-class lifestyle, her movements, her clothes, her hair and hands, particularly her hands, refined, slender and white, even after several years as a farmer's wife, a role she knew nothing at all about, but which she had nonetheless performed with more or less the same immense thrift and scepticism as her predecessors, Johannes' parents.

But there were no more children. And after a while Johannes began to wonder at this because relations between them were as they should between husband and wife, as far as he could judge. In addition, as the years went by, whispers had begun to circulate through the village about something being amiss in his household, rumours that eventually came to Johannes' ears, no doubt he was the last to hear. Above all, there was the ominous question of how someone like him had managed to get his hands on the unattainable Olavia Storm, one of the few women on the main island who really could choose her mate, from the top shelf, one would imagine, and who furthermore had selected him against her parents' wishes, so it was said. Was Johannes really her chosen one, the man she loved? Believe that if you will.

Mattis had coppery brown hair, green eyes and handsome, almost feminine, features. He learned to talk fluently at an early age, was lithe and sinewy and never ill. He teethed normally, soon stopped wearing nappies and liked to explain and justify things from the time he could speak, from a young age he brushed off scoldings, without being defiant or annoying, he elegantly skated around admonitions and rules as though they didn't exist, he was an independent, self-willed boy.

Even at the age of three he would often tell Olavia in detail what he had experienced during the day and was able to talk about what their neighbours had been doing and describe the traffic on the roads and the boats in the harbour. Olavia called him a chatterbox while Johannes smiled at many a curious observation, and the lad's eye for unusual detail, Johannes felt genuine pride at this.

But when the boy had turned four and his flights of fancy had become even more far-fetched, his father began to feel something approaching disquiet when they were together, and on occasion this became so acute that he wondered whether he had a foreign body in his house and not a copy of himself.

Now there are many explanations for an apple falling a long way from the tree, some of which are even reassuring: for one thing, the fact that Olavia's family had for generations had the time and money to develop a state of refinement far superior to the rest of the population.

As indeed there are also less reassuring explanations, such as the German occupying forces happening to have their quarters on the Storm family estate, or the circumstance that Olavia and her sisters had served in the officers' mess whenever they weren't whiling away their hours, each in their own wallpapered bedroom, waiting to be discovered, the way young ladies of their standing had sat for centuries, when there was no war.

But there had been a war. And then it was over, and people began to talk about Mattis perhaps not being Johannes' biological son. Marrying Johannes was merely a far-sighted woman's ploy, a woman who like so many others – even those with stronger characters than Olavia's – had something to rue, something to rectify or hide, once peace had returned.

The rumours became no less compelling after two other women who had served in the German camp had returned to the Trading Post to resume their former activities as fishwives, in the least flattering sense of the word, two withered old biddies who sat on the milk ramp outside Markus' shop and struck up conversations with all the passers-by, seasoning their language with impressive expletives, and who sent begging letters to the poor relief fund and sang out of tune in the church choir while waiting for the herring boats to come in and the canning factory to re-open, with nothing better to do than sit on that old ramp insinuating that truth is hardly the first word to come to mind when one claps one's eyes on the Merchant Storm's discredited daughter and her son Mattis.

Johannes noticed that the gossip was giving more substance to his alleged gloominess and that the situation was beginning to resemble what he had experienced during the first years after his mother's death, when he'd had to go out with his father as a twelve-year-old, first fishing in an open færing, then on the milk-run, a fate that would now befall his son, with the striking difference that Mattis was only five.

On that first morning as an abandoned husband, walking down to the harbour with his son at his side, to do his duty on this day too, Johannes realised that, strangely, all of this was actually as he had been expecting. Olavia had been too good to be true, for him, she had been a dream, which was now shattered.

This was no easy thought to start the day with, but it was at least tolerable, Johannes felt, just as one can experience a lift by finally being given a sensible diagnosis for some mysterious ailment one has been struggling with for some time, even if it is cancer. And perhaps this paradoxical insight was the reason he didn't immediately move heaven and earth to make enquiries about Olavia's whereabouts, or even search for her or try to find whether she had left anything behind in writing. He knew, after only the first few minutes in the kitchen, when he saw that both her suitcase and clothes were gone, irrevocably, and the front door was ajar, that he wasn't going to find any such message here.

Olavia not having left anything in writing obviously said something about her, and Johannes not immediately searching for such a note presumably said something about him too, and these two facts probably said all there was to say about the Hartvigsen marriage, all this was confusingly clear to him.

*

It wasn't until four days later that Johannes started to search the house's cubbyholes, in order to have something to do on a lazy Sunday, wondering who Olavia really was, the items she had taken might reveal something about her he didn't know, set him on the path towards an explanation.

First of all, her best shoes were missing – a patent-leather pair she hadn't even worn at their wedding, with silver buckles over the arches – which on a couple of occasions Johannes had watched her polish with an earnest expression on her face. And also a small amount of silverware she had brought with her from the Storm estate. Johannes didn't have any silverware. And, like her shoes, Olavia's was never used.

Now it struck him how little she had actually brought with her from her childhood home, the second youngest daughter, the first and most loved of the four girls to be married off. In addition to the shoes and the silverware, only two dresses had gone, not her intricately made toys, a yellow wooden horse, a red boat, an abacus, which for some reason Mattis had never been allowed to play with, he's too small, Olavia would say with the same serious expression she wore when polishing her shoes and silverware.

Also missing was the suitcase that had been beside her shoe box on the top shelf of the bedroom closet and which Johannes now realised he had never seen her open. Johannes had moved it a few times, to reach his milk chits, which he kept in a small wooden box on the same shelf, thinking it was strangely heavy, but without examining it any further.

Was there anything else he hadn't examined further or hadn't been surprised by when perhaps he should have been?

He noticed that everything she had acquired in the course of their married life was still there. Most of her clothes hung or lay in a pile where they belonged, a wall clock and a set of kitchen scales she had shrilly insisted on having last Christmas, a framed photograph of the boy, some checked aprons Johannes had thought were too expensive but which she had bought with her own savings, how much she had Johannes had no idea, not that he was bothered. But it was probably this money that she had used to finance her flight? At any rate there was nothing missing from the cake tin they regarded as their common kitty, the same thirty-three kroner Johannes had counted the previous weekend was still there.

Also, Olavia's way of folding towels and bed linen remained, *her* system with the cutlery and tablecloths and the boy's clothes, her system in the pantry and sitting room, her standards of cleanliness. Olavia was pernickety and particular and tetchy, and Johannes had liked that. The buckets stood where they always had, from the day she first entered the house and declared they should no longer stand where they had always stood before. The same went for the washtubs, brooms and cloths hanging over various lines in the porch, her washing lines, her system.

Johannes went back down to the sitting room and saw that she had also left the two rag rugs she had brought with her, lying crosswise on the floor. Johannes had remarked on this, didn't it look odd, two rugs crossing, didn't that look strange?

Olavia had looked at him askance, shoved the table and chairs aside and placed the rugs next to each other so that both husband and wife could see they were too long for the room, that Johannes Hartvigsen's house was too small for the two rugs from the Storm dynasty to be extended to their full length.

He tried not to let it bother him that the cross was still there, after all who would run off from the family home carrying two rugs?

In the years Johannes had lived alone, he had retained his mother's habit of filling a rectangular wooden box with soil every spring and planting wild flowers in it to brighten up the porch balustrade. Olavia had immediately emptied it and consigned it to the utility shed, where Johannes stored his tools and coke and his father's old fishing tackle. He now went to the shed and retrieved the box and put it back on the balustrade, intending to fill it with soil and flowers again. Although just a brief glance down into the gaping void made him realise that nothing would ever come of this.

At around mid-afternoon on this Sunday, he asked Mattis, who was sitting cross-legged on the rugs in the sitting room, if he wouldn't like to go over and play with Slutter and Ole, he hadn't seen his friends for close on a week, now that he had become a seafarer.

The lad said no.

Johannes couldn't come up with anything sensible to say in reply, such as:

Why not?

Anyway, it was probably time to announce the news to the Storm family. Gudrun, from the neighbouring farm, had already been round twice asking after Olavia, with the usual scowling suspicion in her eternally grey eyes, even though she wasn't friends with either of them. Gudrun was more like one of the fishwives on the milk ramp, who espied opportunities in both war and peace.

Johannes considered whether to write a letter and send it north with the bus the following day, but decided that he should travel in person, it was just over ten kilometres, perhaps he could borrow a horse from the Trading Post, one of the carthorses standing idle today.

But he postponed the trip for a while, paced up and down in the house a couple more times, went into the yard, gazed across the farm he should have taken much better care of – which he always thought whenever he surveyed it – but there was no time, all the while contemplating whether to take the boy along or not, until the decision made itself, he had no choice.

Father and son walked down to the Trading Post, they were allowed to take the oldest horse and a cart, and headed north, Johannes deaf to the lad's continuing silence, preoccupied with speculation as to how the meeting would turn out, with in-laws he hadn't seen for many years, except the girls, on the rare occasions they visited Olavia in Hartvika, though they had generally left by the time Johannes returned from the sea, he barely knew them.

Before they arrived at the estate, he had decided that he didn't want his previous inaction to get in the way of things, so he said straight out to Elisabeth, the youngest daughter, who opened the door, that he had come to take Olavia home.

Elisabeth didn't understand a word. But she guided the guests into a parlour with room for rugs of any length, where Johannes' parents-in-law, both his own age, it is also worth mentioning, sat looking at each other across a huge, polished dining table over a cup of coffee, presumably after consuming a hearty meal. They barely looked up and merely cast furtive glances at Mattis, who stood in his bare feet beside his father, his eyes darting up and down the walls until they settled on the chandelier hanging from the ceiling.

Elisabeth knelt down, hardly able to recognise him, but said that he looked even more like his mother than she re-membered from the previous winter, and added some other comments Johannes didn't catch, absorbed as he was, assessing his father-in-law's reaction to what he had just told them, which was that Alfred Storm's daughter, Olavia, had disappeared, Johannes had thought she might be here, perhaps because she was bored in Hartvika or wanted to see her family again.

23

His father-in-law brushed aside any speculation, stood up and demanded to know exactly when Olavia had left.

Johannes noticed that the old man didn't use the term he had used: disappeared.

Isn't she here? he repeated.

Of course not.

Johannes told him the precise date of her disappearance.

Tuesday, then, Alfred Storm said, counting backwards in time, after which he left the room and returned with a calendar, and declared, standing beside the table like a schoolmaster, that it was as he had thought, yes, Tuesday morning at the crack of dawn a stockfish boat had left from the Trading Post bound for Bergen. In fact, half of the cargo was his, Storm even knew the fish grader, a certain Jakobsen from Tromsø, as if that had anything to do with anything, did Johannes know whether Olavia had contacted the crew on board or had known about the boat's schedules and routes?

How should I? Johannes answered, grappling with a sneaking feeling that the news of Olavia's disappearance didn't appear to be earth-shattering here either, but was received more than anything else with a mixture of resigned expectation and shameful relief, as well as a fair amount of waffle, presumably designed to keep the abandoned husband in the dark.

He asked whether either of the other two had known about her escape plans. They hadn't, his mother-in-law, Amalie, assured him, with some prolix and, to Johannes' ears, vague turns of phrase, still sitting at the table with one slightly trembling hand in front of her mouth. Amalie was from Ålesund and made Johannes feel uneasy by dint of her dialect and that trembling hand of hers, so he asked the question once more, this time directed at Olavia's youngest sister, did Elisabeth know anything?

No.

But at least she did appear concerned, genuinely upset, as far as Johannes could judge, even if the look she sent her parents appeared to be more entreating than accusatory, as though she realised they were hiding something, which they might disclose to her, if only this son-in-law would get out of the house. She collected herself and again laid a hand on Mattis' head and suffused her smile with so much sophisticated pity that the lad was able to smile back.

Johannes felt that he had done what he had to do, at least neither of them seemed to blame him for their daughter's disappearance, although he was ashamed to discover that this had been one of his motives for the visit, to ask the family for their forgiveness, which he now felt he had received, perhaps because he had shown up in person, Johannes was not a good judge of character, all that remained for him to do was say goodbye and leave.

Elisabeth accompanied the visitors outside and stood behind the gate in the white picket fence and said, come back soon, ruffled Mattis' fringe one last time, as though they had been welcome.

*

Father and son went back home in the same charged silence as when they had arrived, Johannes in such a fog of bewilderment that it didn't occur to him to feel annoyed that he hadn't even been offered a cup of coffee.

They returned the horse and cart, walked home in the luminous summer evening and stood gazing in wonderment at the small farmhouse, to study it, as it were, to take in the significance of their home, this is our house.

Johannes Hartvigsen had now spent one whole Sunday piecing together the changes in this home of theirs, all so small that to anyone's eye but his own they were probably invisible. It was only Johannes who could see that the house was no longer his and would never again be so. Or rather that was precisely what it was, it was his house, his alone, and would always remain so.

It's Monday tomorrow, he said to Mattis, who hadn't uttered a sound since his mother had disappeared.

So we'll bi on t'boat worken.

3

Ingrid was sitting on the Bench holding Mariann Vollheim's letter. There was only one reason it hadn't already been torn to pieces or thrown unread into the stove, namely the frightening hope that it might contain some news about a man both she and Mariann had fallen in love with during the last year of the war, a young, Russian P.O.W. by the name of Alexander Nizhnikov, a survivor of the *Rigel* disaster, who had to leave them both to save his life and who, she hoped, had managed to make his way home to the Soviet Union.

Had Mariann been able to trace him?

Mariann had inherited a large estate, she had money, a high level of education and was a teacher at the Cathedral School in Trondheim, a self-confident woman capable of dealing with most challenges, there was only one thing to do, open the letter and read it.

Ingrid opened the letter and read "Dear Ingrid", it was as if they were friends: "I hope you won't mind the personal tone. You see, I've never been closer to anyone than I was to you that strange summer four years ago, both on our Vollheim estate and at your home on Barrøy the following autumn. I can't forget you and I don't know why."

That was quite an opening, Ingrid thought, embarrassed.

Mariann explained that the intimacy of her tone was a result of Ingrid having helped her overcome the loss of her two children, who had fallen through the ice on Lake Tunnsjø. Ingrid remembered their names, names which Mariann had not even been able to utter when they first met, but which now in this letter were mentioned with an unsettling ease, as though the deaths of children were something one could ever completely recover from, thought Ingrid, who herself refused to accept that time heals all wounds, time was so cruel, but this was clearly what Mariann had been able to do.

Then a possible explanation became apparent: not only did she have an "interesting job at the Cathedral School", she had also met a new man, an engineer by the name of Olav.

Olav was described in detail, tall and slim, with blue eyes and fair hair. He was considerate and clever, had been a soldier on the right side in the war, was the same age as Mariann, and had recently inherited a sizeable house in the hills around Trondheim, where the couple now lived in very comfortable circumstances, that was what she wrote, in those very words.

Mariann described her route to school – she went on foot via a bridge across the River Nid – and the trees around the famous cathedral, which Ingrid hadn't noticed when she was in Trondheim. Then there was something about eating habits and an orchard and a soft-fruit garden, and making juice and pickling, all carried out in a town, Mariann called these activities her "hobbies". It was obvious that she was trying to create a sense of peace and success, to contrast as starkly as possible with everything connected with the war.

Ingrid's shoulders sagged, but she picked up again when she read that Mariann often visited her father on the family estate by Lake Tunnsjø, so as not to drown in grief and guilt, but to see again the fields and meadows and the lake where she grew up, her own childhood, not her children's.

Eventually there was also a request: Mariann was writing primarily (Ingrid wondered what *primarily* meant) to notify her (notify?) that at the age of thirty-nine she had given birth to a healthy daughter and would like to invite Ingrid to the christening, which was due to take place in nothing less than the famous cathedral she had mentioned, on the third Sunday in September.

Mariann would pay for her return journey – she had enquired about the cost – and she implored her (?) from the depths of her heart (oh, my goodness) to attend, as they had decided to christen the newborn Ingrid, after Ingrid Marie Barrøy (where had she got my middle name from?).

In short, not a single word about the man who had once brought them together, the Russian, Alexander, he was non-existent, as forgotten as Mariann's children.

Ingrid felt a need to sit looking around for a while. She re-read the letter and realised that the mere thought of Alexander was still enough to bring her out in a cold sweat, indeed, to take her legs away from under her.

She got up and headed north again, but her pace was too frenetic, she could feel that, so she took a hold of herself, managed to make her strides more measured, and arrived at the new quay having reached a decision she couldn't have taken earlier that morning, but which now had been made for her.

Johannes and her cousin, Lars, were sitting on the quay chatting. Lars looked up, nodded briefly and turned back to Johannes, who sighed and said, well, he had better be moving on, the milk'll bi spoilen.

"Where's the laddie?" Ingrid asked.

"With the other kids," Lars said without turning round, he had chased him ashore.

Johannes mumbled something to the same effect, got to his feet and looked around.

"He should just stay here," Ingrid said, turning and starting to walk up to the houses as her eyes sought out the children, all eight of whom were on the beach by the boat shed, she heard their laughter and incoherent howls from Oskar. Kaja, soon to be five, was explaining something to Mattis, and at least he was nodding. The twin girls were splashing each other with water. Hans and Fredrik were up to something serious down a hole in the sand while Martin, as usual, was running from one to the other, not knowing what to do with himself. My God, Ingrid thought, what *has* come over me?

"What do you mean?" she heard the milk-boat skipper say behind her.

He could pick up the boy on his return trip, she called back, she was off to cook some food now.

Johannes mumbled something she didn't catch. When she turned, up by the house, she watched him clamber aboard the cutter and start the engine. Lars was standing on the quay and passed him the single hawser that was sufficient to moor the boat in fair weather. That was the last they saw of Johannes Hartvigsen.

4

Ingrid went inside and asked Barbro to boil some water, lots of it. Walked down to the beach again and fetched Kaja and Mattis, carefully plucked the stinking rags from the new arrival, revealing a lean and bony body. The women and girls bathed him in a tub in the kitchen of the old house – it was like a baptism – led by Barbro, the most practical of them, using cloths and soap, Ingrid's 56-year-old aunt and Barrøy's most steadfast presence, the only islander who had never asked herself whether there were any other islands, any other worlds.

Next in line was Ingrid herself, her hands anxiously planted on her hips. Then Kaja, with envious eyes, she loved having baths. And finally Suzanne, also one of Ingrid's daughters, or her adopted daughter, all according to how one wishes to classify people after fate has played its part. Now Suzanne looked at Mattis and said dear God, what a bag of bones, grabbed his arms and asked if she had looked like this, too, when she arrived on the island.

"Tha was as feit as a pig," Ingrid said.

Suzanne gave a wry laugh and asked what was going to

happen now, did Ingrid intend to send the lad away again with that weird father of his?

We'll have to see, Ingrid said, he's not ours.

Suzanne turned serious and said she couldn't do that.

What, Ingrid said, and Suzanne looked at Barbro, who was now standing in the middle of the floor, arms crossed, as if to signify agreement.

We'll have to see, Ingrid repeated, then asked Suzanne to go to Karvika to fetch some cast-off clothing.

Mattis said nothing, but understood when Ingrid told him to stand up, bend forward, sit down and splash with his hands. She examined his arms, scalp, back, legs and feet, but found no sores or injuries, and he shook his newly washed mop of hair every time she asked if he had any pains.

After the bath he allowed himself to be bossed around in clean clothes, at Kaja's whim and fancy, and when dinner arrived on the table, he ate more than the others, and kept down his food as his eyes wandered back and forth between Kaja and Lars, who enjoyed eating here in their childhood home, rather than in the new house he and Felix had built in Karvika. Now Lars had a question for the silent newcomer:

How old are you?

Five, Mattis said.

Mattis' first word on Barrøy, and it would not be forgotten. He ate slowly, meatballs in gravy with potatoes. Kaja said she was almost five. Lars shifted his eyes from the lad to Ingrid and

33

commented between two mouthfuls that she had received a letter today, who was it from?

Mariann Vollheim, Ingrid said. Lars thought about this and then asked if it was t' lady who'd bin here a couple o' years back. Ingrid nodded.

They carried on eating.

Lars wanted to know what she, t' lady, wanted.

Ingrid said she had invited her to a christening in Trondheim. Lars burst into laughter. The door opened and his wife, Selma, walked in and asked what he was doing here, didn't he like her cooking, this wasn't the first time.

Lars grinned and said that in the old house it was a meat day, he was fed up with fish.

It was you who said we should have fish, she said sourly, and plumped down on the log bin, covering her face with her hands, she held them up like two fans, the sign that the marital tiff was over, or deferred, then she caught sight of Mattis and asked whether the Jerry kid was going to *stay* here.

Ingrid frowned and checked to see if the children had heard anything. Lars continued eating in a telling silence, and Suzanne slowly lowered her knife and fork, bit her lower lip and contemplated saying something that had to be considered so carefully that it was unlikely ever to pass her lips.

Selma did not repeat the question, but got to her feet and just stood there, obviously on the lookout for some reason to leave again, placed a hand on the brass rail on the stove, peered at her fingertips and left, after announcing that the twins had been despatched to the cow barn and the boys chased down to Bosom Acre to move the calves.

Suzanne was still weighing up her plan to say something when Lars got up and for once expressed his appreciation of the food. Ingrid told Kaja to show Mattis her toys and followed Lars out of the door, on down the grassy slope, shouting at his broad shoulders that he'd better shut Selma's gob, that word must never be repeated here.

Lars turned and said:

Which word? Jerry?

Ingrid told him to shut his mouth.

Lars casually walked on, tossed his head a few times, meaning that, yes, Ingrid may well be the lawful owner of the island, unfortunately, but without him and Felix no-one could live here, Ingrid was only the queen on paper.

Ingrid sprang at him and asked if he also called Fredrik a Jerry, Suzanne's son.

Lars stopped, came back and stared her in the face, not entirely at ease, Ingrid knew, he was half a head shorter than her.

Say that again, will you?

Ingrid said coldly that she had just told him that word was *not* to be repeated.

What do you mean?

Ingrid had hoped she had given him something to think about as he had taken Fredrik under his wing from the day he arrived on the island and turned him into a Barrøyer like the rest of them. Now Fredrik always went out fishing with them between the Lofoten seasons, along with Lars' sons, Hans and Martin. Lars didn't have two sons, he had three.

He said:

What about that Kaja of yours?

What about that Kaja of mine?

Trying to sound nonchalant, he mumbled that Kaja must be just about the only kid here without a father.

Ingrid smiled sourly and said she had told him about Kaja's father, the Russian prisoner of war, had he forgotten?

No.

I thought not.

What do you mean?

Ingrid told him to sit down.

What, here?

Yes, here, on the ground.

They sat down, and Ingrid said that she herself had been in some doubt about Kaja's origins until after her daughter's birth, when she recognised her father's eyes, Alexander's.

"Yes, I've heard," Lars said sheepishly, focusing his gaze on the whaler *Salthammer* at its moorings, the island's mainstay and debt-laden pride.

What have you heard?

You know.

No, I don't.

He squirmed. Ingrid asked *whom* he had heard it from, whatever it was he knew or didn't know.

From Suzanne.

But Suzanne knew nothing, so Ingrid asked if he had heard about the time Henriksen came to the island with a German officer and raped her, almost killing her, with the result that she lost her memory and had to spend several weeks in hospital. She had regained her memory, unfortunately, she thought in moments of weakness, fortunately, she thought in moments of strength, like now.

Henriksen? Lars asked in surprise.

Ya, Henriksen.

Suzanne said nothing about Henriksen.

Ya, Ingrid said, because she knows nothing.

She watched as an alarming flush spread across his face and into his black stubble. Lars flung out an arm in frustration and disbelief.

So, it was that Henriksen?

And repeated the name. And said:

He's getting to be a bigwig again now.

Ingrid nodded. She had heard that, after a period of ignominious silence, the former lensmann had begun to circulate among people again, presumably hoping that so much oblivion had descended over the village that even an old Nazi could enjoy peacetime. In the early spring he had even been employed as a verger by the new pastor, a torchbearer of forgiveness and amnesia, not an important job, but at least a means of support. Henriksen hadn't even lost his right to vote, no doubt because nobody dared to testify against him.

Lars released a burst of bitter, angry laughter, got up and set off down the slope. Ingrid shouted after him:

Don't you dare do anything!

Lars replied, without turning, that she shouldn't worry, the nights are still too light.

What? Ingrid said.

The nights are still too light, he repeated and walked on.

They'd had a rainy, windy summer, but this last week the weather had been fine, hay-drying, potato-growing, clothes on the rack, calm sea, tomorrow it would rain, Ingrid could feel it in her bones.

Suzanne was standing on the doorstep when she returned, more curious than aggrieved. Ingrid strode past her into the kitchen and said the children were to go to the cow barn and tell the twins to teach them how to milk.

I already know, Kaja said.

Then you can teach Mattis. We're going to wash some dirty linen here.

Suzanne had followed her and asked what this was all about, she and Barbro had done the washing that morning and had even scrubbed the staircase.

Ingrid told Suzanne to sit down, in a tone which made it

difficult for her to stay on her feet. She sank onto a chair, but the expression of bafflement didn't leave her face until Ingrid reproached her for telling Lars about Henriksen's abuse of her during the war. Suzanne directed a meek glance at Barbro, who was bent over the washing-up, trying to make herself invisible.

Ingrid filled the coffee pot with water and, with her back to Suzanne, said she didn't need to worry about that disgusting word being repeated here.

What do I care about that? Suzanne said.

Ingrid turned and looked at her and said calmly that Suzanne had lied about Fredrik's age when they came, and as a result Ingrid had made a fool of herself by enrolling a six-year-old at the school.

Facing the window, Suzanne asked in a subdued voice if Ingrid had known this all along.

Ingrid said the teacher in Havstein had wanted to see the birth certificate, but she hadn't been able to show him it, so he had investigated the matter himself, and Fredrik's name was nowhere to be found in any records.

Suzanne continued to stare out of the window. Barbro dried her hands and muttered that she had better go and see to the lad.

As soon as she had left, Ingrid made it clear that all talk about where the various children came from was over, not even the Lord Himself knows.

Suzanne sobbed that she couldn't stand it here any longer, Barrøy was unbearable.

You've said that before, Ingrid said drily.

But the weather was good.

Come with me.

They took their cups of coffee outside and sat down on the well cover, where they had a view across the island and were able to see that the boys had moved the calves, but had then gone into hiding to do something no-one was allowed to witness. Kaja and Mattis were playing around the peat sheds, with Oskar in tow, he yelled when Kaja teased him. Ingrid shouted that her daughter should leave the lad alone. Mattis turned and stared wide-eyed up at them. Barbro wheeled today's milk churn out of the cow barn and down towards the well near the Lofoten boat shed where they kept the milk cool.

Suzanne sipped her coffee and asked Ingrid if she could keep a secret, whether the island's highest authority could be trusted with something that needed to be said soon, then it could hopefully be consigned to oblivion.

Ingrid nodded, and Suzanne told her that Fredrik wasn't a German child, but the son of a Norwegian idiot she had kicked out of the house, after which she met a soldier at a dancehall in Oslo, a man the girls from the north swarmed around: domestic helps, child-minders, factory workers. A German soldier, yes please.

But he was kind, to both Suzanne and Fredrik.

There was more talk about this "uncle", as Fredrik had called the man and thereafter some lengthy explanations as to why Suzanne had found it necessary to kick him out too, in the last phase of the war.

Ingrid had heard all this before and given up trying to make any sense of it.

She asked what was so horrible about Barrøy.

Suzanne didn't answer, just repeated pensively that Ingrid couldn't send the lad away again.

Ingrid asked if she was thinking about her own childhood, about the time she came here after her mother had abandoned her and her brother, Felix.

No.

Are you sure?

Suzanne shrugged.

Once more Ingrid yelled at Kaja to stop bullying Oskar. And again Mattis was the only one to stare up at them. Kaja took his hand and guided him to the gate in the first stone wall. Oskar ran after them. They speeded up. Oskar was left behind. Ingrid shot a glance across the sea looking for the milk boat and was struck by a feeling that whatever she had done this day she was going to regret it. But her reply to Mariann Vollheim had at least been formulated, however long it might take to put the words to paper, Ingrid was not going to any christening in Trondheim.

She gave her cup to Suzanne and walked down to the new

quay, where Lars and Felix were putting the finishing touches to some herring barrels, and said it didn't look as if Johannes was coming back. Lars didn't even let go of the hammer:

So the lad'll just have to stay here.

They couldn't exactly chuck him into the sea.

5

Ingrid did a few rounds of the beach, noticed that the water in the well where they stored the milk was too warm and carried up two pails of seawater, sending frequent glances across the sea, without seeing any sign of Johannes Hartvigsen's easily recognisable fishing cutter, without hearing the familiar sound of his boat, the archipelago's timepiece, everything was quiet.

She walked up to Bosom Acre and spent more time than usual rounding up the children, a demanding but pleasurable game, chased and grabbed each one of them and pushed them over, even Fredrik. The sole exception now was fourteen-year-old Hans, who had become extremely quick on his feet, but still didn't know whether to ally himself with Ingrid or continue to be chased, a dilemma Ingrid knew how to exploit, to the full.

Come on! Catch us if you can!

Ingrid ran like a young girl and knew exactly where to grab and tickle each one of them in order to release the laughter from the deepest recesses of their bodies and that shriek she loved to hear, the tickle-border between what they enjoyed and what was more than they could stand. None of the other adults had the energy to round up seven – now eight – boisterous children on such a beautiful summer evening that it had made all of them giddy. Not even modest Hanna, who drew her strength from the Lord. Hanna was too stiff and serious, she had forsaken fun and games long ago to immerse herself in hard work and the Scriptures. Moreover, Ingrid was bolstered by memories of the emptiness that reigned when there were no children on the island, a childless island is no island at all.

When the game came to an end with gasps and groans, she ordered Hans and Fredrik to carry Martin between them to Karvika, while the twin girls had to carry their little brother Oskar, who had no wish to be either carried or scolded. And they did as they were told, knowing full well that Ingrid had her limits, although they liked to stretch them a little, also this evening, even Ingrid was forgiving on this light summer night.

Ingrid put Mattis in Kaja's room, where there were two wooden pull-out beds along opposite walls, between them a stool, which she sat down on before reading aloud from *Three Little Pigs*, Kaja's favourite book, until the little girl fell asleep before the heroic pigs had managed to get into difficulties at sea.

Mattis lay staring at the ceiling. Ingrid asked him what he was thinking about.

He blinked but didn't answer.

He should sleep now, Ingrid said, and Mattis uttered his first connected words, he asked Ingrid to read the book again, please.

She noticed that his language was faultless, read the book once more and said that now he should sleep. He nodded.

Ingrid went down to the kitchen, where Barbro was sitting in the motionless rocking chair, her mouth agape, while Suzanne was darning the heel of a sock. They looked at each other. Neither of them said a word. Ingrid went back upstairs and into the North Chamber, lay down and slept dreamlessly until she was awoken by screams. Mattis was having nightmares. Ingrid crept in and sat on the stool between the beds, but didn't wake him, and sat there listening to a boy she hardly knew crying for his mother, a saw grinding through stone, which both he and she had to endure, to discover how strong they were.

Kaja woke up. Ingrid placed a hand on the boy's sweaty body, roused him and lifted him out of the blankets, held him in her arms, examining him once again, still without finding any sores, scrutinised his scalp beneath his tangled curls, which she saw would have to be cut, but still didn't find what she had failed to spot with Nelvy, a little girl from Finnmark who had died here during the war, under Ingrid's care, by now the boy had calmed down.

She took both children with her into the North Chamber and lay between them in the double bed. They slept peacefully until Ingrid was wakened by the sun once more, and the sound of Barbro, who was clattering about at the stove down in the kitchen.

She let the children sleep, got out of bed, went down and

saw that there wasn't going to be any change in the weather after all, today it was as windless as it had been the day before, and the day before that, the sea was as calm, the grass as erect.

Suzanne came into the kitchen.

They laid the table and ate and drank coffee in silence.

The children were still asleep when they went out, Barbro to the cow barn and Suzanne to the wash house to attend to the clothes. On a morning like this it would have been natural for Ingrid to wander through the gardens to see whether they could get going with the second round of mowing.

Instead, she walked down to Karvika and knocked on the door. She always knocked on this door. Selma came out as angry as always that her guest hadn't walked straight in, and Ingrid followed her into the kitchen, where two families were seated around a table that was twice the size of the one she had up in the old house. The twin girls in identical skirts, with red woollen threads in their plaits, on one side of the table, and Oskar between them. On the other side sat Hans and Martin and Suzanne's son, Fredrik, who didn't belong here, but had stayed in the same room as Hans and Martin ever since the house had been built. Everyone had a chair.

Lars and Felix, wearing only cotton underwear, at either end of the table. Hanna and Selma standing by the worktop, a cup of coffee in hand, a palm supporting an elbow.

Here Ingrid should have run through the day's chores and duties for the inhabitants of this paradise on earth, such as grumbling about the confounded smoke oven that urgently needed to be dug up. That was Lars and Felix's job, one which they kept putting off because they hated digging. Or by taking advantage of the prolonged fine weather to sail over to the village to do some necessary shopping, what did they need in the house?

Not to mention the mowing.

But Ingrid didn't touch on any of this. She sat down on the chair Hanna pushed forward for her and said they would have to decide what to do with Mattis.

Felix asked why and received a silent nod from Lars.

Ingrid said that his father wouldn't be coming back.

What do you mean?

She didn't know.

Lars asked if she had become psychic, and those who understood the word laughed half-heartedly. Ingrid didn't. Hanna had given her a cup of coffee and she used every last drop to help her think, took a last swig and placed the cup on the only available space on the table, rose from the chair of privilege and said she would be going into the cow barn with the girls, now at least she had spoken her mind.

They looked in bewilderment at both her and one another.

Ingrid took the twins up to the house with her and sat with them to milk four cows, a few drops less with every passing day. They led them into Rose Acre, cranked the separator, carried the cream into the house and lowered it into the cellar beneath the floor and wheeled the milk down to the well next to the Lofoten boat shed and poured it into the half-empty churn they kept there.

Ingrid said that now they were going out in the boat, and the girls cheered.

They clambered aboard the færing and rowed out between the skerries, Anna at the oars, Ingrid and Sofie each with a hand line. They caught a small saithe and a cod probably weighing four kilos.

Ingrid said they should row back home now.

Only one fish, Sofie said, disappointed.

Yes, one each.

They didn't want to go back, they wanted to be with Ingrid, even if they were in a boat.

Ingrid talked about the strands of wool they had woven through their plaits. Yes, they braided each other's hair, red wool which they dyed themselves, taught by Mamma. Ingrid asked if they were looking forward to starting school again. Sofie said yes, and Anna hesitated. Ingrid stared at Anna. Anna gazed across the sea. An auk was bobbing up and down in the water a few metres from the boat. Anna raised the blades and the bird paddled lazily away. Ingrid leaned back against the gunwale, looked into the blue sky and asked what they thought about the new boy, quickly straightening up again to watch their faces as they reflected. They eyed each other and shrugged.

Ingrid asked if the boys had said something.

Again, they eyed each other and seemed puzzled by the question.

Ingrid laughed and said that now the others would be waiting for them.

They rowed ashore. Ingrid split and salted the cod and told the girls to go to Karvika and tell Selma and Hanna to dig a trench for a new smoke oven.

That took them the whole day, they dug a channel and built an oven with bricks at the far end. It looked like an eider duck house. They covered the top of the trench with sheets of slate, like the roof of a tunnel, shovelled the earth back and completed the construction by placing a herring barrel on top, it resembled a small church with an imposing, rounded tower, or a temple for subterranean beings.

They lit a fire in the oven using twigs, and peat to control the airflow, stood around it in deep silence and watched as the smoke disappeared beneath the earth like a snake and rose from the church tower, satisfyingly white, not to anyone's surprise but to everyone's satisfaction. Sofie and Anna rowed with Ingrid over to Skogsholmen and cut juniper branches. Ingrid rinsed the salt from the cod and hung it from a line she stretched across the barrel and placed the lid on top.

They fed the fire with juniper.

By now the day was almost gone and no-one had mentioned milk-boat Johannes, or his son Mattis, who had been playing with Kaja and Oskar the whole time, and today, too, had eaten

49

more than the others, which Ingrid had noticed Suzanne had also noticed, she asked what she was thinking today. Suzanne asked what Ingrid was thinking.

Ingrid said she didn't know.

Suzanne asked if she was afraid.

Ingrid didn't know that either, and Suzanne repeated what she had said the day before, that she couldn't stay here any longer.

They carried out a long wooden trough and placed it on the well lid and ordered everyone to wash the earth from their hands before sitting down to eat. Even in calm weather a man can be lost at sea. The sea is inscrutable, as a rule it breaks a man down with raw power, once in a while it silently draws him to its bosom.

6

A search for Johannes wasn't launched until several days later, the time it took to be surprised that no milk had been collected, the time it took the dairy to be surprised that no milk had been delivered. But the world is full of surprises, and at length the cutter was found adrift, a ghost ship on the horizon. No-one on board, no note here either, no goodbyes or any sign of drama, a skipper-less vessel with eighteen churns of sour milk in the hold and two empty bottles of spirits in the wheelhouse.

A herring fisherman towed the boat to the village and secured it using Johannes Hartvigsen's mooring ropes, which had also been his father's. A new milk skipper had started up with a new boat and an extended route, but he was nowhere near as punctual or reliable as Johannes, so Johannes would be remembered not only for what he lost, in life and at sea, but also for his punctuality.

In a terrible storm, a good month later, a færing landed on the northern shore of Barrøy, with great difficulty, observed Ingrid, who was there to welcome it. And the new priest stepped ashore, the former Pastor Malmberget's youngest son, Samuel, standing erect, legs akimbo in the buffeting wind, a seminary graduate and doctor of theology, fluent in German after many years' zealous study in Paderborn. It was said that Samuel knew all there was to know about both civilisation and barbarism, after all, he had grown up, and could not only expound his way through Luther's bible but was also able to take delight in the Reformer's wonderful handwriting, down to the smallest individual letter, in something he called a facsimile.

Samuel was as different from his father as a son can be, with respect to his sermons and body shape and happiness and fears. The old pastor was a plump landlubber, a chicken-hearted fellow. Samuel was sinewy with good sea legs, around forty years of age at the time, with a predilection for confrontation and stormy weather, he liked to wake a crew of idle barbarians and put to sea whenever it suited him, perhaps especially when he should have stayed at home, in order to weave their way through the swell, the sail drawn right down to the boom, and surprise his parishioners with visits when they least expected them. He had gained a reputation for impulsive missions, he's one of us, the islanders thought, and so he must have something he wants to say.

Then the crew drag the færing ashore, shove blocks under the hull and moor it with extra hawsers and seek shelter in the boathouse to enjoy their packed lunches and a pipe, while Ingrid and Samuel struggle up the slope into the teeth of the gale and reach the porch, where their oilskins come off, and on into the kitchen, by which time it is at last possible to say something.

Samuel says, what a wonderful world, throws out his arms and gives Barbro a wet kiss on both cheeks, followed by a third on the first, a habit he learned in Paderborn, which draws a giggle from Barbro, she likes this devil-may-care young cuckoo of a pastor, who in addition to all the strange things he says has assigned her a central role in the church choir, where Barbro now sings with a strangely innocent face every last Sunday of the month, weather permitting.

Ingrid has filled the coffee pot and put it on the stove. She did this as soon as they caught sight of the tiny sail in the whirling snow to the north, after first thinking it was a seagull.

Blast me, is it a gull, no, it's a . . . it's a flippen boat.

She adds the right measure of coffee to the pot, and without asking, Samuel sits himself down on the chair by the window, Ingrid's chair, and says, as is his wont, now I've taken your chair, Ingrid, I beat you to it, is it really true that you all grew up here without any chairs?

Ingrid smiles and says no, each one of us had our own chair, all through our childhood. But Barbro can remember further back and protests, she is asked additional questions by an eager Samuel, who doesn't get down to brass tacks until cup and saucer are on the table, with steaming coffee and two lumps of precious sugar, and the brass tacks happen to be the poor lad, where is he by the way?

Ingrid tells him that the little ones can't be outside today, they have to play inside the quay house under the supervision of Lars and Felix, who are repairing nets, herring are on the way, they have been told.

I see, but the boy needs a guardian, this now fatherless boy, so maybe it would make sense for Ingrid to take on this role?

Ingrid has been expecting this and considers waking Suzanne, who uses every storm as an opportunity to sleep her life away, but rejects the idea, Suzanne shouldn't be mixed up in this matter, so Ingrid says, oh my goodness.

Don't worry, Samuel says reassuringly, it is no more than what he calls a "mere formality".

Doesn't the boy have grandparents, Ingrid asks, as well as an impressive number of aunts up there on the Storm estate, she knows the youngest daughter, Elisabeth, who is both a dependable and pleasant woman, don't any of them want the lad?

No, they don't.

Ingrid asks him why and would like an honest answer, but the pastor acts as though it were not necessary to repeat what everyone believes they know about Mattis' origins, a war baby, the result of a misunderstanding, but nonetheless a human being like you and I, Ingrid, he needs a guardian, as do we all, mine resides in heaven, figuratively speaking, the pastor philosophises, at which point he thinks his message has struck home and he concludes by asking Ingrid to sign three identical sheets of paper, which he nervously produces from a canvas folder, one for Ingrid to keep, one as an enclosure for the parish register and one for the civil register, as far as Ingrid can make out, all still damp, down here, at the bottom, on this line.

Pen and ink.

Well, I'm not sure, Ingrid says, wanting to ask what this has got to do with the pastor, she knows Samuel spent the war years in Germany, can that have anything to do with all this hifalutin urgency?

But the pastor acts as if the matter is settled, gets up and glances over Barbro's shoulder at the slices of bread she is preparing, and praises the butter, which is of such a high standard, out here in the middle of the sea, would you believe it?

Ingrid sits down, takes the pen and twiddles it between her fingers while preparing the next question, which is a paraphrase of the first.

Now at least she gathers that there are pecuniary reasons for the Storm family not to take in the lad. Their business still manages a lot of the fish in the area; however, the difference between X – what Alfred Storm has to pay the fishermen for their catches – and Y – the amount he sells the fish on for – has been reduced to an absolute disgrace, the Fishermen's Association has seen to that. On top of which his other daughters have to be married off, and weddings cost money, all of these are poor excuses to Ingrid's ears, she simply doesn't understand why, but Samuel rounds off by saying that he trusts her good judgement, and that is the deciding factor.

Ingrid dips the nib in the ink and signs the first piece of paper, the second and the third, then blows on them, a kind of private ceremonial act, and leaves them lying on the table until Samuel casts an eye over them and grunts his approval.

The boy will have a good life here, he says. How is he coping with all this, first the loss of his mother, then his father, one incomprehensible disappearing act after the other?

Ingrid says they haven't told him about his father. Mattis doesn't ask either. He talks about his mother, but less and less frequently. He still has nightmares, but those too less often, he eats, he has found his feet, he has found Kaja.

And the other children?

Fine. If there's any problem, Hans will sort it out.

If there is any problem?

Yes, when they quarrel. Kids do quarrel.

A lot?

Oskar can be cruel. I think he's jealous.

Because of Kaja?

Maybe.

Don't they ask where he came from?

Ingrid wants to answer: Where does he come from then? But she just says:

He was on the milk boat.

Good, the pastor says.

Ingrid wonders whether they should call him Mathias, which is indeed his name in these papers, she sees, that's a much finer name, isn't it.

Samuel says it will end up as Mattis, no matter what, that's what people have got used to.

But it may be worth a try, he adds, backtracking. And then there's the surname. If you care to look here, Ingrid, he places a finger under Mathias, you will see that there is nothing else, so you can decide yourself whether it should be Hartvigsen or Barrøy, Storm was out of the question.

Storm is out of the question in Ingrid's world too, but what about waiting with the surname, surnames have consequences.

Samuel looks up with interest and discerns a steeliness in Ingrid's eye, which he has learned to be wary of whenever Ingrid grows tired of being simple-minded or has exhausted her supply of servility.

In a milder tone, he asks why.

Ingrid shrugs, stands up and brings more coffee.

Samuel leaves the documents where they are, says it's of no importance to the Church and it may be a good idea to delay the civil registration too, or decide now, right away, that Mathias should keep the Hartvigsen surname so that no-one can contest the legality of the estate.

The estate?

Yes, obviously the estate has to be settled in the courts, although a certain amount of time will have to pass before they can finally determine that Johannes is deceased, but they should definitely sell his boat as soon as possible, it needs repairing.

Ingrid screws up her eyes, here is something else that doesn't add up. What doesn't add up is that the Storm family isn't interested in raking in whatever there might be of value after Johannes' death.

No, the Storms aren't entitled to anything here, the pastor says in an authoritative tone, and they are fully aware of that. Furthermore, the daughter is most probably alive somewhere or other, have you heard anything?

Ingrid knows nothing about Olavia, but is Samuel sure?

Yes, Mattis is the sole heir to his father's estate, so he ought to be called Hartvigsen and not Barrøy. To be on the safe side?

To be on the safe side.

Just a manner of speaking, Ingrid. You can never tell.

Mhm.

Not that there's a lot of property, he continues, the small-holding is tiny and neglected, crags, knolls and bogs, but the fishing cutter's fine. Samuel can try to get it sold and put the money in an account, which Mathias Hartvigsen will have access to when he comes of age, with interest.

There is still something that doesn't add up.

Ingrid collects her thoughts and says the pastor shouldn't have all the bother of selling the boat. But isn't there still a load of gear in Johannes' shed, lines, nets, ropes, tubs, he was a fisherman before he started transporting milk, wasn't he?

It would seem so.

Mhm, Ingrid says again, adding that she will have to have a word with Lars, there is little she does here without his advice and consent.

Barbro smiles at this, and the pastor understands why. Whereafter, he says he will take a stroll down to Karvika and say hello to Hanna. Ingrid says he should watch out going over the hummock, they have started calling it the Oskar Hummock, as the wind has blown Oskar off it several times.

Ha ha, Samuel laughs, puts two of the documents into his folder, pulls on his boots and oilskins and shakes both of them by the hand. Barbro and Ingrid thank him, not for their new status as guardians, but for the visit.

Then the herring arrive.

7

The herring arrive as soon as the storm abates, in surges and vast quantities, several of the nets tear and much of the catch is too big to gut, they have to chop off the heads and rip out the entrails before they can salt them in barrels, one layer of fish pointing north and one west, the island works against the clock for almost two days and nights.

Hanna and Selma are especially excited, catching herring is not only a welcome release from the kitchen and the land, but also a return to their childhood in Lofoten. And the work has to be done double quick, for nothing is in such a hurry as a dead herring. Even the youngest children pitch in, each one filling a quarter-barrel, under strict supervision, as the small barrels are to be stored in the island's larder.

For once, Oskar has something to be proud of and, like a man, accepts both instructions and censure. So has Mathias, though he is more modest, but he is also tough and persevering, standing shoulder to shoulder with Kaja, who wants to do everything her own way, and has to be kept in check by Hanna, Kaja respects "Aunty" Hanna, who has the softest voice on the island.

It takes only two days for the sea to be emptied. But by then twenty-seven full barrels are standing side by side on the mighty stone quay. They are drilled open, filled with brine, plugged and have to be rolled, half a turn, once a day, and topped up with more brine. Nets need to be mended, sinkers fixed, the boat and quay and oilskins hosed down before everyone can stagger home and fall into the deepest slumber of the autumn.

Lars and Felix are the only ones to stay awake.

There is a new moon, the sea is dead calm, the clouds are low and visibility is poor, and unseen by the sleeping population, the two men launch the færing onto the water, sit at the oars and vanish into the silence, intending to transgress Pastor Malmberget's precept regarding the need to forget after the war; Lars and Felix were not so spiritual by nature, nor philosophical.

Ingrid sees no flames in the sky above the main island when she first ventures into the yard the next morning, the clouds are just as low and visibility is as poor as before. She sees the closest skerries and Oterholmen as usual, she notices the dark two lines in the dew on the grass outside the Karvika boathouse, but pays no heed, just registers that the weather today is going to be calm.

The children have to be scrubbed after their exertions with the herring, so she goes into the wash house, fills the boiler and stokes up before returning to the house, where she puts the coffee on and sinks onto her chair by the window, on a day when no-one wants to be wakened, what about the cows?

They aren't giving much milk now, Ingrid waits and thinks about the letter she still hasn't written, to Mariann Vollheim, who christened a daughter in Trondheim several weeks ago. Ingrid has written three letters without sending any of them. But she hasn't burned them either, they are serving as a draft for something beginning to emerge clearly before her eyes.

She walks into the parlour and pulls out the top drawer of her father's bureau, sits down and writes "Dear Mariann", as if they were friends, and apologises for not having replied to the invitation, not blaming this on her lack of time or the invitation not arriving until it was too late, but writes the truth: she had been so confounded by both the letter and the newborn Ingrid that she couldn't take it all in, she can't make Mariann out, she writes.

It seems an odd thing to say, but it is close enough to the truth, so it will do.

She doesn't mention Alexander, but does say how well the children are doing, the ones Mariann got to know when she was here. She had especially taken to Kaja, but also the twin girls and Fredrik. Ingrid mentions Barbro's new role in the church choir, all the herring they have caught and how she's become the guardian of a five-year-old lad, his name is Mathias. But she provides no further details, she sends her best wishes from an island in the sea where life is just as peaceful and happy as Mariann's in her elegant house with a soft-fruit garden in the rolling hills around the town of Trondheim.

Is the war over on Barrøy too?

Not quite.

The door opens as Ingrid seals the envelope and in walks a newly washed and red-eyed Lars with a strange gravity about him. He says it might be time to raise the issue of the sale of the milk boat with the pastor, the weather is good, was Ingrid serious about it?

Ingrid wonders whether it might not be a bit early and maybe there are more herring on the way?

Lars says he wasn't thinking of staying over there long, he just wanted to have a few words with the pastor, maybe the mayor too, and perhaps have a look to see what tackle there was in Johannes' shed.

Ingrid nods and asks him to post this letter.

Lars reads the address on the envelope and mumbles: T' lady, I see, mm.

Ingrid looks at him, her eyebrows arched.

Lars looks back at her, anything the matter?

No, just go. Ingrid knows that boats plying deeper waters are still being asked to keep a lookout for Johannes, or what remains of him, but no, just go.

Lars leaves with an earnest smile on his face, joins Felix in the yard and they walk down to the new quay. Ingrid, looking through the window, can't see anything unusual about their bearing or gait, she drains her cup of coffee and heads for the cow barn.

*

Felix steers the *Salthammer* into the fjord while Lars sleeps, puts in at Johannes Hartvigsen's quay with its shaky, dilapidated landing stage, on the seaward side of the milk boat, two fenders, no jolting, the weather is still calm. The silence of the engine wakes Lars, they exchange a few words, and Felix takes his turn on the bunk while Lars walks up to the rectory and asks if Samuel Malmberget is at home.

He's not, says a housekeeper Lars has never seen before, he's over at Henriksen's.

Oh, why?

Well, there was a fire in the village last night, Henriksen's house has burned down, the old lensmann's been taken to hospital on the mainland, coughing his head off.

Really, Lars says and wants to know more, but the house-maid can't help him, so he walks to Margot's shop, where Margot herself is sitting on a stool beside the stove, knitting socks for a considerable number of grandchildren, while her son Markus has taken over behind the counter, wearing a leather apron spattered with bull's blood and molasses, two chewed pencils poking out of his breast pocket. They say hello and exchange views on the subject of the fire. In Markus' opinion the old bugger set it alight himself to get his paws on the insurance money.

Lars manages a vacuous smile before a customer at his side says, no, he wasn't insured. Which Markus doubts, that's not like Henriksen, but time will tell.

Lars buys molasses, coffee, pearl sago, sugar, overhears a bit more speculation about the fire, and on his way to the Trading Post bumps into an old acquaintance. They discuss the herring situation and agree that it has been good, just far too short a season.

Has Lars heard about the fire?

Ya, nasty business.

Oh, I don't know about that.

Lars carries on down the slope and talks to the foreman, and then the owner himself, a new man by the name of Vig, young, straight-backed, with a smile intended to be misunderstood.

Yes, Vig is interested in the barrels of herring from Barrøy, when?

They agree on a date and price, then Lars walks back to the rectory, and asks the housekeeper, whose name is Lise, he now discovers, whether Samuel is back yet, he would like to sort out an agreement they have about the tackle in Johannes Hartvigsen's shed, you see.

No, the pastor is still busy at the fire.

Lars asks if he can come in and wait.

Please do.

Lars sits down on the pastor's leather sofa and then in one of his leather armchairs and counts the minutes on the clock face next to the door until it is almost eight in the evening, gets up and goes into the kitchen and tells Lise he can't afford to wait any longer, would she kindly mention the agreement to the pastor, they don't want to jump the gun.

Yes, of course, she'll pass on the message.

Lars leaves and walks down to the *Salthammer* with his purchases and wakes Felix. They go up to Johannes Hartvigsen's smallholding, where they find the front door unlocked, like all other doors on the coast.

Felix is the only person who can make Hanna laugh, folk say this is why they got married. The fact that Felix reads books and is as much of an unbeliever as Hanna is a believer is neither here nor there, one of them is master of the waves and the other the mistress of a rock-steady house, but at this point Felix feels a tinge of almost religious disquiet, aren't they pushing things a bit here?

Don't fret yourself, says Lars.

They enter a house where no man has set foot since Johannes and Mathias left it early one morning at the end of August, it will soon be November. It is dead and soulless and damp inside, a grave with a leaking roof. They stand in the doorway between the kitchen and the sitting room, gazing at two rugs lying criss-cross on the floor, and are filled with more disquiet. This is what remains of the life of a man approaching sixty, a man's house and a man's life, frozen at the moment father and son left the place, unaware that they were doing so for the last time.

Would anyone ever light a fire in these cold stoves again?

Would anyone ever again clean, dust, fill the cupboards with food?

The cupboards do contain food. Covered in mould.

Would anyone remove the old food, bring in fresh goods and only allow the tins and the preserves to remain, the jars of jam with Olavia Storm's handwriting on the labels: Gooseberry, blackcurrant. Could that date be wrong?

No.

They don't need to go upstairs and look at the beds to know that this house's days are irrevocably done. Lars says that no-one has ever really lived here, as if swatting away a swarm of flies.

What about the shed?

No-one has ever lived in the shed, either. But here at least there is a wealth of useful objects, tools and equipment that are still in good working order, and will be so for many more years, with correct care and maintenance: net hangers, nets, tubs and ropes, bailers, net floats and gaff hooks and bow-rollers and knives, all the implements people on the coast had used to scrape together a livelihood, a civilisation, for a thousand years.

Mm, Lars says, and after a pause brings up the subject of the fire.

He's not dead, he announces, referring to Henriksen, but at least he's in hospital.

Felix smiles and asks whether that is a good or a bad thing.

Lars shrugs and says the old boy probably wasn't insured either.

Again, Felix asks whether that is a good or a bad thing.

Lars says it should be regarded as an example of God's grace.

Felix laughs, takes two steps inside the shed and grabs a net hanger, sees that the hooks are not rusty, the buoy lines are strong, replaces the hanger and runs his fingers along the net straps hanging on one wall and picks up a coil of rope.

Lars says they had better wait, he has a gut feeling. Felix says nothing.

But then they see an anvil.

They find a badly maintained forge buried beneath soot and dust and scrap iron, with an anvil at the side, so massive that it could have been stolen from a modern workshop in a town, it is an item that doesn't belong here at all.

They brush the dirt and rust off it.

Felix says he thinks he spotted a cart outside. They go out and assess the cart, judge it worth a try and with the aid of two sets of block and tackle, a hook hanging from the rafters and a sturdy rope, manage to hoist the anvil onto the cart, which is on the point of collapsing, but it doesn't, until they come to the slope opposite the quay, and the steel cable on the milk boat's crane can reach this far. However, it is designed for lifting milk churns, so they pull Johannes' boat forward, to be able to manoeuvre the *Salthammer* to the quayside, since its crane is capable of hauling on board ten-ton minke whales, then they

drag the monster anvil over the quay planks, which groan alarm-
ingly, and right up to the very edge, then lift it like a snowflake
down onto the deck between the hold hatch and the wheelhouse and go to the galley for a cup of coffee.

Lars gives a rundown of his activities in the village and
suggests that Felix should make his presence known there too,
pulls Ingrid's letter from his pocket and says he can go to the
post office and buy a stamp.

Felix looks at the envelope, he can remember the lady
from Trondheim too, a remarkable woman, Mariann Vollheim,
who had once given him a list of books to read, books which
Felix had borrowed from the library and with growing wonderment had ploughed his way through. She had also encouraged
him to do the coastal skipper course, which he completed
without missing a single day at college.

He takes the letter to the post office, but first shows his
face in Margot's shop and greets his friend Markus, who has
no customers at the moment and suggests they go together to
the scene of the fire, meanwhile Margot, with her knitting, can
keep an eye on the business.

Only a blackened chimney remains of what was once Henriksen's quite imposing house, the first on the main island to be
painted – by Henriksen's father, during the previous war – and
was therefore referred to as the painted house, by the old folk.

Now all that is left of the painted house is soot and ash and embers, half of the woodshed has also burned down, a few last tongues of fire shoot into the air, but have long since ceased to impress the twenty-odd spectators who are still standing there, at least they won't be getting cold.

Felix hears some speculation that the fire might have started in the parlour, where it was said the old boy kept the stove going all year round so he could have his midday nap in the warm, he must have forgotten to extinguish an oil lamp.

Felix contemplates the spectacle with the same stoic calm as the other onlookers and listens as an elderly man explains that some time ago the old fool had taken home some old parish registers in order to draw up a family tree, the Henriksen genealogical table. Now these registers have no doubt gone up in flames too, the pastor had gone to the hospital to find out more, claiming the history of the parish was at stake.

Aha, Felix says, so that's why we couldn't get hold of him.

Of who?

The pastor.

He walks back to the shop with Markus. Markus insists this is a case of insurance fraud, Felix doesn't react, he doesn't know Henriksen, he says, he wasn't here during the war, he doesn't even know what Henriksen looks like.

They part company and Felix goes to the post office, where he buys a stamp and is struck by an idea. From behind the counter he is given a pen and ink by Svetlana, a voluminous Russian woman from Finnmark who has stayed on here with four sons and no husband, she too a vestige of the war. He adds his own message to Mariann Vollheim, in a corner on the back of Ingrid's envelope: Kind regards from Felix too, if you remember me, regards, Felix.

But then his name and his regards are mentioned twice, but he is a well-read man, and this will not do, so he underlines the second "Felix" as if to draw attention to an intended joke, and it immediately looks better. He pushes it across the counter to Svetlana, who rolls her eyes, stamps it and lets it fall into a sack.

On the way back, Felix makes a foray down to the house where he and Suzanne spent their first years, the most elegant house in the village, the bastion of the previous Trading Post owner, where Vig now resides with his wife and daughter. Felix wonders whether it is sad to see the house again.

It has been painted recently, the windows now have grey frames, and a burnished copper lantern hangs above the entrance with the same leaded-glass windows he remembers the sun shining through when he himself sat on the floor inside, amid all the colours of the rainbow, and wasn't allowed to go out because his mother was afraid of the sea – the only thing Felix remembers from those years. Perhaps also a few flashbacks of his father, the Trading Post owner, who went bankrupt and fled south in shame, who knows where, who cares? Felix has no wish to delve into these memories and knows that he could never have lived in this house, that if he'd had to choose between

Barrøy and this, he would have gone for Barrøy without a second thought.

What's missing on Barrøy?

Is it the light and shadow of childhood?

No, all of this exists on Barrøy too, where he and Suzanne grew up under Ingrid's wing. Felix is no sentimentalist, what he feels is more like an exquisite glow of satisfaction at a job well done, the actions of the night, and with life in general. Then his thoughts turn again to the impressions Johannes Hartvigsen's house made on him, the significant features that distinguish these houses from one other and the insignificant features that unite them. He leaves it at that, this hazy musing about life and death, and walks along the beach back to the *Salthammer* and wakes Lars. They start the engine, and Felix gets an hour's sleep while Lars steers the boat homeward, with an anvil on the deck.

8

The following week more herring arrived, which they only discovered as a result of birds gathering above the turbulent sea, conditions were so terrible that the children had had to stay on land, even Hans, which infuriated him, he was fourteen and due to go to Lofoten next winter, and now he couldn't even take part in the herring fishing!

We need you in the bait house, Lars laughed.

The lad told his father to go to hell.

Ingrid, who was working at the next barrel and had been musing on the question she had asked the twins, but still hadn't put to the boys, at first displayed some sympathy for Hans and then asked him what he thought of Mathias.

Hans was heaping herring into the barrel and shovelling salt on top, like muck on a field, he didn't understand what Ingrid was driving at.

Ingrid said he wasn't lining up the herring properly.

Alright, alright.

You can keep an eye on the children.

Hans looked at her.

Ingrid said he would be going fishing soon enough, and he still didn't understand what Aunty Ingrid was trying to say.

Yes, Aunty Ingrid said and told him again to look after Kaja and Mathias, and wanted to know what he thought of the new islander.

He's a prick, said Martin, working at the next barrel. Fredrik, who was standing beside him, just grinned.

Ingrid asked what he meant by "prick". Martin looked at Mathias, who was struggling with his new firkin and Fredrik said, precociously, that Mattis was a clever little lad.

His name's Mathias, Ingrid said.

Alright, alright, Hans said.

Do you think that, too? Ingrid asked Hans.

Do I think what, too? he said, and sulkily began to take a little more care with the rows of herring. Ingrid noticed that Selma had overheard the conversation, if indeed that was what it was, and was leaning over to Mathias and praising him. He looked at her, just as baffled as Hans had been, so Ingrid decided this would have to stop and told Kaja to listen to Aunty Hanna, causing Kaja to look up in bewilderment too, this was how it should be, if everything was as it should be.

Lars and Felix sailed the *Salthammer* around wildly in the raging spray, not bothering about the grapnels and sinkers, and dragged the trail of nets in circles wherever they thought they saw signs of herring in the troughs between the waves, an improvised dance-like form of fishing, bordering on madness, but they drew in an enormous haul and towed it to the quay, where the islanders stood, eyes agog at the sight of a bag of silver dangling like a trawl net behind the line-setter.

They ran a strap around the bag and started pulling, the storm lashed it against the quay, bursting it, to the sound of howls and screams, for there went their riches, and the islanders had to get down on their knees and pluck the squirming catch from the water with their bare hands.

They fetched new nets, went out again and made more forays, managed to haul ashore another catch, of which they salvaged a greater proportion. But this took its toll on the tackle, and it was turning dark too. Lars decided they would have to wait with the next sally, maybe the weather would calm down, now they would get themselves that bloody radio, no-one can survive here without a radio, as they had always done.

Most folk went home and had a few hours' sleep, while Lars and Felix went out again, this time with Hans and Fredrik, who was a little on the young side, but the wind had dropped, and Fredrik had been here since he was five – or six? – and worked like a man. This time it was Martin who felt left out.

But the herring had gone. It wasn't until later that they found a shoal north of Skogsholmen, in Barrøy's waters, so to speak, which meant the whole day had been spent burning up fuel, and what about an echosounder, that brilliant Norwegian invention, a sonic telescope that let you see right to the bottom?

It was too expensive, like the radio, like most of the other equipment they didn't have.

But the last catch ended up on the quay too and in barrels. And with this herring fishing was over for the autumn, very probably, in their frenzy and madness they had ruined more tackle than had been necessary, the mainstay of all serious fishing, but there has to be a balance between frenzy and wisdom, so Lars was in a sombre mood as he passed between the tattered nets they had hung up to dry in the quay house, objects of ridicule rather than items they imagined could be repaired, it was embarrassing, even with forty-six barrels of herring standing in all their splendour out there in the rain, all eyes were on Lars this day, especially those of his eldest son, Hans, who was really beginning to understand what this was all about. But so were those of Fredrik and Martin, the latter even displaying a hint of malicious pleasure. Martin was ten and was hoisted above his father's head and held there until he begged for mercy.

Needless to say, Pastor Samuel puts in when everyone is asleep. And he doesn't come in the færing this time, instead he has managed to get a fisherman to drop him off, he climbs up the ladder and stands unseen on the quay wondering whether the island has met with a disaster, although an impressive number of herring-filled barrels lined up on the splendid pink granite suggests quite the reverse.

Beneath the blue sky Samuel trudges up the slope, the sun low over sea and land, a gentle breeze, one last peaceful sigh of autumn, and is halfway to his destination when the porch door opens and out comes Ingrid, fumbling with her woollen jacket, almost breaking into a run, on the verge of apologising as they proffer each other a hand.

Samuel's handshake, he gauges his parishioner's well-being with this handshake, Ingrid's is firm, as usual, she is surprised that he has come in fine weather, it is not like him.

They laugh and walk up to the house and into the kitchen where Barbro is on her knees in front of the wood-burning stove, blowing on the glowing embers, she gets to her feet to receive her usual three kisses. Then come the coffee grinder and the coffee and the chair game and two lumps of sugar, all before the purpose of the pastor's visit is revealed.

Johannes Hartvigsen's boat.

The search has now officially been called off, Johannes is to be regarded as lost at sea, he has even been assigned a grave in the churchyard with a cross, which is white.

Samuel delivers a monologue on the subject of the unortho-dox ceremony he conducted in the rain, alone, last Tuesday, it is as if he feels a need to get his head around the matter again, with an audience this time, this tradition which is lacking on the coast, burying, metaphorically speaking, also those who have gone missing, burying the memory of a person.

Not that Samuel has had a spade in his hands in Johannes'

case. On the Finnmark coast there are many cemeteries where "unknown" is inscribed on the crosses after human remains have been found on the shore, floating in the water, unidentifiable objects, which the local inhabitants have buried in a dignified manner. So there is at least something beneath these crosses, which will turn into earth, albeit not the actual memory of a specific individual, for nobody knows who this person might be.

But tell me, Ingrid, shouldn't those who have gone missing also have a grave, an Archimedean point, so to speak, on dry land, which the bereaved can visit to assuage their grief?

Yes, Ingrid thinks this is a nice thought, she is just a little unsure that the idea should be introduced in the case of Johannes Hartvigsen of all people, the least missed man on earth.

The pastor: When you walk through a churchyard, Ingrid, do you feel as though you are trampling on corpses? No, so there you are. People only avoid treading on fresh graves, where someone has recently been interred. It is too early, we feel, the bodies have not yet become earth. But when they have, this earth is bound up with a memory, the same type as the memory of Johannes, Samuel says. Looking around, as if searching for an intelligible conclusion, he takes a sip of coffee. And again Ingrid is reminded of Nelvy, who died here during the war and whom Ingrid had to all intents and purposes buried with her own hands, and tears, a grave she continues to tend with feelings of guilt that will never leave her, Nelvy was too much like herself, Nelvy who was never given the life that Ingrid has.

Samuel believes it is his modern theology that has moved Ingrid to tears and lays a hand on her arm and repeats that we are mere mortals, Ingrid – now is the time to weigh his words – we all have our crosses to bear – one can say something reasonable, yet to others it is like rubbing salt in open wounds – until he finally manages to close his mouth, and Barbro can sit down.

Sit down in the presence of the pastor?

Yes, in the presence of Samuel everyone can sit down, he is the first among equals, how long has he been here now?

Four years and nine months, Ingrid says impatiently, and Samuel confesses that he never imagined he would thrive so well in these wild parts, now he will probably have to stay here until his dying day.

Barbro is on the point of asking him whether he has any plans to get married, she thinks she has noticed that he has a twinkle in his eye when he looks at Olavia's elder sister, Anna Karina Storm, who likewise sings in the choir. Anna Karina is at all events attracted to Samuel, but who isn't, so Barbro thinks better of asking him and contents herself with sitting at the same table as the pastor, drinking coffee with him.

The boat? Ingrid breaks the silence.

Yes, the last weeks of summer had been hot, and the boat was beginning to be affected by mould. Samuel has been on board and run the pumps a few times, but he has better things to do, it has to be sold, unless the Barrøyers want to keep it themselves?

Ingrid says they don't.

No, I thought not. In which case, he has a ready buyer at hand, do they know Daniel from Malvika, Adolf's son?

Oh, yes, Ingrid knows Daniel well enough to be certain he is no seafarer, so he doesn't need Johannes' gear, she'd like to keep it.

Samuel eyes her.

Ingrid realises she shouldn't have used the word "keep", that is the word the pastor used, and instead says they would like to make use of Johannes' tackle.

Samuel nods.

Ingrid pours more coffee and asks whether he has noticed the iron rails on the beach beside Johannes' quay, rusty and buried in seaweed and kelp, there had been a slipway there once, Ingrid would like to make use of those too.

Scrap iron?

Yes, it's scrap.

Lars told her about these rails when they arrived with the anvil, they have never had a slipway on Barrøy and have always wanted one.

Fine, fine, Samuel says, nothing could interest him less, it was the price of the boat, Daniel is willing to offer the rightful owner twelve thousand.

Ingrid almost falls off her chair.

The rightful owner is Mathias, I've opened an account in his name in the savings bank and can arrange the sale, then you fetch the bank book and sign.

Ingrid pulls herself together and nods, but again foresees new problems with the surname.

Samuel reassures her that the guardian has full power of attorney over the account until the boy turns twenty-one regardless of the fact that she is called Barrøy and he Hartvigsen.

Ingrid has to stand up. Even though much is still undecided, one thing is clear, Barbro should not have heard the sum mentioned.

Ingrid has an idea: she offers the pastor some cream in his coffee, which is in the cellar adjoining the well, so Barbro has to go out, and, in her absence, she convinces the pastor that the buying price should remain between the two of them and Daniel, if the pastor wants to see this money lasting for the next sixteen years, that is the way of the world, people are no better than that.

Samuel seems annoyed he didn't think of this himself, gets to his feet and takes Ingrid by the hand, but sits down again after this unprecedented action, and waits for Barbro to return with the cream. They quietly drink two more cups, accompanied by slices of bread, they are having breakfast together in the middle of the day, while the rest of the household sleeps. And Samuel shows his human side again, he asks Ingrid how the lad is getting on.

Fine, but he doesn't talk much, she says, and almost only with Kaja, and both of them whisper in other people's company, as if they are hiding something.

Samuel nods and says the boy is lucky to be here.

What?

Yes, times are difficult for the children on the mainland just now, peacetime is, in fact, hell for them, so it's good he's here. Samuel also says something about reconciliation and the need to forget. To Ingrid this sounds like it isn't she who is the saving of Mathias but being on an island could be, and that ever since the day the boy uttered his first word on Barrøy, it has been a blessing he isn't part of the rest of the world.

9

Lars is in a better mood, standing outside his house in the last rays of the sun this year, after a full night's sleep, when he sees a fishing smack heel around the North Reef and set a course for the village. But his mood darkens as soon as he begins to wonder whether the weather has affected him, whether he is the same person in a raging snowstorm as beneath a clear sky. But there is Ingrid, coming over Oskar Hummock and shouting something to him.

What?

Ingrid doesn't want to come down, she calls from the top that they should go over and get Johannes' slipway rails. And while they are at it fetch whatever tackle they needed. The milk boat has been sold.

Lars shouts back, what did it go for?

Four thousand, Ingrid shouts, it's Mathias' money.

Stone the crows, Lars says, goes inside and has breakfast and sails over to Johannes' quay with Felix.

First, they walk up to see one of the neighbours, who goes by the mystifying name of Gått, a recluse who has managed to live where he lives for years and years without anyone noticing, a shadowy figure people bump into once in a while and say, oh yes, that Gått fellow, yes, only to forget him, until sometime in January when he reappears, and they think, ah, it's him again, Gått.

With Gått as a witness Lars and Felix tear out six lengths of rail and hoist them on board the *Salthammer*, smash the rotten woodwork of the cradle and remove the rollers and iron, including the bolts in the sleepers. After that they walk up to Hartvigsen's shed, still with Gått as a witness, and carry down nets, lines, ropes, tubs and tools. But they don't venture inside the farmhouse today, they avoid this forever-lost home, as do Gått and everyone else. Gått helps them by carrying down two floats, holding one in each hand.

Meanwhile Ingrid convinces Barbro she has misheard the price of the boat. She achieves this by waiting until Barbro mentions the sum herself, just imagine, twelve thousand, as they are topping up the brine in the herring barrels.

Twelve? Ingrid says in surprise. You've got it wrong. I jotted down the amount on a slip of paper, didn't you notice? Look at this: a note Ingrid pulls from her apron pocket: four thousand kroner written in letters. This is a dirty trick, and Ingrid feels ashamed, as Barbro can't read, so she says in a friendly tone that the four thousand will come as a surprise to Lars, should he get wind of it.

Barbro asks why it would be a surprise, and especially to Lars of all people. Ingrid has no answer to this and says Lars will be pleased that Mathias has four thousand kroner in his account, four thousand, however hollow this sounds, now it must have stuck.

Lars and Felix return as darkness is falling, unload the iron and drag it into the quay house, sort it into three piles in the light from the Petromax lamp Ingrid is holding and find that the rust is superficial, except on the rail mountings. One arm on the frame is broken, but it can be welded. They discuss the sleepers: use driftwood or buy new? Felix's mouth gushes with new information about the fire, which he has heard from Gått.

The fire, asks Ingrid, who cancelled her newspaper subscription when the milk route was suspended for the year and hasn't been to the village for several months.

Yes, Henriksen's house burned down this autumn, didn't you know?

Ingrid says nothing.

Now the investigation seems to have been dropped, Felix explains, Henriksen had either fallen asleep and left an oil lamp burning or attempted insurance fraud, neither shows him in a good light. At the moment, he is staying with one of his sisters on the mainland, suspicion still hanging over him, he has to pay rent, they say, he has to be a tenant in a house owned by a member of his own family.

Felix chuckles and Lars has lost interest, he thinks they have enough driftwood for at least eighteen sleepers, the question is whether the cradle and the wagon are strong enough to bear the weight of the *Salthammer*, a boat sixty-two feet in length, but perhaps they could first haul up the bow to clean that and then the arse?

Hm, Felix is sceptical. The winch?

Ingrid still says nothing, just shines the lamp on the hope-giving iron. She passes Lars the Petromax and walks out into the darkness up to the house, where she sits on her own chair by the window, immersed in thought, weighing up whether it was wise of her to show so little interest in the fire. As if she had any choice.

Then she begins to wonder what else she might have missed out on this autumn, in the village, here on the island?

But, looking at herself in the windowpane, these convoluted thoughts give way first to a kind of indifference and then to a feeling of relief she would prefer not to acknowledge.

On the other side of the table, Barbro sits with Kaja on one knee and Mathias on the other, singing softly without words and making faces as an accompaniment to her silvery tones. While Suzanne is half-lying on the log bin with Oskar on her lap, the boy who is only quiet when Barbro sings, she hugs him as if he were her own son, Suzanne who throughout the autumn has been listless and sullen and didn't even allow herself to get excited by the herring adventure, that climactic display of febrile human energy, Suzanne hates herring, herring are worse than yuk.

The table has been set.

They eat in reverent silence after the singing, and Ingrid casts her eye over Suzanne, this out-of-place stepdaughter and daughter, it all boils down to the same thing, while Suzanne chews with her mouth closed, and occasionally places a hand on the head of Oskar, who looks at her as if she is to be trusted, this obstinate little tot, now he is probably the only thing that binds her to the island. And it is Ingrid's job to do something about this situation, she realises in a blinding flash, and wipes away a tear without anyone noticing.

10

On the last Tuesday before Christmas, Ingrid is standing beside Felix in the wheelhouse of the *Salthammer*, wearing the finest clothes she possesses, the women on Barrøy no longer go shopping in a færing, at least not in winter.

Next to her is Hanna, more meticulously and sombrely dressed than usual, this is serious business, Hanna hasn't been to the village since early autumn.

And Lars?

He has his hands full collecting driftwood in the south of Barrøy, while the question of whether any of the youngsters should join them has been resolved in the following way: No, they shouldn't, they should do some baking with Barbro, Suzanne and Selma, the Lofoten season is just around the corner.

Above the rolling bow, they see the church spire and the churchyard and the Trading Post and the village approaching. Hanna says she is going to be sick, and Felix grabs her around the waist, making her laugh with embarrassment. Ingrid counts the eleven free-standing barrels of herring on the deck in front of them, the rest are in the hold, she wonders whether she is sufficiently prepared for this journey, which she hasn't really got time for.

While Felix is negotiating the price of the herring with Vig and his enigmatic smile, Hanna goes to the shop and Ingrid to the savings bank, which is in a converted storehouse and adjacent to a telegraph counter, post office and library. The former mayor is the bank manager and is sitting in his coat reading a newspaper Ingrid hasn't seen before.

She greets him, sits down unbidden and says she would like the bank book belonging to young Mathias Hartvigsen, she is his guardian, here, look, Pastor Samuel has probably told him.

The manager raises his eyes, mildly surprised, clears his throat, puts a pair of spectacles on his nose and squints at the document Ingrid has placed on the table, more to give himself time to think, Ingrid suspects, than to ascertain that Ingrid really is Mathias' legal guardian, he then removes his spectacles and says, as if it's any of his business:

Well, is he finally dead then, old Johannes?

Ingrid isn't so badly prepared after all, it transpires, and refers to the stone cross bearing Johannes' name that Samuel erected during his simple ceremony in the churchyard. She also emphasises that she has no intention of stealing the bank book, on the contrary, it is her duty to take good care of it, either until Johannes reappears or his son turns twenty-one.

By now Sund's resistance is insufficient to prevent him

from opening a drawer, taking out a blue booklet and laying it on the table.

Ingrid doesn't lean forward to grasp it, she remains calmly sitting with her hands on her bag and says she would also like to take out two hundred kroner, in Mathias' name, he needs some clothes and shoes and something she can't remember offhand, she just wafts an arm.

Sund is even more clearly behaving as though they are talking about his own money and says he doesn't think he has that much ready cash in the safe, nodding in the direction of a black iron box on four tall legs resembling train rails.

Ingrid eyes him.

He gets up and plods towards the safe and turns his back on Ingrid. She hears some metallic clicks. The iron door opens, and Sund sorts through something or other, it takes him a long time, emitting a few coughs and various other noises, half-turns and gazes out of the window, contemplating, has an idea and bends down to a lower shelf, more clattering and coughing, a ritual Ingrid knows all too well from when she worked at the Trading Post during the war, when it was so endlessly complicated to get your hands on your own money.

But the door clanks shut, he comes back and sits down clutching a wad of banknotes, which he is loath to place on the table. Ingrid says she should probably count them, to be on the safe side and to make sure he isn't trying to fob her off with some old notes that went out of circulation during the First World War.

Sund looks up in surprise and laughs aloud and says she has a damn good memory, but she is mixing up the wars. No, this is legal tender. Count it, ha ha, and sign here.

Ingrid counts and signs, and he scribbles something in the bank book. Ingrid asks if he has an envelope.

He shakes his head, smiling, and nods towards the post office door. Ingrid returns his smile, stuffs the money in her bag and without thanking him walks over to see Svetlana and first buys two envelopes and writes on them, one letter is addressed to Mariann Vollheim.

But Svetlana looks at the second envelope and rolls her eyes the way only a Russian can: Daniel Malvik? He lives only five kilometres away, doesn't Ingrid want to save the postage and hand it over herself?

They agree that the letter can stay where it is, Daniel will be dropping by before Christmas, by the way, since the milk boat has stopped, there is a stack of post for Ingrid.

It turns out that this stack consists of one letter, from Mariann Vollheim in Trondheim, and a pile of old newspapers Svetlana has been keeping for her. Ingrid asks how her sons are. Svetlana rolls her eyes again, and Ingrid walks out into the last rays of sunshine she will see for three weeks and two days.

On the journey home Felix complains that Vig, the owner of the Trading Post, is just like all the other bloody Trading Post owners, it's as though they go on a course to learn how to be like each other. Hanna hums as she steers the boat and Ingrid leans back against the bulkhead, reading the letter from Mariann, no surprises there, and Ingrid is formulating a reply when she is interrupted by Hanna, who, out of nowhere, says she didn't come along just to go shopping but to have a few words with Ingrid in private.

This sounds ominously formal in the mouth of a willing and uncomplaining workhorse, who stands there now, confronting her with an irrefutable demand. Hanna doesn't want her children to go to school this winter, if they do, she can't live here, alone on an island, the previous winter was dreadful.

Ingrid says of course the children have to go to school, they have been slack enough this autumn, but Hans and Fredrik only want to go to sea, and Lars and Felix haven't been much help here.

But Hanna turns her back on her, rejecting outright Ingrid's arrogant standpoint, and gazes out over the rolling bow as it ploughs into a sleet storm.

Ingrid tells her to turn round.

She doesn't.

Ingrid stares at her back and glances at Felix, but he agrees with his wife.

Could Fredrik go to school on his own and the girls stay on Barrøy, keeping their mother and Oskar company?

Still no answer.

Felix states into the sleet that Fredrik is going to Lofoten

and can attend school there, with Martin, and do some baiting with Hans in the afternoons, they need help in the baiting
house.

"He's only ten years old!" Ingrid shouts.

He's twelve, Felix says flatly, at least, and adds that Ingrid
seems to have forgotten how old her father was when he left
school, and her grandfather too, not to mention himself and Lars.

Ingrid wants to say that times change, but if there is one
thing that doesn't change, it is folk, so she says nothing and
wrestles with a silence, which makes her more and more angry
with herself, she is like a lackey, until she feels a plan forming,
a desperate plan.

11

That year saw the greatest exodus from Barrøy of all time, in pitch darkness and sleet sweeping in from the west, the whole of Karvika boards the *Salthammer* on the morning of the third of January. Hanna and Selma are to spend the winter in their childhood homes, the children are on their way to school in Lofoten, including twelve-year-old Fredrik, when he is not doing the baiting, that is.

Ingrid gives the twins a hug and a few warnings that are lost in the wind. The only person to cry is Suzanne, who is not only about to be separated from her biological son – he lost interest in his mother long ago – but also from little Oskar.

Ingrid has had a great deal of trouble organising this extra-ordinary event whereby two thirds of the island's population will be leaving, temporarily, it is claimed, but who knows?

The fishing tackle and equipment were loaded the day before. One last chest of food is hoisted aboard, an extra rug, a mitten, a cap.

Have they got everything?

Lars shouts down from the deck that he is sick of all this palaver every time they have to go somewhere.

Ingrid walks to the edge of the quay and shouts up to him, in a tone he cannot disobey, to come forward to the foc's'le, passes him the moorings as if they were a gift and says she wants to thank him for the fire.

Lars eyes her in surprise and shouts into the wind that he hopes she will go to Karvika and light the stove from time to time, houses that aren't heated die.

They leave it at that.

Felix is in the wheelhouse, the engine is running, the *Salthammer* puts off and tacks to the north in heavy seas and darkness, and even though as usual those remaining stand out in the vile weather until the stern lights have stopped swinging in this soot-black stovepipe of a night, Ingrid shouts to sobbing Suzanne, telling her to be quiet and go up and pack.

You're leaving too. Tomorrow.

Suzanne wipes away her tears and the sleet and breaks out into even more sobbing. But Ingrid has started walking up the slope with Barbro and the children, so Suzanne has to run after her and ask what in heaven's name she means.

Ingrid stops and says, in a tone she has never used before, tomorrow, Suzanne, tomorrow you're leaving Barrøy.

She couldn't have said this in a more solemn and menacing manner, in a fury she knows she cannot constrain.

Suzanne insists on having this repeated and explained, she has lost control of her face and voice. Barbro is mystified too, but at least she has Kaja and Mathias to hold on to and drags the children the last part of the way up to the house, where they dutifully take off their coats and oilskins and hang them on the lowest hooks to the right.

Ingrid leads Suzanne into the parlour where oddly enough the stove is lit and explains in the same solemn tone of voice that she has a present for her, a Christmas present, she glibly lies, which she hadn't been able to give her last year as, firstly, the others would have seen and, secondly, Suzanne can't keep a secret, or hide anything, not even her own shame.

But enough of that. Daniel will take you to the town. From there you'll catch the express boat to Trondheim, where you will see an acquaintance of mine, Mariann Vollheim, maybe you remember her, she will help you on your way.

Suzanne is struck by lightning. Thrown out? Of her own home? Does Ingrid want to get rid of her? She behaves in such a heart-rending manner that Barbro comes into the hall and yells at the top of her voice, is anything the matter?

In response, Ingrid yells no and glares with barely disguised contempt at a creature who is in all but name her own daughter and says: Stop making a scene. She only just manages to restrain herself from adding that Suzanne can't keep on poisoning the island with her constant yearning and endless whining.

But why the fury?

Well, yes, because with the fury it is established, once and for all, by Ingrid herself, the head of the island, that it is indeed possible to leave an island, on top of which the whole crowd of them have recently moved north, this is the final curtain for Ingrid's world.

She flings the banknotes in her hand across the floor like fluttering leaves and Suzanne asks whether she has taken leave of her senses.

Quite possibly. Ingrid is in a rage and shrieks that she has saved up this money (for God's sake, don't make it seem like a sacrifice) so that Suzanne can go to Oslo, she deserves much more (for God's sake, don't make it seem like a payment).

Again she has to pause for breath.

Suzanne gets up, grabs a log and puts it in the stove, but stays on her feet summoning strength, to what end? Ingrid knows that something has to give. She yells at the door that Barbro should come in with the children and help them to eat up what remains of the Christmas biscuits, biscuits for breakfast in a heated sitting room, to mark the islanders' departure for Lofoten.

Hesitantly, they come in, and Ingrid tells them how nice it will be for them in the winter, Barbro can sing a song, can't she, what's the time, half past seven, goodness me, so we can sleep as long as we want.

Had it not been for the barn, with the four cows and the sixteen sheep, which need feeding, and for the tattered nets they have out between the Lundeskjære skerries. And quite a lot else.

*

In calm, clear weather, late the following morning, the old milk boat puts in at the new quay. It is unrecognisable. And a good thing too, as Mathias is also there to welcome it. Daniel has cleaned and painted it, mounted a line-setter and converted it into the fishing cutter it once was, even giving it a new name, after his young wife, Malin, shiny brass letters emblazoned in an elegant curve across the mahogany plaque on the wheel-house. Ingrid can't even remember what it was called when it transported milk, oh, yes, it was Olavia. The engine now has a healthier sound, a soothing purr, and Daniel excitedly announces that he has done it all himself.

He fixes his eyes on Kaja and Mathias and jovially asks if the nippers are going to Havstein.

Daniel is under the illusion that he has been summoned to take the Karvika children to school, and is unaware that the trip has been cancelled so that Suzanne can be ferried to a town on the mainland.

Oh, right, I suppose I can do that.

Suzanne is ready to go, wearing the same clothes she arrived in during the war, which haven't seen the light of day since. With the same diminutive suitcase next to her stockinged calves, and a moss-green coat with a collar which to Ingrid's eyes resembles a tern's wings. She has a woollen bobble hat on her head, but is also holding a bonnet in her hand to replace the hat as soon as she arrives in town. Suzanne's sobs are more controlled today, but her tears are nonetheless copious enough for Daniel to ask if she is going to a funeral, and this is not even meant as a joke.

Suzanne ignores him, waves for a helping hand, and is supported, stiffly and clumsily, down onto the deck. A word from the war occurs to Ingrid, lady-like, one she'd forgotten but which now at any rate calls forth a welcome smile on her face.

Only now do both of them realise that they haven't given each other a hug, and maybe it is just as well, although Suzanne appears to be considering climbing back up to at least embrace Barbro, she has no axe to grind with her. But with Ingrid standing next to them, watching, wouldn't one of them attempt an awkward embrace? What kind of farewell would *that* be? And she has already hugged the children, several times. So, Suzanne contents herself with the thought that she has managed to get down onto the deck unscathed, that it is too late now anyway, she is already on her way, and looks up at the four remaining people and gently waves the bonnet she will don as soon as she steps into civilisation.

12

Mathias had begun to talk, all of a sudden, a lot and quickly. Ingrid first noticed this about a month before Christmas, when she overheard a stream of words coming from inside the small bedroom, which they heated on stormy days so that the children had somewhere to play.

Instead of going in, she placed her ear against the door and listened to Kaja's usual chatter, now interrupted by Mathias' words and some shouting from Oskar. Mathias was chuntering on about something he must have picked up from Lars, about how stupid fish were, they stick their heads into nets and get caught, fish must be blind. Kaja:

What does blind mean?

This.

Ingrid realised that Mathias had thrown a blanket over her. Oskar said: Me too. Another silence, two shouts. Mathias explained that it was dark at sea, no-one could see a bloody thing. Kaja protested that *she* could, the sea was green and clear. They began to squabble over a toy Kaja claimed was hers, a doll's house, Ingrid gathered, which apparently had to be thrown against the wall.

She was about to intervene, but Mathias beat her to it: No, no, it'll break. A brief tussle. And Mathias explained *why* things can break, in great detail.

Is he the explainer type?

All autumn Ingrid had held back from exploring further, but now in the new year with only four of them around the table, it was natural for her to ask him about all manner of things, for example, why he didn't want to hold a knife in his right hand.

Mathias said he couldn't, his arm wouldn't do it.

Kaja laughed and said that *she* could, cut off a piece of fish and was about to put it into her mouth with her fork when it fell onto the table, she shoved it in with her fingers.

Mathias grabbed the knife with his right hand and awkwardly cut through a potato, used his left to stab it with a fork and elegantly dipped it in butter, guided it to his mouth with ease and proclaimed he was made differently.

Ingrid laughed and asked how he was made then.

He squirmed. Kaja said she was made too. She asked what was different about him. Mathias said: I'm strange.

Are you strange?

Mathias laughed, and Barbro said quickly that in this house I'm the strange 'un.

And me, Ingrid said, annoyed that she hadn't got in before her aunt.

In that case, Kaja said, everyone was strange. And Mathias didn't say any more, but he smiled and displayed better table manners than Kaja, despite holding his knife in his left hand. He had gained weight since he arrived, a lot, and was now taller than Kaja.

When the weather was good enough for the children to be outside, Ingrid took them with her to see the sheep, which she led down to the wide beach to graze on seaweed. She noticed that Mathias was wary by nature and generally let Kaja take the lead, even though he showed no signs of anxiety when they jumped over stone walls or struck out on new paths through the gardens, he just seemed more alert, watchful and pensive.

While the sheep grazed, Ingrid pointed out the shells and pebbles and conches, told the children about all the treasures she had collected here in her childhood, and they agreed and disagreed about what was worth keeping and what could be tossed into the sea.

Snow lay over the trampled grass, and Ingrid said they should grab the woolly coat of the biggest sheep, which Kaja called Mother, and let it drag them uphill. Mother was as strong as a ram, they only had to lie on their backs, in their oilskins. Ingrid showed them how. Mother tossed its head, kicked out and shook itself and set off on a run as soon as Ingrid let go, and towed the howling children up the hill and down into a green hollow, where it picked up speed and the screams grew even louder. Kaja had to let go, but Mathias hung on and Mother ran like the wind over the frozen tufts of grass in one garden and then another, not stopping until it was by the pond in the peat bog, where the animals usually quenched their thirst after grazing on the salty seaweed.

Mathias stood shaking with delight beside the breathless ewe, which stamped its front feet and glared, waiting for Ingrid to smash a hole in the ice.

Ingrid called Mathias a plucky little chap and asked if he had held on with both hands or only his left.

When Mathias didn't answer, she explained the difference between left and right, which of course the children knew, she had forgotten that, but what about port and starboard?

Kaja was allowed to ride Mother up to the cow barn. Ingrid held her and steered the sheep with soft, well-aimed kicks and Mathias walked beside it on the starboard side. In the house, Barbro had dropped off to sleep while intending to cook, happy that the peace of bygone days had once again descended over the island.

They still had the small, flat-bottomed boat, and this winter Mathias and Kaja learned to row. On clear days they took lines and jigs, and Ingrid also taught them how to fish for cod and saithe in the sound between the island and the skerries. They learned to bleed and gut fish, Mathias holding the knife in his left hand while Kaja held it in her right. Two fingers into the cod's eye, a thumb under its jaw, turn the belly up, knife through the white skin under the gills to make the blood run, then an inch below the gullet and down to the anus, but no further, so that the intestines spill out, save the liver, the rest is chucked into the sea. Kaja thought it was disgusting and Ingrid took note of her overreaction. Mathias gritted his teeth and said it was fine. Ingrid observed that he was exaggerating too, the concentration, the exultation, a woman and a man, she thought, here at any rate things were as they should be.

In good weather Daniel Malvik sailed south of Barrøy to do a spot of fishing and at the end of January he came by with a parcel, wrapped in brown paper and tied with string, from Svetlana at the post office. It contained mainly some well-thumbed newspapers, but also a letter and an old Russian children's book.

Svetlana was born in Archangel, but during the Revolution she came with her family to Vardø as a thirteen-year-old, she attended a Norwegian school, married a Norwegian, became a Norwegian widow and regarded herself as Norwegian as everyone else in the Arctic town. Then, during the last war, she became a refugee once again, and that was enough for anyone, so she didn't go back, but stayed here, where fate had landed her, for good, she thought.

When Ingrid was still passionate about Alexander and all things Russian, she had asked Svetlana to teach her the language, and she had not only rolled her eyes, but answered testily, no, Russian was the language of Stalin, the greatest criminal in the history of mankind, she didn't even speak Russian with her own sons, and was proud of it.

Ingrid had been surprised by her outspokenness, well acquainted as she was with Stalin thanks to the portrait of him that had hung for years in her grandfather's room, beside that of his friend Lenin, and Karl Marx.

She opened the book and saw that it was a school reader, with drawings, poems and stories, presumably for the second or third class. Above the Cyrillic words, Svetlana had written a transcription in Roman letters and above that a translation into incoherent Norwegian, three lines for each original line, the pages looked like sheets of music.

Ingrid read the accompanying note.

Svetlana remembered how she had flatly refused to teach Ingrid Russian, she wrote, but had been told how she had helped Russian prisoners of war after the *Rigel* disaster, and this had touched her.

Ingrid had in fact helped only one, inside her head she corrected Svetlana as she showed the book to Kaja and Mathias, who didn't give a hoot about the Cyrillic writing, they loved the drawings however, small dancing bears and an eagle that was obviously kind and helped a lost boy to find his way out of a forest and as a reward was allowed to live in the boy's room, sitting on a perch like a hen, it ate porridge with a spoon, snow falling in the background, outside the cottage windows decorated with wooden carvings of dragons and flowers.

There was also a story about two hares and a spruce tree with a mouth, it was probably telling the hares a fairy tale. On the next page, the hares were holding a map, which they used to find a hole in the ground, they peered down into it and saw five other pairs of hare eyes. In the last drawing, all seven of them were dancing around the hole, a reunited family and, on the last page, readers were left to admire a seven-armed candelabrum and a Russian cross.

Ingrid told the children to be gentle with the book, it is precious, she said, place it on the table when you turn the pages, treat it with care.

Afterwards Ingrid opened the letter from Mariann Vollheim, who had received a visit from Suzanne, whom she called "quite a handful", an expression Ingrid didn't need to have explained in order to understand. Suzanne had spent three days in Mariann's house, as arranged, before Mariann put her on the train to the capital, believing she would never hear from her again.

But within a week Suzanne had rung and said she had met a friend, she was staying with her now, looking after her children while waiting for a bedsit (?) and she had found a job in a factory that made curtains and bed linen and towels and paid a good wage.

Mariann suspected that Suzanne was laying it on a bit thick, she wrote, an expression Ingrid thought she had heard, but didn't understand in this context. But Suzanne sounded both happy and cheerful, she only had the snow in the streets to complain about, it was so heavy that the traffic had come to a standstill, and it slid off roofs onto people's heads, roof avalanches they were called.

But, and this was Mariann's main point, Suzanne didn't want to write to Ingrid until she had settled in (this is how she put it) in her own place (the bedsit?), until she had more to say than that she had just arrived safe and sound, Ingrid was so demanding.

Mariann concluded with news of the happiness in her own household, and of nine-month-old Ingrid, who had to go with her to work, where a secretary kept an eye on her while Mariann was teaching. Little Ingrid crawled about and was hyperactive (?), pulled books down from shelves and knocked over flowerpots.

Olav says hello. And here's Suzanne's address, so you can write to her yourself.

Ingrid made a mental note of the address and the new words, "demanding" in particular had made a great impression on her, and an idea struck her, she pulled out all the bureau drawers and piled them up on the dining table, emptied the cupboards and with Barbro's help manoeuvred the carcass up into the North Chamber, a rearrangement that felt both necessary and right, the bureau was perfectly positioned between the windows. She fetched the drawers and the contents of the cupboards, put them all back in place and sat on the bed wondering why this piece of furniture hadn't always been here, in life improvements are often only seen as such when they stare you in the face.

Ingrid didn't learn much Russian from the book from Archangel. But she pronounced the words in the middle line, and practised them, and the children never grew tired of the drawings. Kaja was enthralled by the interpretations Ingrid came up with when they read together, all those variations. Mathias was as critical as always, but wanted to go even further than Ingrid and added his own embellishments to the story. Ingrid decided that what she could do was to teach them the Norwegian alphabet.

It went like a dream.

The only slight snag was that Mathias insisted on using his left hand and objected when Ingrid forced him to write with his right on the brown paper she had cut up and made small notebooks out of, even though he wrote more neatly with his left hand than Kaja did with her right. The situation was complicated by the fact that in the course of only the last two months he had become an inseparable brother to Kaja, a true son in this family, it was as clear as daylight. And it was winter, it was dark. So, when Daniel came by next time, Ingrid left the children with Barbro and sailed over to the village with him.

Once there, she didn't go to see Markus in the shop, nor did she visit Pastor Samuel at first, which had been the original plan, instead she went to the library, which was in the other half of the storehouse, where the savings bank was. Sund, the former mayor, was the librarian as well as the bank manager, and handled the books with the same healthy scepticism with which he managed other people's money, however, he did allow himself to be persuaded by Ingrid and unlocked the library to show her an encyclopaedia.

Ingrid read that being cack-handed, or left-handed, as it is properly called, may cause problems for children, especially if they are forced to act against their nature. There then followed some unclear explanation of the difference between congenital and inherited left-handedness, which Ingrid couldn't make sense of, no matter how many times she read it.

At times, she had wondered whether to believe in God with a little more conviction or even trust in some other God that had a little more power than the official one. So, without even saying hello to Svetlana and thanking her for the book, she hurried off to meet Samuel, who seemed glad to see her and apologised for not visiting them this year.

He led her into his office and patiently listened to the mystery of Mathias' hands, could this have anything to do with his wretched origins, Ingrid asked.

The pastor's expression changed, and what was more he sat down behind his father's enormous desk.

My goodness, Ingrid, do you believe in original sin?

What?

Do you think, he said in an unnecessarily loud voice, do you think, my good woman, that children inherit the misdeeds and sins of their parents?

What? Ingrid said again, ashamed that she hadn't given this matter any thought, but also aware that she would have had problems getting to the bottom of it anyway.

Samuel seemed to realise what was going through her mind and said calmly: Leonardo da Vinci was left-handed. As were a multitude of other geniuses. Mathias may turn out to be a prodigy or he may be a very ordinary boy, normal, like most of us, a human being.

Ingrid was about to ask him who Leonardo da Vinci was, but instead she thought aloud, so the boy is not strange after all?

Strange?

Yes, he says that himself, and he *is* strange. At any rate, he has an imagination which . . . she couldn't find the right words, and told him about the Russian children's book and the stories which Mathias had embroidered on in wilder and wilder flights of fancy, and about how often he varied and adapted them, while Kaja wanted Ingrid's version repeated word for word.

That's quite something, the pastor sighed, in such a resigned tone that Ingrid took it personally and fell silent. As she stood in the unchanged study of Samuel's father. With all those reminders of the war, of when Ingrid had been here, assigning refugees to chairs and sofas. And of the time before the war, when she sat opposite old Malmberget and had difficulty understanding both his words and motives.

Now his son was sitting in the same chair with an expression befitting a meeting with his sorriest parishioner. Samuel said she should go home and let the boy be.

He had rebuffed her.

But Ingrid hadn't finished, what about Mathias' independence, at first he had clung to her like a kid to a goat, but now he has become more and more his own self, if I can put it like that.

And?

To Mathias, the bears in Svetlana's book were just as likely to kill as to dance. Mathias could take off his clothes in the middle of the day and want to have a nap, and then Kaja did too. What else? Well, yesterday he called Ingrid stupid because she had happened to mix up port and starboard.

The pastor laughed and asked if he still got seasick.

No, not even in bad weather.

Does he wet the bed?

Rarely, no more than Kaja.

Nightmares?

Less and less often, but then Ingrid had to switch on the light.

Light?

Yes, if he wakes up and is afraid, it's not enough to take him into the North Chamber and cuddle him, he says he has to have the light on and be able to see the whole room. So, Ingrid lights a lamp and he looks around, cautiously, as if he is counting everything inside the room, then he settles down and falls asleep again.

The pastor nodded reflectively and asked her if she loved the boy.

What sort of question was that?

Ingrid was on the point of mentioning Nelvy, but as usual she had difficulty uttering her name.

Well, everything's alright then, the pastor said.

Ingrid leaned back and looked around, recognised the lamp again, recognised the picture again, the same chandelier she recognised when she came in, the pattern on the same door.

She got up, said thank you without looking at him and walked down to the Trading Post, but couldn't find anyone to take her home. The sky above her was so very strange, so inscrutable and menacing, and yet perfectly still above the wind.

The staff came out of the Trading Post at the end of the working day and strolled two or three hundred metres up to their evening meals and beds, while Ingrid sat and stood on a windblown quay for an hour, and then another, with the ridiculous mystery of the words "congenital" and "inherited" churning around inside her, all she had to do was ask Svetlana for a bed for the night, but, no, here was a boat that could take her home, a fishing boat heading out to deeper waters.

Then it was a thrill to step ashore onto your own quay, to

come home after a bout of enormous mental exertion, home to Barrøy. She walked slowly, enjoying every step, up the slope to her house and into the porch and then the kitchen and during the evening meal reconfirmed that Mathias was eating with the knife in his left hand. For her, this was the second time he had come to the island. On the first occasion, he had been starving and couldn't speak. Now he was eating normally and talked with food in his mouth.

13

A month later the whole family sailed over to the village, one mild, peaceful Sunday morning. Ingrid had been up since five o'clock preparing breakfast and a packed lunch and getting their clothes and other essentials ready, and as soon as they had eaten, they walked down to the boat shed and put out the færing.

A gentle south-easterly, the land was white and the sea as green and clear as Kaja could wish for. She was sitting next to Mathias on two rugs in the forepeak, beneath sheepskins, the way Barrøy children always sit in a færing, while Barbro attended to the sheet-ropes and sail and Ingrid steered, progress was slow.

Halfway over the fjord, the wind dropped, and they had to use the oars, but still made it to the church service in good time, this was Barbro's day, her first public performance since October.

The eldest of the Storm daughters, Anna Karina, also sang in the choir, she was one of Mathias' aunts, for better or worse. Anna Karina was regarded as the family's least desirable proposition, and bore a certain air of having given up, a fate which befell a surprising number of well-to-do daughters when they reached the age of perdition, as it was called, between thirty-two and thirty-four, when everything on two legs in the way of husband material had been weighed and found wanting by those who did the weighing, the woman's family, by and large, on the basis of two criteria, the amount of money they had and their degree of stupidity. And the Storm family had come to the conclusion that they were probably stuck with Anna Karina, yes, probably, people said.

Ingrid hadn't come solely to listen to Barbro singing, but also to study folk's expressions when they set eyes on Mathias. So far only Johannes' old neighbour had seemed to recognise him and raised her eyebrows, but Gudrun was who she was, and fortunately there weren't too many of her kind.

Ingrid noticed that Anna Karina exchanged several whispered words with Barbro up on the podium, but never once glanced in the direction of the Barrøy pew, the third row, nor when the choir paraded down the central aisle singing "Lovely is the Earth", an idea at the end of the liturgy that Pastor Samuel must have come up with himself, or brought along from Paderborn, nor did she look at Mathias, even though Ingrid had moved him to the aisle end of the row to make him as visible as possible.

After the refreshing acid bath of a conversation about left-handedness, Ingrid had hoped to have a word with Samuel, so she accompanied the other churchgoers out of the white-walled temple in order to take her turn shaking the hand of the pastor, that famous handshake of his, this priest who was once again gauging the temperature of each one of them, forgetting no-one, the priest who exchanged trivial or profound words with high and low, answered questions, drew a few individuals aside for more serious discussions, though brief, as the queue was waiting, a personal communion between the lay and the learned, which had attracted more people to the church than ever before, in spite of all this peacetime and, one would have thought, a much reduced need for Our Lord.

When it was Ingrid's turn, she expressed her sincere gratitude for Samuel's enlightenment regarding left-handedness, stupid woman.

A comment Samuel didn't respond to, but smoothed over with a sympathetic smile, then he leaned over to the children, got right down on his haunches, so his gown crumpled up in the slush, and coaxed out of them first their names, and then their ages, and some shy nods, listened to Mathias describe how they had been allowed to steer the boat on the way over, and, when they'd had to row, how they had sat with the tiller between them. Samuel laughed more loudly than was strictly necessary, and each of them felt his heavy hand on their heads as he got to his feet again, as if supporting himself on them, like crutches, after which he looked at Ingrid once more, she was still standing there, mumbling almost inaudibly about whether she couldn't adopt Mathias, wasn't that far more reassuring and dependable than being a guardian?

The look on the pastor's face told her all she needed to know.

No, no, there's no rush, she quickly added, and Samuel nodded and turned to face the next in the queue.

Barbro was waiting at the wrought-iron gates with Svetlana and another woman, whom Ingrid didn't know, it was Lise, the pastor's housekeeper, a mild-mannered and well-rounded individual who claimed to have heard a lot about Ingrid. They nodded to each other, and Svetlana said something in Russian, laughed out loud at Ingrid's confusion and said the book she had sent her hadn't been much use, had it, so now she had a box for her.

Ingrid said wait a minute, drew Barbro aside and asked her what Anna Karina had said in the choir, I saw you two whispering.

Barbro thought for a moment and said Anna Karina had asked how things were going on the islands, how the children were.

Mathias?

No, the children.

Did she mention his name?

No . . . Barbro said.

Are you sure?

Barbro wasn't sure.

But you were talking a lot. I saw you.

Barbro smiled and said Anna Karina had praised her voice, perfect pitch.

Ingrid gave up and went back to Svetlana, who had sat down on her three-wheeler, a moped that had a carrier-board mounted above the front wheels, with side-fiddles, on top of the board stood an object resembling half a beer crate, from Mariann Vollheim in Trondheim. The lid had been nailed down, and Svetlana had no idea what it contained. But here are two letters, also from Mariann, and one from Fredrik in Lofoten. It was now March, winter was on the wane, and this was the first sign of life from the Karvika gang since they had left Barrøy.

The children were allowed to sit on Svetlana's carrier, she took them down to the shore while Ingrid and Barbro went to see Nelvy's grave, thought their thoughts and followed them down.

The sky was blue with a scattering of light clouds, the same gentle breeze from the south-east. They found a cosy inlet, shared their packed lunch with Svetlana and chatted until after it had got too cold, drew out the time even longer, loaded the crate on board, wrapped the children in sheepskins and sailed home at a leisurely pace.

14

The wooden crate turned out to contain eight litre-bottles of apple juice, packed in wood shavings and securely corked. And this wasn't concentrate, they found out after Ingrid, with a lot of effort, managed to twist a screw down into a cork and then prise it up with a crowbar.

It tasted heavenly, so sweet and fresh and delicious that Ingrid immediately knew they would have to ration it.

But there was something strange about both of her letters.

Mariann had again spoken to Suzanne on the telephone, she wrote, and had also received a letter from her in Oslo, here, I am enclosing it.

Ingrid read Suzanne's letter in the kitchen, she and Mariann had apparently become very close, and Ingrid's mind could now be put at rest, Suzanne had not moved into the "bedsit" after all, it was too small, she was sharing a two-room flat with a friend from Øvre Foss, walked every morning to her job in the factory and was having a great time. There was something about clothes and shoes and two restaurants, about dancing and having fun, in what Suzanne called her "leisure".

Suzanne clearly had a great deal of it, but she assured Mariann she worked overtime one evening a week and every other Sunday.

The main part of the letter, however, was about her concern for her son, Fredrik, who had written to her from Lofoten about a memorable day at sea because one of the crew had broken his arm and consequently Fredrik and Hans had had to help to do the splitting and fix the floats.

An experience which seemed to have frightened the wits out of him. They had been caught unawares by a storm, had to spend sixteen hours far out at sea, and he was covered in bruises and sores on his hands that wouldn't heal because of the salt and the wet. But, fortunately, Lars had managed to bring them back to land again, where for a time they'd had to call on an extra baiter because of their damaged hands.

So, they were baiting full-time? Ingrid wondered, what about school?

The *Salthammer* left the quay at four o'clock in the morning and didn't return until between six and twelve in the evening, when three men had to clean one or two or sometimes even four tons of winter cod before there could be any talk of sleep, preferably before they had to go to sea again.

But the baiters could sleep until six. When their terrible sores had healed, they managed three whole tubs, Fredrik wrote to his mother, in a mixture of clumsy block letters and normal handwriting, four pages. So, Mamma, you don't need to be worried.

But Suzanne did worry anyway, though not so much about their schooling, but why on earth write to Mariann Vollheim?

Second point: Fredrik's account of his adventures at sea, in all its artlessness, was probably a lot more accurate than the missives Ingrid had received – dry, lapidary notes about catches, no accidents, bye, Lars, and before Lars, bye, Hans, Ingrid's father. And before him, bye, Martin, Ingrid's grandfather.

The *Salthammer* was a robust ship, Ingrid knew, which accordingly meant that it was hardly ever laid up, sixteen, even eighteen hours at a stretch, in pitch darkness and ten degrees of frost, the sea breaking over open decks, the bilge pumps going nonstop, six days a week.

But she had to read about all this in a report not intended for her eyes, via Suzanne, via Mariann Vollheim, a circuitous route whose implications she was unable to fathom.

Straight after the meal she went up to the North Chamber where she re-read Suzanne's letter. And her state of mind wasn't improved when she finally opened the letter Fredrik had written to her. Dear Ingrid, it was a replica of Lars' terse style, good catches, good weather, bye, Fredrik, oh yes, Hans and Martin say hello too.

Had Fredrik written to Ingrid at someone else's behest?

At the direction of Lars and Felix, so that the womenfolk at home wouldn't fret?

At least that made sense.

Ingrid looked at the postmarks and did some simple mental

arithmetic. Yes, Fredrik had written to Suzanne more than a month before he wrote to Ingrid, perhaps before he was told to paint a rosy picture of their life in the fishing waters?

But at least it was some comfort, wasn't it?

We-ell maybe. Ingrid was sitting at the bureau in the North Chamber. The top right-hand drawer was locked, it was where she kept her letters, as well as birth certificates, marriage certificates, letters she had written but not sent, those she must have regretted writing, the ones that hadn't passed the writer's muster and therefore had to accept being laid aside, a record of second thoughts and regrets.

Here there were also letters she had received and not burned, children's drawings, conveyance deeds, grant of probate. But, oh, there was also a pile of receipts from various purchases she had made, which she now sat staring at while something began to stir deep in the recesses of her mind.

What was going on?

A receipt for a coat, bought after selling eider down at a good price. A sales chit for twelve and a half tons of cod. The purchase of herring nets, boat fuel, a pallet of slates . . . Had Ingrid Marie Barrøy really imagined that one day there would be cause to complain about a batch of Alta slates?

Ingrid looked down at the three recent letters, put them on the pile of important things, crumpled up all the unimportant things, thereby removing the rubbish from a private, locked drawer, then went downstairs and threw the lot in the stove with a feeling that she had achieved something useful, Ingrid liked this feeling, and did her best to seek it out, this feeling of achievement, but she still couldn't get away from a sense that she had lost something, Fredrik and Suzanne, had they turned away from her? And what about all the others?

The following morning, she was back at her bureau – outside it was raining, slanting down, hard – with paper and a pencil, replying to two letters, one to Mariann and one to Fredrik, almost in parallel. Neither of them caused her problems of any kind, thank you for the juice, everyone is well, spring is on its way, looking forward to seeing you again.

But there was still one unused address, Suzanne's, in Øvre Foss, Seilduksgata, Oslo. This was a harder nut to crack.

Ingrid realised that she would have to take the traditional approach and reel off the same, well-worn formulae, the winter formulae, some trivial and preferably euphemistic words about the terrible weather, the meagre catch she and Barbro had managed to hang on the drying racks this winter, shall we say a couple of hundred pairs, now that there are only two of us, we have to fish so close to land that we can keep an eye on the children, who had been told to stay in sight, but they don't, of course, we're in good health.

Ingrid erased the bit about the children staying in sight, added a more truthful remark about the weather, and her pencil took on a more conciliatory tone: the loss of Suzanne was huge, we miss you, all four of us. Ingrid finished off by saying she had recently received a letter from Fredrik, and as a result the boy's mother would be happy to know that he was having a great time in Lofoten, was getting on well with Hans and Martin and the twins, and the four of them were going to school and looking forward to returning home.

She rubbed out the bit about school and their looking forward to returning home too, and wrote that she really hoped Suzanne was doing fine, she thought about her all the time, as if she were her daughter, and hoped to hear from her soon.

But should she send it or leave it for later?

She left it, set about her daily chores, took a decision and sent all three letters with Daniel when he came by at the end of the week with coffee, sugar, flour, two trays of eggs and again some old newspapers from Svetlana. But there were no letters for Ingrid this time, and she was pleased.

15

They had spent the whole day preparing the houses for the eider ducks that once again would soon be waddling out of the sea, building their miraculous nests, laying their pale olive eggs and sitting on them until new life revealed itself beneath them sometime in May, June, baby chicks with only one thought in their heads: the sea.

Where is the sea? thinks the chick as it pokes its beak out, into freedom.

As a rule, it is downhill to the sea, perhaps they navigate with the help of gravity or else they are guided by the tail of their mother, who, emaciated and dutiful, waddles ahead of them.

The sea is their salvation.

Ingrid told Kaja and Mathias about this mysterious, annual ritual which human beings can set their watches by, it was a mixture of what we understand when we observe animals and what we make up about them.

Ingrid knew that she wasn't sticking to the facts, encouraged by Mathias' inexhaustible creativity, this is what we have to do, she thought, and we enjoy it and want to tell our children and grandchildren what we ourselves have learned and experienced, we are just doing the best we can for them.

What are grandchildren? Mathias said.

Eh? Ingrid said.

The weather was terrible – sleet, snow and the devil himself – but the gusts of wind had not been strong enough to prevent the children from going with her. Barbro was singing. Ingrid placed the slate on top of the eider houses, which were refurbished old fish crates, put straw and dry seaweed in them as the basic materials for what would become nests, or rather thrones, the thrones of queens. Ingrid rejected the children's pleas for her to sing along with them, she had no singing voice, listen to Barbro. But at least she could push them over into the cheerless, brown heather and hug them warm, and she acted the fool to such an extent that even Barbro had to roll her eyes.

Then home again, coats off in the porch and hallway, hooks to the left and right, port and starboard, into the kitchen. Hell, it's freezing in here! Light the stove, cook some food, four rationed glasses of apple juice, it's getting warmer, another jumper off, some more letters of the alphabet on the white sheets of paper Ingrid has managed to get her hands on, two crayons, while Mathias wonders whether eider ducks are as stupid as fish, fancy allowing themselves to be caught in these ramshackle houses.

Ingrid wants to say something wise about the difference

between being caught and being taken care of, eider ducks are man's (or woman's) most faithful friend, in summer tamer than a hen, in winter as wild as an eagle. But a flicker of light flits past the wet windowpane, from a Petromax lamp, there is a clatter in the porch, and in walks Pastor Samuel, beaming with joy and soaking wet, he kisses Barbro and Ingrid on both cheeks and shakes the children's hands. Ingrid insists that he hang his oilskins and reefer jacket above the stove, here, he can borrow a pair of socks, would he like a bite to eat?

Yes, he'd love a bite to eat.

Ingrid thinks he has come with a solution regarding the issue she mumbled to him outside the church a month ago, the answer that would bind Mathias' fate to Barrøy's once and for all. But Samuel has quite different reasons for coming, and says over a cup of coffee, that Ingrid no doubt knows he is not only a theologian but also a historian, and for that reason cannot spend his whole life on these fair shores without leaving his mark in written form.

No, Ingrid didn't know that.

He reins in his enthusiasm and seems to be considering how he can explain to a simple soul that life on the coast deserves to be chronicled and preserved for posterity.

Ha ha, no, how crazy is that, what nonsense has he got into his head now?

Samuel says that this coast is of great significance.

This is enough for Ingrid to look just as puzzled as before.

He regroups: How many tonnes of fish did you deliver to Vig last year?

Ingrid doesn't know.

Eleven, he says. That's what you Barrøyers dried and salted in the spring. Here on this one island. On top of that comes the whale meat and what the menfolk land in Lofoten in the course of the winter, in good years close to a hundred tonnes. Plus the herring and saithe. But eleven tonnes from one single island! Does Ingrid know how many islands there are like Barrøy?

No.

As I thought. Shall we say a thousand? Ten thousand? At least they are round numbers, ha ha. And does Ingrid know the kilo price of this fish in Italy, Portugal, Spain, the "bacalao" countries? In Hungary?

Ingrid hasn't thought much about the price of fish in Hungary.

Now she is told.

And it is shocking information.

Well, I'm blowed.

Ingrid laughs uncomfortably, a laugh which she usually emits when she is skating on thin ice.

Samuel deliberately introduces a solemn pause, which he utilises to eye the children playing on the floor, with a smile reserved especially for them.

Ingrid asks him if he would like some more coffee.

No.

Then he says "yes" after all and gets to the point: that idiot of a verger, Henriksen, the former chief of police, managed to burn his house down last autumn and, while he was at it, two parish registers, irreplaceable source material for a historian. For that reason, Samuel now has to travel around asking people to show him their documents and for permission to copy them.

Ingrid waits.

Samuel nods towards a large, black suitcase which came in with him and stands next to the log bin. He places it on the table, opens the lid and pulls out a camera, which looks expensive, a flash gun, a shutter release cord, a small tripod, and explains that he can't really tell people to hand over their birth and marriage certificates, but perhaps they will allow him to photograph them. He has already been around large sections of the village, and a score of islands, and people have been extremely cooperative, a few of them proud even.

Ingrid immediately sees her opportunity and acts as though she is considering his words, hesitates a little longer and then says she doesn't know what she has in the house, but promises to find out.

Well?

The pastor looks at her, waiting.

What? Now? Ingrid says in surprise. This minute?

Samuel heaves a sigh of frustration. Ingrid mumbles, well, alright, it might take a bit of time, actually it was something completely different she wanted to have sorted out, this adoption matter?

Aha, Samuel says, gets to his feet, fiddles with the camera, shows it to the children, opens the body, explains what's what and inserts a roll of film. But Ingrid stays in her chair with no plans to go upstairs and look for some old marriage certificates.

Samuel gives up and gestures to the children. Ingrid tells them to go up and make their beds, which normally they are not allowed to do without her being there as they would end up under the same eiderdown.

They run off, and Samuel says in an undertone that Olavia might be an obstacle, Olavia Storm Hartvigsen, who by all accounts is more alive than her missing husband, in which case Ingrid needs her consent. But this could possibly be solved by means of a missing-person announcement, formally and publicly, it should be time-limited, and if the person in question has not reported her existence before the deadline there might be a chance, via a statutory notice.

Ingrid knows what a statutory notice is.

And will the Storm family have any objections?

Samuel can't imagine they would, but says that just for safety's sake he can have a word with Anna Karina, whom he knows well, maybe he can get *her* to report her sister as missing.

And if the family already knows where she is?

Samuel smiles in acknowledgement, but believes this is highly unlikely and adds cryptically that in any case the war is too recent for Ingrid to expect any problems from that quarter, why the rush anyway?

To Ingrid this sounds promising. She doesn't mention either the boy's, Kaja's or her own feelings about this, the fellow will have to work all that out for himself, if he has eyes to see, over a long autumn and an even longer winter, she has hesitantly come to the conclusion that Mathias is no Nelvy, that Mathias is alive and will remain so, Ingrid is his mother and he can never leave Barrøy.

Samuel appears to recognise her determination and promises to look into the matter.

Look into the matter?

Ingrid glares a rather more binding commitment out of him, from her point of view, and makes Pastor Samuel promise to do his utmost to arrange the adoption.

Nonetheless, she drags it out a little longer, smiles at the children as they come downstairs again, at Kaja, who says she is too big to sit on Ingrid's lap, she has her own chair, oh, the significance of chairs in this house. And another delay: How is the pastor going to get back home? Maybe he would like to stay the night?

Samuel has met his match and smiles and says he would, the fishermen who dropped him off won't be back until late the following day.

Ingrid nods and says that Barbro can make up a bed in Suzanne's room, after which she goes up to the North Chamber, unlocks the right-hand drawer of the bureau and sorts the letters into one pile and the documents into another, puts back that which neither God nor man must set eyes on, locks the drawer and goes back down.

In the kitchen, Samuel is busy photographing the children, each standing on their own chair, Barbro between them, gets them to smile on command, to laugh on command, look serious, Mathias, lie down on the table and pretend you're dead, you too, Kaja.

Ingrid, too, is told to join the group, and stands beside Barbro with what might be termed a smile on her face. Next, Samuel mounts the camera on the tripod, points the lens down at the tabletop, attaches the shutter release cord and weighs it in his hand like a weapon. One by one, Ingrid arranges her parents' marriage certificate, birth certificates, grandfather's and grandmother's, her own, Lars', Kaja's … Most of them signed by Samuel's father, just a slightly different colour of ink, but the same florid handwriting, whereafter his son, Samuel, presses the button and immortalises them with bright flashes of light: godparents, dates, addresses, Barrøy's history, to the extent that it has left its imprint in official documents, in truth this isn't wonderful, in truth it is rather meagre, the pastor says suddenly, such lean pickings from all these lives, and it is precisely this which is the very stuff it is the historian's imperative to record, if Ingrid understands what he means.

But all this is unbridled joy for the children. Samuel lifts them onto the table to look through the lens with one eye and read signs and symbols they don't understand, but they marvel at their sharpness, the clarity, press the button, he says, press again.

After the last document has been photographed, he asks Ingrid if she has any letters to or from her parents, her grand-parents? From Lofoten?

Ingrid says she doesn't keep letters.

Samuel finds that hard to believe.

Ingrid puts on an appearance of being offended by his scepticism, and he seems to understand that once again he has reached the limit, Ingrid's limit.

He asks what time the children go to bed.

Ingrid takes Kaja and Mathias up with her and ensures that they sleep in their own beds, but after the spiritual experience in the kitchen this takes longer than usual. She reads aloud neither a Russian book nor *Three Little Pigs*, but tells them about an island in the sea where no-one lives, only birds, until eventually people arrive in a rowing boat and are amazed by how wonderful it is, they discuss all the things they can do with an island, what people in general can do with an island! This is grist to Mathias' mill, there is no limit to what you can do with an island, the imagination sets the only limits, as with the sea.

Ingrid rises early, lights the stove, washes, and then makes breakfast. Boils five eggs and puts them on the table with the pointed ends facing each other, so they resemble the petals of a flower.

Barbro gets up and comes downstairs and washes and they drink coffee. Ingrid slices some bread, Barbro fetches butter, rolled mutton sausage and brown cheese from the larder, lays the table.

Knives.

The children wake up and appear, in various degrees of dress, and Ingrid asks if they have slept well. They can't be bothered to answer.

But there is no sign of the pastor.

They have a priest sleeping in the house, for the first time in Barrøy's history, and he hasn't woken up.

They wait.

Ingrid asks if Kaja has used the chamber pot during the night. Yes.

Go up and get it and empty it you know where.

Kaja goes up, returns and walks into the yard with the pot, screaming her head off in the driving rain. Mathias has crawled up on the table to watch her through the window, laughs and gesticulates frenetically with his left hand.

Ingrid tells him to be careful not to knock the eggs onto the floor. Mathias sees them, moves back onto his chair and sits admiring them.

Kaja comes in and gives the pot to Barbro, who rinses it under the tap, dries it and hands it back. Kaja takes the pot upstairs, and Ingrid and Barbro eye each other, shrug, pull on their thick woollen jackets and go to the cow barn. They feed the animals, shovel the muck through the hatch, feel the stomachs of those cows with calf and return to the house.

One of the eggs has fallen on the floor.

Pastor Samuel Malmberget wakes up in a strange bed and has no idea where he is. Heavy spring rain pelts against the window and he decides to take this as a source of inspiration.

Where am I?

He is on one of the islands that some day he will write a book about, one of the thousands of islands whose importance he is slowly discovering. He falls asleep again and sees his father and all the brothers he has lost contact with, scattered to the four winds as they are, except for his eldest brother, who lives in Bergen, but, in his dream, they are gathered together as they were before, and they belong together, they are one.

Samuel wakes a second time beneath this caress of an eider-down and still doesn't know where he is.

But now at least he gets up and pulls on his clothes and walks into an empty room, steps into what the poor folk on the coast call a parlour. This is where the most precious objects they own are to be found, the finest furniture, chairs and tables they have made with their own hands, a cupboard they have inherited containing Polish porcelain behind two glass doors, pictures on the walls of people who are no more, curtains in front of the windows and a clock showing ten past ten.

16

Ingrid Marie Barrøy had finished thinking. She got up from the Bench and walked northwards, the long grass tickling her calves, soon it would have to be cut a second time, if the weather held, hopefully they could dry it in the field, it was too short to be hung on the racks. And it is worth noting that she didn't walk along the coast now, but through the gardens, and she didn't leap over the stone walls, as in her childhood, but went through the wicket gates, closed the third one behind her and was about to smile when her foot struck a rock. She bent down, picked it up, studied it, placed it on the nearest wall and walked on. If everyone who stumbles over a rock bends down, picks it up, studies it and places it on a wall, the walls will not only be kept intact but grow twenty centimetres a century, and the meadows will remain meadows. There are eight gardens on Barrøy and five stone walls.

II

17

The sea, this vitreous film enveloping the globe, has never been thinner, for the fifth day now, so the Barrøyers have decided to go on a "picnic", a term they have used before but which they now call a holiday, they are going on a holiday, to Træna.

It is not all wasted time. Lars and Felix have to fetch a winch from Træna, it might easily take a day or two, so what could be more natural than for the whole island to go along in the recently overhauled *Salthammer*, as the radio on board has announced that the wonderful weather will continue. But an island cannot be left unpopulated, so they have drawn straws to decide who will stay at home to look after the animals. And Barbro has drawn the short straw. Barbro is not going on holiday. She was not the only one to react negatively to this outcome, Lars in particular would have liked to take his mother with him, to enjoy the good food and abundant laughter, only people who have experienced the fury of the sea at its worst know how to appreciate it when for once it takes a breather.

But the result is not negotiable. Ingrid, after intense

deliberations as to whether she should offer Barbro her place, has come to the conclusion that in that case Kaja and Mathias would also have to stay at home, which is inconceivable, given the way they are looking forward to this, and it was equally impossible to send them off without a mother. This was a dilemma that was so agonising that she gave up thinking about it out of pure exhaustion.

They emerge from the old house and the newer one in Karvika in two separate columns and march down towards Noah's Ark. Leading the way is eight-year-old Oskar, who ventures the first critical step down from the quay to the gunwale, using a ladder with three wooden rungs that Felix has knocked together for the occasion, and stands there looking triumphantly up at the rest of the gathering.

Note those unruly locks of his, which his mother Hanna can't bring herself to cut, as they are unique in the family, it is also a cheering thought that later in life he will be remembered not only for his curls but for how sociable he became after he learned to talk, a likeable lad who was quick to learn, a boy no-one sneers at any longer.

The next person to set foot on the gunwale and be welcomed on board with a solemn bow by Lars – he is wearing a tie and a waistcoat and stands there to guide them down one by one onto the newly oiled deck – is Kaja, the princess of the island.

Like Oskar, Kaja has one year of successfully completed schooling behind her and is a sartorial replica of her mother, unfortunately this means in Ingrid's drab costume from when she was eight, clothes she has moved in and out of cupboards and drawers over the years, waiting for a golden opportunity like this. The girl looks as if she is in mourning, but her outfit is nonetheless the prettiest the Barrøy family owns, and Kaja is in no doubt about her status as "Uncle" Lars gallantly helps her down onto the deck so she can stand next to Oskar and form a reception committee for the expectant crowd still waiting on the quay.

First some hampers of food are handed over, an enormous pot of lobscouse, rugs, blankets, sheepskins, more food, before the next holidaymaker is allowed on board.

This is Mathias Barrøy, also eight years old, Ingrid's son since October last year, when the adoption papers were finally agreed, he too has completed one year of schooling, more successfully than Kaja, this well-adjusted boy, whose origins most people have forgotten, Mathias is one hundred per cent Ingrid's and has lived on the island for more than three years without causing problems of any kind.

Mathias acts as if he doesn't need the solemn assistance of the skipper, so Lars quickly withdraws his hand and lets the boy place his left foot in front of his right, until he almost loses his balance, whereupon Lars lifts him above his head with an elegant flourish and puts him down next to Kaja, where he stands wondering what impression his entrance has made, reconciles himself to the fact that he is after all among friends, even including Oskar, who is clinging rather too much to Kaja, causing Mathias to keep threatening to do him in, but these are for the most part empty phrases, and returned in kind.

The other Barrøyers are ready to board.

Suzanne is home on holiday in new town clothes, which she refuses to change for the "rags" Ingrid wants to foist on her before they go into the cow barn. Suzanne is not going into the cow barn, she might at a pinch rake some hay and cook some weird food and tell her she is pregnant.

Suzanne no longer lives with her friend in Øvre Foss in Oslo, but with a certain Bjørnar, until they can climb another rung up the prosperity ladder, she and Bjørnar are on the waiting list for a three-room flat in a housing cooperative, with running water and central heating, at a development where Bjørnar is on "dugnad", as it is called, doing unpaid work as part of a local community scheme, together with several hundred others, after his normal work. Bjørnar has already invested six hundred hours in this building enterprise, where they will move in a year or two, hopefully not too long after the baby is born.

Needless to say, Suzanne has no objection to being helped down onto the deck.

Bjørnar, however, has. Lars makes no attempt at gallantry in his case, but uses the opportunity to attend to something in a knife-holder on the gunwale.

Bjørnar is a burly bear of a man, a digger operator, who has spent the first week of his stay here drinking spirits he brought with him and looking down his nose at the local population, an attitude that changed when the grass-mowing got into full swing and he revealed himself to be a slumbering workhorse who was more than willing to don the old rags worn by the island's forefathers. He even worked barefoot, got up with Lars and Felix when the dew fell at three or four in the morning and good-humouredly allowed himself to be made fun of because he couldn't handle a scythe, but he didn't give up, and actually passed the husbandry test with flying colours, eventually, not least because he distinguished himself as the most courteous man anyone could imagine confronted by a character like Suzanne.

Now Bjørnar clambers aboard unaided in a white shirt with rolled-up sleeves, trousers with a crease, and a suitcase, joins the others on the deck and wraps his arm around his sweetheart.

A suitcase on board the *Salthammer*?

Yes, that is how far things have come.

The last time the *Salthammer* had transported a suitcase was during the war, and the suitcases then contained all that remained of the Finnmark refugees' possessions, but the war has been forgotten.

The idea that a suitcase on board a boat should bring bad luck in the same way as brown cheese, heart-shaped waffles, the sound of whistling and so on, all that kind of thing also no doubt disappeared with the war, it is superstition.

*

Then there is a kerfuffle in the queue. Hanna and Felix's twin girls can't agree on who should go first. They are teenagers with budding bosoms under overly tight dresses and pouting mouths, they don't consider this journey any more exciting than milking a cow or bottle-feeding a lamb. But Anna pushes Sofie so close to the edge of the quay that there is no way back. Lars grabs Sofie around the waist like the child she is and lifts her down amid her squeals of disapproval.

But now, of course, Anna is left standing alone on the quay. And insists on boarding the boat unaided. She rejects Lars' hand and climbs down onto the deck without attracting much attention, allies herself with her sister and they are free to make their way to the foc's'le and sit in the sun below the harpoon gun with their backs turned to those still boarding and start a whispered conversation that none of the others are allowed to hear.

As for Hanna, well, her clothes have become brighter since she returned from Lofoten, after her winter visit there a few years ago. Meeting the family again had not lived up to expectations, it was said this had something to do with her mother, whom Felix describes as an old battleaxe. So Hanna has felt more at ease on Barrøy, no longer resigned or easily offended, and last winter she did some offshore fishing with Ingrid and managed to hang a considerable number of tail-tied fish before the men returned from Lofoten and could act as if they weren't impressed.

Hanna has been on board a boat before and performs the least dramatic embarkation so far, carrying a basket in one hand, filled with food and clothes, and a Bible in the other, but doesn't join the others on deck and goes straight down to the cabin she and Ingrid had scrubbed from top to bottom the day before, all the cabins are provided with aired woollen rugs and blankets, pillows even.

Selma will soon be the shortest on the island as one youngster after the other outgrows her, she is small and neat in a flowery dress, still with cascading fair hair, and hardly has a foot on the gunwale before Lars seizes her around the waist and swings her in elegant waltz-time down onto the deck, where she giggles and brushes the hair from her face, and Ingrid passes a basket down to her, which she immediately takes with her into the galley.

What about Barrøy's menfolk?

They are growing in number and are already on board. Felix is standing with Hans and Fredrik on the wheelhouse roof watching the farewells from aloft, leaning over the railing with the white tarpaulin. Whalers also have a helm on the roof of the wheelhouse, from which the skipper manoeuvres the boat when they are on the hunt for whales, while two or three of the crew are stationed in the crow's nest, fifteen metres above, but of course no-one is there yet.

Martin is in the wheelhouse, this thirteen-year-old boy, leaning out of the lowered window, skipper-style, waiting for the signal from Lars. Which means that only Ingrid is left on the quay, Ingrid and Barbro.

Ingrid hesitates, not that she needs a hand to climb on board, so Lars places his hand on the small stepladder ready to pull it away, does Ingrid need it? as he turns to the wheelhouse and yells at Martin to start the engine.

Martin disappears from the window, the engine roars. Ingrid shouts to Barbro that they won't be away for more than two days, three at the most, as if she hasn't heard all this before. Barbro goes over, lifts the stern hawser and stands there with it in her hand, shouts to the men on the wheelhouse roof, should she chuck it in the sea?

Fredrik climbs down, catches the rope and coils it while trying to find some suitable parting words for Aunty Barbro, but, failing, he valiantly smiles up at her instead, Barbro doesn't smile back, she turns and walks past Ingrid to the front of the boat, where she picks up the bow hawser and bellows at the girls below the harpoon gun to stir their stumps and catch it.

After some hesitation Sofie gets up, sulkily grapples with the rope, but is unable to control it until Anna comes to her aid. They both tussle with the hawser until they can more or less manage it, but before that happens Ingrid has swung herself on board under her own steam carrying the kitbag. Martin engages the clutch, edges the boat away from the quay and sets a course seawards, while the passengers assemble at various visible places on the deck or the boat's superstructure and wave to Barbro, who grows smaller and smaller and doesn't wave back, but turns and walks up to the house as if she has urgent matters to see to, the hay has been brought in, it has dried in the field this year, and is lying in the barn, almost green, the sheep are on the islets, the cows have been separated from the calves, and no milking needs to be done for six hours.

18

The Trænfjord sea is calm and vast. Only a few lazy puffins shatter the illusion that the *Salthammer* is ploughing through air and not water. The girls below the harpoon gun have wrapped themselves in blankets, but now throw them off and pull up the hems of their dresses to get the sun on their legs and arms as they lean against the base of the gun and close their eyes without speaking to each other.

Ingrid and Hanna are lying on their rugs on the foc's'le and have also pulled up their skirts. Lars and Bjørnar are sitting on the wheelhouse roof enjoying a dram. Lars is explaining and pointing while Bjørnar smokes and every so often he says that he really hadn't expected this idyll, force-fed as he has been with Suzanne's tales of woe from her childhood in hell. Lars smiles and says, well, it isn't exactly like this all year round.

But Bjørnar can't imagine that. And, in fact, neither can Lars, miracles are what they are, however well you might know a place.

On the bait-house roof four young men are sitting around a pack of cards, which Bjørnar has brought with him, he is a keen bridge player, but he hasn't managed to teach them the game yet, so they are playing whist and trying to explain the rules to Oskar. They would have preferred to have Mathias or Kaja join them, because the two of them know how to play, but they have other matters on their minds.

They have asked if they can climb up the rigging, first Ingrid says no, then Lars, but they still have a foot on the lowest ratline, on either side of the boat. The rigging is as strong as iron, but they have to walk along the outside of the gunwale to reach the rope-rungs. And all is well as long as Ingrid's eyes are closed. They take a step up, and one more, smile at each other across the deck, daring each other to go higher, the third rung, the fourth, the seventh, until Ingrid opens her eyes and screams at them, come down this minute, right now.

At least this stops them in their tracks, but they are so high up that they are out of Ingrid's reach. In addition, she has to make the impossible choice between helping her son or daughter, and instinctively strides towards the rigging where Kaja is, even though Mathias is nearer.

Felix also realises what is going on as he emerges from the galley with a cup of coffee. He puts it down on the hold hatch and calmly climbs up after Mathias and stands behind him on the lower ratline, encapsulating him, and says, aren't you scared?

Mathias whispers no.

Ingrid has performed the same manoeuvre on the port

side, wrapping her body around Kaja, and calculates the distance down to the deck, three metres, four?

Leave 'em be, Lars calls from the wheelhouse roof.

Ingrid shakes her head.

Felix asks in a whisper whether Mathias dare go higher. Mathias nods and slowly clambers up, three more rungs. Felix follows. On the port side, Ingrid guides Kaja in the opposite direction, more slowly, to Kaja's angry protests, she wants to climb as high as Mathias, but to deaf ears. Ingrid gets some assistance from Hanna, who, at the right moment, grabs the little one by the waist and swings her around the rigging and down onto the deck.

Ingrid laughs with relief, but stays where she is watching Mathias and Felix, who have climbed up a few more rungs and now find themselves six, seven metres above the gunwale. Mathias lets out a triumphant shriek, his knuckles are white. Felix tells him to move one hand after the other onto the shroud, the mast stay, a true whaler doesn't hold the rigging but the shroud, you're a big lad now, it's just like at home, you don't crawl up the stairs, you hold on to the banister.

Mathias does as instructed, with even whiter knuckles, his body is trembling, he defies Ingrid's ever louder screams and scales three more rungs. Felix whispers that they should pause and get accustomed to the height, it's still five or six metres up to the crow's nest.

Are we going right to the top? Mathias manages to stutter.

Felix laughs and says it's a bit too soon for that, but we can stay here for a while.

Ingrid is back on the deck and has adopted her hands-on-hips stance, she screams again, come down now, for Christ's sake, d'you hear me, Felix!

Hanna shouts too, but not so loudly.

Can *you* hear what they're saying? Felix whispers.

Mathias smiles and dares to look down at these people who are now no more than small faces and narrow shoulders, standing on a deck shaped like the sole of a shoe. He steers his gaze out across the sea and once again up at the prized crow's nest.

Felix says he wants to show him something and shouts down to the card players on the bait-house roof, they have taken a break to enjoy the drama on the rigging. Martin is told to find a sinker stone and throw it into the sea, a white stone.

Martin clambers down and goes into the bait house, re-emerges with a light-coloured stone and holds it up with an enquiring expression. Felix shouts yes, that'll do, and whispers to Mathias:

Now watch carefully.

Martin walks over to the windlass and throws the stone. It breaks the surface of the water with a splash, but doesn't sink. It floats, swaying from side to side, like a feather in the air.

Felix explains that they don't go to the crow's nest just to see far into the distance but also to look *down*, from up here the sea doesn't behave like a mirror, you can see a kilometre into the water.

Mathias nods solemnly.

And the stone isn't moving. He can't take his eyes off it. Slowly it becomes greener, and also slightly smaller, but it doesn't move or sink. It turns even greener and darker and is still there. The *Salthammer* begins to hover, in the air.

Mathias is dizzy and has to vomit.

Close your eyes, Felix says.

Now you can open them again.

The stone has disappeared and the *Salthammer* is no longer hovering but locked in the firm embrace of the ocean. Mathias smiles, impressed.

What was *that*?

Felix says that now he's learned something important, is he frightened?

Not anymore.

Then let's go back down, and hold on to the banister, not the stairs.

Mathias takes one painstaking step after the other, encapsulated by Felix, down to the gunwale, where he is snatched and lowered onto the deck by Ingrid and hugged for much too long, until he is left in peace and can shake with euphoria. Ingrid glares at Felix, who takes his cup of coffee and praises the boy so that everyone can hear, to applause from the young ones, Idiot, from Hanna, who goes into the galley to help Selma with the cooking. Kaja asks Mathias what he saw and for once he is lost for words.

Felix pulls on some leather gloves and climbs up the rigging once more, like a cat, leaps into the crow's nest and is lost from view. His head bobs up again, they can see him outlined against a solitary cloud, and can feel the *Salthammer* swaying, the mast is a pendulum in the sky. Felix is holding a tin box, which he lowers to the deck, they watch it and see another pendulum in the works of a gigantic clock, hear him calling to them to refill his coffee cup and put it in the tin box, a bit of cake wouldn't go amiss either.

But the tin box and the rope hit the deck before anyone can react, amid wild screams.

Shark! Shark! Basking shark!

And a torrent of obscenities, which the young men on the wheelhouse roof laugh at and whose significance only Lars understands. Bjørnar realises at least that he has to get out of the skipper's field of sudden, frenetic energy, and sneaks down onto the deck, where the young ones are gathering around the mast and shout up:

What? Where . . . ?

Felix's outstretched arm points to starboard, more swearing, Lars pulls at the levers, full throttle, the *Salthammer* tilts to one side, straightens up and steams ahead towards something no-one can see.

I've got her, Lars mumbles, and shouts: Is she a big 'un?

This is enough for the man in the crow's nest to haul himself over the edge, he slides down the outside of the rigging, in his boots and gloves, jumps onto the foc's'le, pulls Sofie and Anna away and tears open the ammunition box while bawling at Hans: Harpoon! Harpoon! Shark!

Hans runs into the bait house and returns dragging a one-and-a-half-metre-long monster weapon with a section of wire cable attached to a wrought-iron eye in the middle. Felix opens the end of the harpoon gun and loads the cartridge, slams it shut, tightens the wing nuts, swings the gun around and inserts the harpoon in such a way that the cable is hanging out of the barrel.

In the meantime, Lars has ordered Hans up onto the wheelhouse roof and races down to the deck, rips the tarpaulin from the winch, takes a roll of cable and passes one end to Felix, who snaps the shackles together and turns the gun around again. Lars coils the other end of the cable around the winch, tests the handles and clambers back onto the wheelhouse roof, where, from this critical moment on, he stands instructing Hans while Felix returns to the crow's nest.

Shell-shocked, Suzanne asks what is going on.

Ingrid knows, she is furious and has repeatedly shouted that they are on holiday, for God's sake, but nobody pays any attention to her.

You're not going to shoot a whale now, are you?

The basking shark is not a whale but indeed a gigantic shark.

It is not shot in the back with a cold harpoon, neither is it drained of its blood in ten minutes, to be dragged on board, dead, after an exhausting struggle. With a shark, a harpoon is shot right through the fish, the barbs end up forming a kind of T on the other side and the animal is hauled in with raw power, by means of a winch and an engine.

Unfortunately, Ingrid knows this too.

Lars tells Hans to slow down. The *Salthammer* glides slowly forward, those on the deck stare with bated breath in the direction the boat is heading. Martin is the first to spot the creature, the dorsal fin that cuts slow, gentle curves through the surface of the water, a keel against the distant sky, two or three hundred metres ahead. Lars estimates its trajectory and speed and orders Hans to change course and accelerate.

Over there.

Felix signals with both arms. Yes.

Lars tells Hans to change course again. And now the young man is beginning to get irritated with his father. Lars takes the hint and nods, your responsibility, from now on, and I mean it. Hans opens the throttle, and the *Salthammer* surges forward but not towards the shark.

Lars grunts his approval.

Hans slows down and peers up at the crow's nest where Felix is giving directions with only one arm. They hold their breath. Ten long minutes later, the *Salthammer* crosses the course of the shark fin, a hundred metres ahead.

Hans eases back the throttle without Lars needing to say anything.

They turn and watch the shark glide slowly into their wake, they see it veer to the side and hesitate, at first once, then again, until it decides to follow the boat.

We've got her, Lars mumbles.

Hans steers gently forward, gradually changing course and begins to cut a huge circle in the sea, he completes a whole circuit to encouraging nods from his father. Describes a slightly smaller circle. The boat and the shark are in a round dance on the sea, following each other in ever decreasing circles until they find themselves at either end of a diametrical line of less than a hundred metres.

Now, Lars whispers, unable to restrain himself.

Hans turns the boat and heads for the shark at full throttle.

Felix swings himself over the edge of the crow's nest, slides down onto the deck and glares furiously at Ingrid, who has failed to move the children out of the way. Suzanne has sought refuge in the cabin, the twins stand with their mother in the galley doorway. Oskar is sitting on the console in the wheel-house with his hands over his ears. While the holiday guest, Bjørnar, is wise enough to know he has to stay at the stern, where he lights another cigarette in the certain knowledge that he is about to experience something unimaginable.

What about Ingrid?

Ingrid is standing alongside a petrified Kaja and an undaunted Mathias in the middle of the deck and is the slowest to react. Trying in vain to catch Lars' eye on the wheelhouse roof, trying to communicate with Felix, who is standing with his back to her, behind the harpoon gun, legs apart, ready to fire.

A rendezvous at sea. The *Salthammer* glides slowly forwards to the broadside of a shark, a six-or-seven-metre-long beast, now they can see it in the crystal-clear water, six tonnes? Eight?

Again, Ingrid tries to meet Lars' eyes, but he is on the way down to the deck. Hans disengages the clutch. Lars is by the winch, he just has time to send Ingrid a resigned glance before the roar of the gun shatters the quietest day of the year.

A monumental shower of water in front of the bow. Lars starts the winch, screams up at Hans – who has been joined by Fredrik on the wheelhouse – full speed astern.

Sea and blood wash over the deck. Every nail in the *Salthammer* quivers. Everything movable clatters. The engine thunders. The *Salthammer* buries its bow in the seething water. The girls have slammed shut the galley door and Bjørnar sticks another fag in the most disbelieving gob he will ever exhibit.

Drenched to the skin by the deluge, Lars winches in one metre of cable after the other. The bow rises again. Felix climbs onto the gunwale with an iron bar and uses the slack in the cable to lever it from one hawser-hole into the next and from there into a third. The tremors don't subside until the fish is right up against the side of the boat. Then they increase in strength and the *Salthammer* heels to one side again.

Felix takes over the cable and the winch. Lars climbs up into the wheelhouse, disappears and reappears with his Krag rifle, fires two shots into the foaming water. Then another. He raises an arm to Hans, who disengages the engine.

A soaked and stunned crowd approaches the starboard railing. Felix reels in a few more metres of cable and they look down at the almost-eight-metre-long monster, a leviathan weakly flapping its fins and drowsily rolling from side to side, and Lars fires another shot.

Oskar has come down on deck.

You shot her in the nose.

Lars laughs and says that's where the blighter's brain is.

He sends a nod of acknowledgement to the young ones on the wheelhouse roof and tells them to come down and take over, it is their turn, focuses his gaze on the man from the city and asks him where he keeps his hard stuff.

Bjørnar goes down to his suitcase in the cabin and reappears with his wife and a full bottle, pulls out the cork and flicks it into the sea, takes a good slug and swears, impressed at what he has witnessed. Lars takes a swig and passes the bottle to Felix, who gulps his way down to well below the label and holds out the bottle teasingly to Hans, who sticks out a hand two or three times before Felix takes pity on him. Hans drinks and splutters and passes the bottle back to Bjørnar, whereupon Lars reasserts his authority, this wonderful giving of orders, which is no longer necessary when all the cogs are running smoothly, but it is a joyous ritual.

19

Ingrid is still in a state of shock, but realises that the show-down with Lars and Felix will have to be postponed, perhaps for ever, there are other matters to see to.

She wrenches the soaking wet, bloodstained clothes from the children and tells them to dry off in the sun on the foc's'le, from where they can study the art of handling a dead shark while she herself stands stiff and ill at ease and notices something new in Kaja's eyes, doubt?

Fredrik and Martin tie a rope around the tail fin of the creature and attach it to the rearmost rope cleat, hoist the fish as high as they can with a cable, the white belly facing upwards. Hans slices it open with a flat scythe blade lashed to a boat hook, a clean cut from the gills to the anus, so that the liver can spill out, the enormous liver of a basking shark, which is worth more per kilo than cod, haddock, whale or anything else. This liver constitutes almost a quarter of the fish's body and contains glycerine, which is sold at sky-high prices to people who know a lot about how to make perfume and dynamite, somewhere in the south of the country.

They fetch the basket from the hold and mount it on the crane. Hans operates the winch while Fredrik and Martin guide the basket down into the belly of the fish, so Felix can cut off one piece after the other, these are then lifted amid a wild swarm of squawking birds and dropped into six herring barrels and eight re-bunged line tubs, which are lowered one by one onto the ballast block in the hold. All while Lars struts around like a whinnying beast of prey enjoying this, the sight of youth at work in all its glory.

Felix calls for more line tubs, bungs them up, there might be a thousand litres, maybe eleven hundred.

What are they going to do with the carcass?

The carcass is not hoisted aboard despite some light-hearted comments about sending it to China since basking shark meat is full of uric acid and tastes foul. They finish the butchering process, loosen the ropes and pull out the harpoon. The whole crew leans over the side and sees the monster lying motionless like a white stone in the sea, watching as it turns ever greener and darker, and then even greener and smaller, until it is swallowed up by the planet.

In Træna they load the winch at four o'clock in the morning. Lars is up in the village, making enquiries over the telegraph line, returns and says they have to go to Røst to sell the liver.

They sail to Røst on yet another calm day and drift into Glea, where they see, as expected, a basking shark boat from

Hareide with an all-white crow's nest, in contrast to the black band around the middle of the crow's nest on whalers.

Lars and Felix take Bjørnar and the last bottle of spirits with them when they go ashore, board the Hareide boat, talk to the Sunnmøre folk for just short of an hour, after which they return contented.

However, by then the Barrøyers are either sitting on the foc's'le or have sought refuge on land because of the stench, in the course of the rolling trip across the sea this precious gunge has become pure oil, and stinks worse than, well, shite.

But the Vestlanders are not affected by bad smells, they have tanks on board, and pay in ready cash. And the *Salthammer* steers its bow south again, after a short visit to the local Fishermen's Rest, where everyone is served a dish of lobscouse and crispbread. They make a few purchases before heading back to Vestfjorden again. They hose down the deck and the hold. The pumps are going, they rinse everything down again, leaving behind a wake of blood and stench that attracts killer whales and dense swarms of birds, puffins, hawks, petrels, gulls . . . But not even a killer whale can rouse Lars. He is asleep in the chart room behind the wheelhouse. Felix is sleeping in his wife's arms in the cabin. And on the wheelhouse roof Hans and Fredrik are showing Mathias and Kaja how to steer a whaler home.

Ingrid is sitting with the twins on the foc's'le, handing out juice made from apples in a garden in Trondheim, which she is sent every year. The girls still cling to Ingrid, often without having anything to ask or tell her.

They haven't now, either.

Ingrid asks them whether they themselves have knitted the pretty socks they are taking off, but even such a simple question as this can be met with reluctance. Of course, Ingrid knows this.

Being children, they did all they could to be like each other, with such success that even Barbro and their own brother had difficulty telling them apart. Now it seems as if they *don't* want to be like each other, to no avail.

They are above average at school, by and large in the same subjects, apart from drawing and arithmetic.

Ingrid has begun to look upon the twins as different individuals, since this is evidently what they want, but don't know how, nor does Ingrid actually. What, however, she does know is that she can see herself in them and that it is easier for her than the others to smile when Hanna tries to get them to go into the cow barn or into the fields with a rake. Selma says openly that she is glad she doesn't have any daughters and Ingrid might have had the same thought had it not been for Kaja, who is beyond any such speculation.

Sofie is good at arithmetic. Anna is good at drawing.

A future accountant and a future artist?

Ingrid hasn't thought along these lines, but there is certainly one difference, in addition to features the others have also noticed and responded to accordingly: Sofie has a slightly crooked upper tooth whereas Anna the illustrator gets her way as a rule and is the leader and spokeswoman for a population of two. Ingrid asks if she has brought her drawing materials along.

Nope.

Ingrid has two of Anna's drawings on the wall in the North Chamber, one of the Swedes' boathouse with an eider duck in a nest between the posts and one of the old wheelhouse in the southernmost garden looking somewhat out of place in the swaying grass. A wheelhouse on land, one that washed up here in a storm and has been used to play in by two generations of children.

But it is neither the eider nor the wheelhouse that has given Anna's work such a prominent place in Ingrid's North Chamber; it is the extraordinary sense of movement in the grass and the magical play of shadows in the eider ducks' plumage, techniques Anna hasn't been taught anywhere, but which cause the observer to look and look again and to continue to stare in wonderment, it seems to be alive, it seems to be art, where does all this come from?

Her teacher in Havstein, on the other hand, is not so enthused by these drawings, he thinks Anna has a "flawed style", trained illustrator as he is, so Anna has given up pursuing her talents at school. However, every year Felix brings her some drawing materials from Lofoten, she keeps at it on Barrøy, where praise for her skill is all the greater, giving rise to a certain envy on the part of Sofie, who doesn't think so much more fuss should be made of a "flawed" drawing than an accurate calculation.

Ingrid says it is a shame, if Anna had brought her materials, she could have drawn the revolting shark, which Ingrid still has her doubts about, even though no-one has made a comment, not that this makes the situation any better.

Nah, Anna smiles, but adds she has drawn a picture of her little brother, Oskar, with his blond curls, which makes him furious, because he looks so odd, he claims, while Felix says it looks uncannily like him.

Ingrid suggests she draws a portrait of her too.

Anna eyes her sceptically.

I mean it, Ingrid says. Anna should draw everyone on Barrøy.

Sofie scoffs at this idea and Ingrid is about to say something about the importance of being able to do calculations, but is interrupted by a voice from above, it is Felix, who is now awake and is on the rigging again, he signals to Ingrid that she should climb up on the opposite side, he wants to show her something.

What, Ingrid shouts.

He shushes her.

Ingrid warily gets to her feet and climbs as high as she dares in the port rigging and looks across at him. Felix points down behind her, Ingrid turns and stares down into the crystalline depths and sees whales, three gigantic finback whales frolicking around the boat, all bigger than the *Salthammer*, as well as a slightly smaller fourth whale, blue planets twisting and turning, as smoothly and soundlessly as birds in the air.

Ingrid clings to the rigging, watches as Felix smiles, and asks him in a hushed voice if they are intending to shoot them too.

Felix shakes his head, they weigh forty tonnes, maybe fifty, the minke whale they hunt is a herring compared to these.

Ingrid asks whether these monsters can topple a boat, toss this eggshell of a ship over the horizon.

Felix shakes his head again. And Ingrid's gaze caresses these wonderful creatures, six of them now, she feels the boat rise and hover, the chilling sensation and the tears, for she will never see this again, life is too short, she knows this, as she also knows that she won't be able to keep anything for ever, nothing.

She sees the disaster before it strikes, she sees the end of all things, life's fragility. Ingrid has become weak, not from war or life's tribulations or the loss of love and Alexander, but from being a mother, another tremulous spectre that the ocean reveals to her.

Now Fredrik, too, has discovered the whales and is transfixed too, at the helm on the wheelhouse roof. Down on the foc's'le sits Suzanne beside Bjørnar, the digger operator, staring equally spellbound into the deep, next to them the twins, Sofie looking up at Ingrid with panic-stricken eyes, as if to ask whether they are going to sink, Anna seems to be sobbing.

Hanna has scrambled up the starboard rigging and positioned

herself next to Felix, looking as if she is praying. Ingrid feels the rigging shake and a hand on her calf, Martin and Hans scurry past her like cats and pull themselves over the edge of the crow's nest. Lars is standing motionless on the hold hatch, this skipper on a grain of sand, then silently makes his way to the cabin and fetches Selma, who is dumbstruck as the sight meets her eyes, the most incredible creatures on earth quietly cavorting around the ship, they see the sun playing on their fins and tails, they see eyes and white bellies, one of them blows only a few metres from the bow, emitting a cosmic blast that forces Ingrid to thrust back her head and close her eyes.

She opens them again and another whale blows. Now Fredrik, too, has climbed up into the crow's nest and sits on the board at the back with his arms around the top of the mast. Fredrik has disengaged the engine without the skipper's knowledge, Fredrik has left the helm without permission, the *Salthammer* is rudderless, Kaja also touches Ingrid's ankles and creeps in between her mother and the rigging, as though all is forgotten.

Mathias is standing on the port gunwale clutching a boat hook, lets it go and balances his way along the side like an acrobat, looking by turns down at the monsters and up into the rigging with a smile Ingrid has never seen before and knows she will never see again. She moves her lips and mouths inaudible words. Mathias vaguely nods back as if to seal a pact, jumps down onto the deck and climbs onto the wheelhouse roof, where he stands like a man at the abandoned helm, but doesn't touch it, nor the clutch or the levers, in a crowd of fourteen people there is always one person who doesn't understand, but on this day there is no-one.

III

20

Then Olavia Hartvigsen turns up again, dead. Olavia Hartvigsen died of a viral infection at a hospital in Aachen, in North Rhine Westphalia, West Germany. Her husband, now a widower, Ottmar Ehrlich, served during the war as a Stabsfeldwebel billeted on an island in the north of Festung Norwegen. Now he is making arrangements to have the body returned "home", as he writes in a letter to the Storm family, in surprisingly good Norwegian.

Olavia hasn't left a will or anything in writing, but in the days when they knew which way things were heading, she repeatedly asked Ottmar to send her home when it was all over, so that her family could lay her to rest in the graveyard by the sea where she grew up. She doesn't want to be buried in Fuchserde, a dreary place, where people are moreover arch Catholics, a point Ottmar emphasises in his letter, as over the years Olavia became more and more religious and was active in a small Lutheran community.

The Storm family regard this matter as inappropriate. That is: Olavia's still unmarried sisters shed many a tear over the sad tidings, they had long hoped to see her alive again, provided that the shame had receded into the past, provided that the damned war was sufficiently forgotten, a hope their mother Amalie had shared, in a more controlled manner.

Alfred Storm takes Ottmar Ehrlich's letter with him into his study and needs to open the lowest drawer in the desk and take out a silver-framed photograph of his next youngest daughter to remember what she looked like. Then he, too, sheds a tear. Not that this makes him any more kindly disposed towards Olavia's final wish, so he sits down and pens a letter to Ottmar Ehrlich in the limited German Storm Senior picked up in the course of the war, to mark a linguistic distance between them.

In actual fact, Alfred remembers Ottmar as a gentleman, a high-ranking officer with a high-ranking officer's natural aptitude for figures, words and supplies. Ottmar Ehrlich hadn't waged any personal campaign here in the north, but nonetheless he had been here, and he was and is a German. Accordingly, Storm perceives this sudden son-in-law of his expressing himself in Norwegian as an undesirable attempt at fraternisation, Norwegian, the mother tongue of the Storm family, so mediocre school-German flows from Storm Senior's pen as he refuses to fulfil his daughter's final wish, for practical reasons.

Practical reasons?

Yes, he can't really say straight out that he doesn't want old wounds re-opened, nor to be inconvenienced again by an unruly daughter who seemed to be constantly in heat from the age of fifteen and had the nerve to make off in the way she did, moreover with a German officer, high-ranking or no. Storm also well remembers – even though at the beginning he had neither encouraged nor otherwise given his consent to this inappropriate match – how, as the relationship with their daughter degenerated, he had given up on her, both he and his wife had.

They had even had the young man over for dinner and praised his manners. Amalie had in fact liked him too, and wasn't ashamed to say so, between the four walls of the house, for these dinners were held behind closed doors, but the question is still whether it is reasonable to accuse Storm of trying to ride two horses at once during those fateful years.

But who didn't, who doesn't prepare for the worst, who doesn't stockpile when danger is imminent and all outcomes equally possible?

Storm doesn't think he has anything to be ashamed of. He was hardly a collaborator, nor a profiteer, he had just kept the wheels turning, with the highest patriotic motives, at times he might have oiled them a little too well, perhaps. But we ought to have had two sets of laws, as Alfred Storm sees it, one valid for war conditions and one for peace, and neither of them applied retroactively.

This would have been far more democratic than one timeless, overriding principle adopted by those idiots over in London, who spoke on the radio and drank wine and didn't even have shoes on their feet, they were sitting there in their bloody socks.

This was Storm's favourite image, an exiled government in stockinged feet, completely oblivious to where the shoe pinched for the people back home, a haunted population in its daily struggle not to defile itself in circumstances for which it was in no way responsible. Now he writes Ottmar Ehrlich's address on the envelope and sends the letter, hoping that the matter is thereby resolved for good.

But it isn't. He omits to take account of the fact that Amalie and his three surviving daughters have also read Ottmar Ehrlich's letter, which he now locks in a drawer, to distance himself from it. Burning it – his first thought – strikes him as being simply too vulgar, and one never knows.

His youngest daughter, Anna Karina, in particular, reacts to this stubbornness of his, and without informing her father, calls on the pastor in the village, and asks Lise, who opens the door, whether Samuel is at home.

He isn't. He's visiting the islands.

In this weather?

Yes, Pastor Samuel likes blustery weather. Lise will tell him she called.

Anna Karina leaves the rectory thinking that postponing her discussion might be a blessing, knowing herself as she does, she will now either change her plans, hopefully for something better, or become even more sure of her intentions. The latter proves to be the case and when she finds the pastor at home the following week, she soberly summarises the contents of the disconcerting letter from Germany and insists that Samuel persuade her father to relent. Olavia should be laid to rest in the family grave in the churchyard by the sea.

Before Samuel has a chance to reflect, she adds that this arrangement will probably cost a lot of money and that neither she nor her sisters have any to speak of, so he will also have to get her father to pay.

Samuel has known Anna Karina for many years and is aware she has had her eye on him. He has had his eye on her as well, but he hasn't really made his mind up yet. He knows he mustn't let his feelings run away with him, so now he poses the most relevant and hitherto unanswered questions of all to the Storm household: Did the family have any knowledge of Olavia's escape plans at the time? Were they in any way involved in the planning or financing of it? And have they over the years had any contact with her?

That is at least two questions too many. Anna Karina soon finds a way out:

No, the family did not assist in any way with the escape, but they assumed, or hoped, that Olavia had run off to Germany to live her life with Ottmar Ehrlich, they knew the man, or at least they had met him. But there hasn't been any contact between them since.

No letters?

No letters.

The pastor muses philosophically on the theme of letters that arrive and those that do not, and what that may mean for those waiting for them, if none arrive for years, won't those waiting become both impatient and anxious?

In short, Samuel asks himself whether life in the Storm household has been on hold for all these years. Have they been sitting up there all this time, in reduced circumstances, holding their breath? In particular, he dwells on the fact that nothing has happened on the marriage front with respect to the three remaining sisters and that only one of them, Gyda, has a job, as a nurse in the town.

Anna Karina says she understands what he is driving at and tells him that their father has strictly forbidden them from trying to find Olavia, and the sisters have obeyed, albeit reluctantly.

Why?

We hoped time would change things.

That the war would fade into the past?

She nods, something like that.

Samuel realises that there is no way around this, he will have to ask Alfred Storm to relent. Storm is not a man for relenting, but he is beginning to get old and children shouldn't die before their parents et cetera, so there must be something somewhere that can soften even an old stick-in-the-mud like Storm, Samuel reasons.

Then he invites Anna Karina to have dinner with him, eating alone every evening is tedious. She accepts. Lise serves roast pork with prunes and is terse with the guest. But Anna Karina notices that, at an early stage in the meal, Samuel moves the vase on the table between them so that they can see each other better and wonders if there might be some advantage in being a little less stiff, a little more relaxed.

Samuel Malmberget's expedition to the Storm estate was both bruising and complex. Alfred Storm worked himself up into a violent rage, first directed at Anna Karina, then at the pastor.

But rage often wears a man down, especially an old man, so after a while Storm takes a seat to recuperate. Samuel, who has hitherto stood in front of the old man, is petulantly motioned to take a seat as well. He sits between Anna Karina and Elisabeth on the opposite side of the table and waits for Alfred to reel off a few obligatory remarks about what a curse it is to have only daughters, can the pastor imagine this?

No.

They are deceitful.

And you're King Lear?

Eh?

Samuel prefers to wipe the literary smirk off his face rather than to elaborate about Cordelia, perhaps because he can't see a Cordelia around the table, Elisabeth perhaps, but he doesn't know her.

Instead, he says he presumes this is urgent.

What does the pastor mean?

Well.

The old man understands what Samuel is hinting at and works himself up again, and it slips out that Ottmar Ehrlich has sent him another letter, in answer to his rejection of the idea that Olavia should come home, for practical reasons.

With fumbling fingers, he takes the new letter from his jacket pocket and is about to read it aloud, but before he has even unfolded it, Anna Karina suddenly leans across the table and snatches it from his hand with a loud shriek, what is Father trying to hide from them?

Alfred Storm stands up, strides around the table and demands the letter back, again with mounting fury, presumably because he has remembered there is more in these lines from Ehrlich than he, Storm, would want the family to see, Anna Karina realises this, runs away and reads the letter aloud, impervious to her father's bellowing.

Not that there is any rush, Ehrlich writes, for practical reasons, for now Olavia's coffin is being kept in a modern cold-storage facility. But there is a limit to how long she can stay like this, it is undignified, does Storm have any special wishes in the event that they have to find a solution in Germany, Fuchserde being, as mentioned earlier, out of the question?

That's exactly what I said, the old man shouts, again trying to get his hands on the letter, which Anna Karina takes as a sign that it contains even more he would like to censor, so she quickly reads on and sure enough: The Ehrlichs have two children, five-year-old Stephan and three-and-a-half-year-old Eva, and Ehrlich feels certain that both, asleep upstairs at the moment, would send their Norwegian grandparents all their love if they knew what a Grandpa and a Grandma were, Ehrlich's own family is no more, neither his brothers nor his parents, they were all victims of the war.

Oh, my God, says Amalie, the frail-limbed and crook-backed materfamilias in this household, who has so far sat in loyal silence at her husband's side, pretending to knit.

She puts her knitting down on the table, rises to her feet and walks calmly over to Anna Karina, who, with tears in her eyes, hands her mother the letter and is embraced by Elisabeth, who is sobbing loudly. With a look of calm authority, Amalie slowly reads the whole letter, checks the other side to make sure there is no more, folds it, walks over to her husband and delivers a stinging slap, turns and leaves the room, carrying the letter in her hand.

21

Olavia Storm Hartvigsen Ehrlich came home in a reefer ship and lay on pallets in Trading Post-owner Vig's storehouse in the time leading up to the funeral, Samuel Malmberget's most challenging to date.

Here lies a long-lost child of the village, who has returned home in a coffin, with three surnames, which all evoke awkward and unhappy associations with the war, a war that is really beginning to get on the pastor's nerves.

For all these names give rise to further discord in the family. They are not only about to take leave of the family's most spirited daughter, a wild child, and a ray of sunshine throughout her childhood, as far as they can remember, for God's sake let's not talk about all those strange ideas of hers. Olavia's name will also be carved in stone and remain there for eternity, as inerasable as the written documentation of lives the historian cum pastor travels round the village photographing, a man who wants to both forget and remember, he calls it reconciliation.

Which names will the family choose?

"Olavia Storm" is Alfred's unshakeable standpoint.

But Alfred Storm is not unshakeable any longer, after the to-do over the letters he is a mere shadow of his old self. Anna Karina, Elisabeth and Gyda – the nurse, who has come over to be with the family at this difficult time – all want "Olavia Storm Ehrlich" on the gravestone, they know Ottmar Ehrlich to be a gentleman, albeit in the wrong uniform, and they are heartily sick of all this peacetime sugar-coating and fakery and are actually captivated by the thought of the second-youngest sister in the bevy having had the courage and stamina to fly in the face of both war and peace and family and fatherland, for love, is there anything more beautiful than that?

Or anything more mind-boggling? Amalie adds.

Amalie too has harboured a secret respect for her daughter's life choices. She has even come to terms with the course of action Olavia took with regard to Johannes Hartvigsen, the fellow was worth a try, a desperate try, Amalie thinks, undertaken by a daughter whom the family immediately disowned, they actually ought to be ashamed of themselves, but all three surnames should be inscribed in the stone out of respect for Olavia's strength and courage, so what she is remembered for is as true as possible in the impossible times we live in.

At first, Amalie has difficulty getting her daughters to accept this line of reasoning, they are not so keen on Hartvigsen. However, they move slowly but surely over to their mother's point of view, first Anna Karina, then Gyda and eventually Elisabeth. Storm Senior hasn't got a chance. On two occasions he has also been thoughtless enough to talk about money, trans-port, what is this German oak coffin going to cost them, he has no intention of making such a mistake again.

Fortunately, the family is united in their scepticism about Ehrlich's wish to bring the coffin to the house himself, person-ally, it is too early, for practical, compassionate and political reasons.

Strangely enough, it is Alfred Storm who makes the most noise in the church, he sobs loudly during parts of the service as if he has finally understood something so profound that it will be the death of him, a reaction which doesn't pass unnoticed by the many in attendance. Pastor Samuel hasn't had a fuller church since he was appointed. Here sit all those who for years have been grappling with the mystery of Olavia and Johannes, are they finally about to get an answer?

Hardly.

In the case of Olavia, there is still a multitude of possible interpretations and unanswered questions, motives and actions, and fragments of information that can be pieced together to form the narrative that fits their individual needs. It isn't one person's life they are paying their last respects to but rather as many lives as there are people in the church, a deeply moved congregation, they are here not only out of respect for the deceased and her family but also for highly personal reasons, to bury a hypothesis, and thereby to keep it alive.

In row three sits Ingrid Barrøy, next to Svetlana, who as usual has been keeping a beady eye on the incoming post and the telegraph line between Norway and Germany. Svetlana has her own reading of this drama: Olavia loved Johannes Hartvigsen too, of that she is absolutely convinced, a reasoning so Russian that Ingrid is staggered.

Loved?

Yes, insists Svetlana, Johannes tried to save Olavia at a time when her family had disowned her, and took care of a child that wasn't his, there was a chivalrous side to Johannes that Olavia could see and appreciate, therefore it is only right to have his name engraved on Olavia's gravestone too, it shouldn't just be written on the puny cross the priest had erected on an empty grave at the edge of the churchyard.

Ingrid has to reflect on this, but there are more pressing things on her mind.

Originally, she reacted quite calmly to the news of Olavia's reappearance. Well, that's *that* chapter over and done with, she had thought, and at first felt something akin to relief, but then shame too. Her feelings of relief didn't leave her, however, as a result of her shame, but lived on, undiminished, both of them.

So Svetlana's information about two surviving children in Germany came as another shock: What implications might this have for an adoptive mother whose son suddenly had two full siblings? Her fear that the widowed husband might turn up in person at the funeral had also loomed over her. Ingrid has still not spotted anyone who might be him, after intensely scanning the gathering, every face, several times, but still she can find no peace of mind.

At Storm's side sits Amalie, all in black, passing her husband handkerchiefs and whispering hush and placing a consoling hand on his shoulder. She is also annoyed at her eldest daughter up there in the choir acting as if she is providing entertainment at a wedding. Anna Karina is putting on too much of a show. Amalie wishes the best for her and has been glad to see her in a more cheerful frame of mind recently, but this is after all her sister's funeral.

In addition, Amalie has been feeling more and more uneasy about that domineering priest, who doesn't have any sense of how to hide his light under a bushel, but evidently relishes his importance, his gravity, his own words, a priest who sticks his nose into other people's affairs offering glib words of encouragement and advice no-one has asked for.

To the right of Amalie sit her daughters, they too in black. Young Elisabeth's thoughts are focused solely on everything going as smoothly as possible without any hitches. She is the one who has created the floral decorations inspired by her mother's revised view of Olavia's long history of suffering, which has made a deep impression on Elisabeth, there is now something sacred about Olavia.

One more thing: even though there has been so much doubt

about Mathias' paternal origins, there has never been any doubt about his maternal parentage, which means that Olavia is survived by no fewer than three children, whereas her three sisters haven't produced a single one, Elisabeth has to admit. Olavia has lived for us all while we have been doing what? Gyda's training and work as a nurse in the town pale into insignificance alongside Olavia's calamities.

Elisabeth has also begun to think about the boy, Mattis, as she calls Mathias, and has cast several glances towards the back of the church, but has only recognised Ingrid of the Barrøyers, sitting beside the coarse Russian woman from the post office, and Olavia's old neighbour, Gudrun.

Elisabeth and Ingrid have also exchanged nods, but why isn't Mattis there, at his mother's funeral? Have the islanders kept him in ignorance, for the boy's sake, or their own?

Elisabeth would have liked to see him again, to scrutinise his face in search of Olavia's features, and wonders whether she should perhaps try to approach Ingrid outside the church with a bit of casual small talk and drop into the conversation what a shame it was the boy couldn't be here to say goodbye to his mother, something along those lines. Mattis is after all Elisabeth's nephew, so an approach of this kind must surely be both possible and natural?

But then it occurs to her that the Storm family hasn't actually given the boy much thought. Apart from her. Gyda and Anna Karina have scarcely mentioned him. While her mother,

Amalie, on a couple of occasions, has sighed over her knitting and mumbled: Well, here we are, with our own flesh and blood walking around on one of those poverty-stricken islands, and we don't care, that is how low we have fallen.

Ingrid senses something going on in the well-groomed head two pews in front of her, something which has to do with her, and her worries are not assuaged by the sight of the thin, gold chain adorning Elisabeth's slender neck, the white lacework on the black dress, the posture, the dignity.

Furthermore, Ingrid has realised that the chances of exchanging a few private words with Samuel are getting slimmer and slimmer with every sob she hears from Storm Senior. On a day like this, the pastor obviously has other matters to attend to than her trifling business, once again she has built up more anxiety than there are grounds for, she consoles herself with this thought, and prays in silence with the others while her eyes continue to focus on Elisabeth's hairstyle, neck and jewellery.

22

Over recent weeks, Pastor Samuel has drawn closer to the Storm family and grown to respect them. Even old Alfred comes across as human on occasion. However, it doesn't take much for him to destroy any sympathy Samuel might have, with his pettiness, irascibility and unreasonableness. The fact that Samuel is beginning to reconcile himself to the family's capriciousness and shadowy side may be due to force of habit, he reasons, inspired by his feelings for Anna Karina, which are growing stronger and deeper with every passing day.

Samuel has known Anna Karina for several years, but has never really been able to make her out, in his mind she has been a blur, nebulous, but since she came to ask for help to bring Olavia home, things have begun to fall into place. Now Samuel has Anna Karina in focus, as he likes to put it, and she is sharply delineated in his inner eye at all times, clear and majestic, so much so that he is forced to confront his own most incomprehensible trait.

Samuel's most incomprehensible trait, in his own eyes, is that, when all is said and done, he is a shy man, if he is honest with himself. With the result that he has begun to have doubts again, even though he surely cannot doubt what he has seen over the years at choir practice, that Anna Karina has her eye on him?

In dark moments he can.

In more optimistic moments, he thinks: Of course, she loves me. He fluctuates between these two extremes, and the thought of how embarrassing it would be to make a decisive move only to be met with surprise, disbelief, a closed door. What has got into this priest?

Samuel knows that such a rejection would floor him, as a man, a priest and a human being.

Nevertheless, he thinks he has found a way out. Three days earlier, in a moment of clarity, he realised that he actually could tolerate a no, so long as it wasn't straight to his face. So, he sits down to write a letter. It takes three days to formulate this letter, even though it consists of only four lines, which however are critical, he can feel the weight of them beneath his surplice.

At the same time, he has been working on his sermon, a worthy tribute to Olavia, and this task has not been easy, either. In Paderborn, he learned there were two schools of thought as regards such delicate cases as this: the first enjoined the speaker to tell it as it is, to speak more or less truthfully about the deceased and to reduce literary turns of phrase to a minimum.

The second demanded total non-engagement: a few general,

superficial remarks about life and eternity, and leave the deceased's biography to take care of itself.

But, as he stands before the congregation, Samuel realises all too late he has committed the sin of trying to combine these two doctrines.

The part about Olavia's childhood goes tolerably well, as she was so indisputably charming in those days, it is when puberty sets in that things begin to go awry. Olavia had to make impossible choices, the pastor finds himself saying, society imposed them on her, not her character but the war, here we go again. On occasion, external circumstances can bring even the strongest of us to our knees, whereupon it is our duty to forgive.

Choices? Forgive?

Is there anything to forgive if there's no personal responsibility for bad decisions and courses of action, what we usually term sin?

Samuel hears all too late that he is getting in a muddle, and things don't improve much as his gaze sweeps the congregation, whom Storm Senior refers to as cattle, and he hears himself state once again that the war seduced so many of us into taking steps we would never have even considered in any other circumstances, the war showed us who we are, showed us in all our naked glory, not always a pretty sight. Our Lord, and Olavia, by means of her example, showed us who we are, thanks be to Him.

Samuel closes his mouth and "Fair is Creation" fills the air.

Another work of art is to follow.

No-one in the family is going to carry the coffin. At any rate, Storm Senior is in no state to do so and the rest are women, so Samuel in conjunction with Amalie has hand-picked locals from the village who had least to do with Olavia, those souls who can be expected to arouse as few awkward associations with the deceased as possible, it is basically a gang of labourers, six men doing a job of work.

The only person not to comply, in some way, with the criteria is old Gått, Olavia's neighbour in the years she lived with Johannes. But Gått is Gått. And then there is Daniel Malvik. He is a friend of the people on Barrøy, where the deceased's son lives, but Daniel has never seen Olavia and he is here not only as a pall-bearer but also to do the pastor a personal favour as soon as they are outside the church.

Daniel is at the back on the left of the coffin and meets Ingrid's eyes as the procession passes pew three, and doesn't quite understand what he sees.

What's up with Ingrid?

Ingrid is standing beside Svetlana and old Gudrun, one of the gossips who for all these years have perpetuated the rumours about Olavia, convinced as she is that Johannes caused her death, there had always been a menacing dark side to Johannes, an unpredictable, spiteful character. As soon as they are outside, she whispers to Ingrid:

What did I say?

What Gudrun thinks she has said is that she knew from the very start that Olavia had left to join her true love in Germany, full stop. Ingrid's mind blackens, whatever is going on in her head has intensified at the continuing sight of Elisabeth's aristocratic neck, the gold, the beauty . . . Mathias' two siblings in Germany. She asks Gudrun:

But what about the boy?

What?

A *mother* abandons her *own* child – for a *man*? Has Gudrun lost her senses? Hasn't she got any children herself? Is she an idiot?

Both Gudrun and Ingrid are taken aback by the violence of her outburst. And Ingrid has to hurry away. She makes for the April-brown grass by Nelvy's grave, kneels down and begins to root about in the earth with a trowel, furious not only at having crossed the line with Gudrun, but also at having lost control of herself again, being a mother really has turned her into a wreck.

Then a shadow falls over Nelvy's cross, someone is standing in the sun waiting for Ingrid to look up. Ingrid sees Elisabeth Storm. Elisabeth takes off a black glove and wants to shake her hand. Ingrid gets to her feet, grasps her hand, says, my condolences, and waits, the silence is so protracted that Elisabeth blushes and sheds a tear and averts her face as if in pain. She is unable to utter a word about what had been brewing up inside her during the funeral service. Courage, dignity, what is natural and what is possible, it has all gone.

Never mind, forget it, Elisabeth says, with a weary smile, bows her head and walks back towards the procession of people following the coffin's last, slow journey to the Storm family grave.

Ingrid watches her, casts a final glance at Nelvy's resting place and visualises the wild flowers that will be growing here this year too, and slowly makes her way to the mourners standing in a semi-circle around the grave, listening to Samuel's final words.

Now the pastor is concentrating hard not to make any more mistakes. He has already passed the crucial letter to Anna Karina and is encouraged by the reaction he thinks he has seen, the moist eyes and the demure smile.

As soon as Samuel has said his piece, Daniel Malvik stands on the other side of the pit with Samuel's camera and tripod and uses a whole roll of film immortalising the coffin with the flowers and wreaths, behind the grieving family, Samuel among them, and behind them again the ordinary folk, an entire village and a host of islands.

However, these photographs will later be censored, by no other than Anna Karina herself, as soon as she is in a position to do so, they will be burned in the pastor's stove because she thinks she is smiling in them. This presumed smile is vague and unclear and doubtless occasioned by the letter she has just received and is temporarily kept in the handbag she is holding in front of her stomach with folded hands. But the smile is obvious enough in Anna Karina's eyes and here for once she agrees with her mother.

Only one vehicle is parked outside the church, the Storm family's recently purchased second-hand car. But a car is still a car, a remote and unachievable thing, which the children like to run after and don't mind being covered in dust by, even if it is a twenty-year-old Ford.

After taking wordless leave of the pastor and sending as neutral a glance as possible to the gathering, Alfred Storm opens the car door and gets in. His wife and two daughters follow him and climb into the back. Anna Karina gets into the driving seat and starts the car, and they leave behind a social event that Storm considers the most humiliating in the whole of his family's history, unaware that he has never before aroused greater sympathy and understanding.

Elisabeth is in the back reflecting on the failed meeting with Ingrid Barrøy, at a graveside she knows nothing about, a simple cross surrounded by shells and small, smooth beach pebbles. She is holding her mother's right hand, Amalie is holding Gyda's right hand, and Elisabeth is wondering what has become of all the emotions and thoughts she had in the church. Ingrid had always seemed to her a pleasant person, easy, reliable, uncomplicated. But in the churchyard a cultural barrier had risen between them, a wall Elisabeth had seen that she would never be able to find her way through or climb over, no matter what she said or did, whoever she might be.

Elisabeth is twenty-seven. She stares out through the dusty car window, at the fields and trees and farms and mountains, a glimpse of the sea to the west, some newly shorn sheep. She turns to her mother and squeezes her hand until Amalie opens her eyes, and Elisabeth says she would still like to apply for the secretarial training course that her parents consider beneath her dignity:

What do you say, Mamma?

Do as you like, Mamma says.

23

Ingrid woke early but didn't get up. The sun was about to disappear from the north-facing window, only a narrow wedge remained, which at this time of the year meant that the clock down in the parlour would soon be sounding seven distant chimes. But Ingrid didn't get up.

There are two reasons on an island for getting up, first to put an end to the night's thoughts with work, and second because this work needs to be done. She lay thinking about Olavia's homecoming, so long ago, about what might have happened and what hadn't happened, yet.

She thought about her mother, who used to say the sound of children playing was God's song. She thought about the dance of the whales in the ocean and heard her mother talk about the art of weeping: only in solitude can tears do themselves full justice. Not a breath of wind in the rowan outside, but a feeling of disquiet in Ingrid, always this sense of disquiet.

She got up, washed and dressed, went downstairs and at the breakfast table told Barbro that perhaps she ought to row over to Havstein and fetch the children herself, as she used to. Barbro looked at her and asked if anything was the matter.

No, nothing, Ingrid said, but Barbro understood, the children changed more in a week in Havstein than in a whole summer on Barrøy.

Ingrid prepared some food for the trip, packed a rucksack and walked down to the færing, sat at the oars and saw herself being rowed out by her mother that first time, the mother who also fetched her, the relief Ingrid felt after a week-long, unequal struggle with a teacher who was obsessed with ridding her of her "bad habits", ridding her of Barrøy, civilising her.

It had been simpler with Felix. On his first journey over, Lars sat at his side on the stern thwart, laughing and joking, and there had never been any talk of Felix and bad habits. Nor had there been with Kaja, Mathias and Oskar, they were not only a threesome but arrived home so close and with such self-confidence it would not have been a problem even if they *had* had a few bad habits.

Suzanne, on the other hand, was a girl who did have bad habits. Suzanne wanted to be on Barrøy and had to be taken to school with brute force, and she spent months screaming at and fighting with other children, so her big brother, Felix, had to step in. There had never been any trouble with Felix, but there had always been awith Suzanne.

She had now written to say that she was living in a three-room-plus-kitchen flat with Bjørnar and a little daughter, Hege, on the third floor of a "dugnad"-built apartment block with central heating. The tenants burned their own rubbish in enormous incinerators, which heated water that was circulated through radiators, they each sat on their own toilet, had a bathtub and double-glazed windows and a balcony and a refuse chute and bomb shelters and hobby rooms and laundry facilities in the basement, all described with great enthusiasm.

Suzanne could certainly write.

They also had gas masks, "folk gas masks", which were kept in what Suzanne called the Centre, without any further explanation. But Ingrid understood that food and shoes and paint could also be bought there, all in one place, there was a chemist's, a clothes shop and a kindergarten, for the poorest, since most of the mothers spent their time at home in their three rooms while the children played outside in what Suzanne called "the street", although in reality this was a sandpit on a "lawn" next to a clothes horse that was called a 'drying rack". The rack, the laundry room, the hobby room and bomb shelter were "communal", as were the sandpit and the refuse chute.

Enclosed in Suzanne's letter was a photograph Bjørnar had taken when he was doing the "dugnad" work, and in it, Ingrid could see more dreadful buildings than it was possible to imagine. Four-storey concrete boxes in all directions on a mud-caked slope, the remains of building materials, three cranes, countless lorries and black-clad men in caps by cement mixers, wheelbarrows.

Suzanne had marked blue crosses on the top two windows

on the right in the second-lowest block. Barely a hundred metres away ran a wide road where no fewer than thirty-one cars were to be seen when the picture was taken. Ingrid had counted them twice and had seriously wondered whether it was advisable to tell Barbro.

Hva's tha got their? Barbro piped up.

The thought of Suzanne sitting there the whole day long, behind the two blue crosses at the top right while Hege was playing in the "street" and Bjørnar was working "overtime" was not easy to entertain, especially in view of the enthusiasm with which it was all described. Of course, Suzanne was free to go out, lock the door behind her, walk down four flights of stairs and up the muddy road to the Centre to buy shoes.

The first thing Ingrid had wondered about in her reply was whether it was right that the women didn't do any work, she had read about this in the papers, but was none the wiser as a result. Hege had to be fed of course, and they washed their clothes outside their flats, "communally". There was generally so much that was "communal" that perhaps it didn't matter so much that people spent so much time inside on their own.

Next question: Wasn't the traffic on the road noisy?

And the third: What were they doing on the balcony that could just be made out beneath the cross on the right? Were they standing or sitting? When and for how long at a time? Ingrid was careful about how she expressed herself and tried to appear interested rather than incredulous.

Last question: Could Suzanne send a photograph of Hege? Ingrid would frame it. Now she had only one framed photograph on the wall above the bureau, of Kaja and Mathias standing on the kitchen table, Pastor Samuel had taken it when they were five, they were eleven now.

Ingrid arrived in Havstein feeling nothing but worry, and far too early, but moored the boat, walked uphill and knocked on the familiar door of the classroom, the parlour on the Havstein estate, where she herself and all the other Barrøy children had sat. She entered without waiting for a "Come in" and was met by the surprised gaze of the teacher and pupils. All three of her children sat there, with eight others.

Ingrid lowered her shoulders.

The teacher asked what she wanted, no-one was allowed in here.

Ingrid hardly knew him, but Kaja and Mathias were looking at her with a smile of recognition, so she walked calmly over to an empty desk by the window and said she would like to stay for a while.

To bewildered giggles from the children. Kaja turned and frowned. Ingrid waved cheerily back. Kaja glanced enquiringly at Mathias, who gave a sly smile while Oskar, sitting right at the front, displaying his long, blond locks, laughed out loud.

It was this teacher who had once said that Anna Barrøy's drawings were sloppy and flawed. Now he was clearly wondering whether to make a fuss and risk causing embarrassment or to back down. Ingrid didn't seem very ready to yield ground, so he chose the latter.

But this obviously caused him a good deal of irritation, which he wasn't initially able to control, he rose to his feet and began to make a scene after all, he said Ingrid had to leave, then had second thoughts as she didn't react, with the result that the pupils took this as a defeat. He couldn't have this hanging over him, so the least he could do was ask who she was.

As if he didn't know.

Ingrid said she was the mother of Kaja and Mathias and Oskar's aunt and just wanted to sit there for a while, she wouldn't disturb him.

The next round of giggles was sufficiently amiable for him to find his footing again. In the constitution, you see, in this, our free and independent country of Norway, which became even freer when it left the union with Denmark, and then Sweden, and then again had to regain its independence during the last war, for the third time, that is, in less than one hundred and fifty years. And a hundred and fifty years, children, you have no idea how short a time that is, for a country, because you are just children, I like to call childhood the age of ignorance, do you understand?

Ingrid let out a laugh, put up her hand and said, well, I suppose two hundred years isn't so long, either.

Flustered, the teacher glared at her and chanced his arm

with a laugh, but noticed that Kaja blushed on her mother's behalf, while an exultant grin spread across Mathias' face, it was as if they weren't brother and sister. The teacher knew of course they weren't, Mathias was adopted, a circumstance he had been ordered to keep secret, with the consequence that many a tale did the rounds about where Mathias came from, most of them harmless, as far as he could judge, the place was swarming with love children, and after all Kaja and Mathias were the best pupils he'd had from Barrøy, with the exception perhaps of one of the twins who had left a few years back and on several occasions had driven him up the wall when doing fractions, what was her name again, the genius at arithmetic?

Sofie, Ingrid said.

Ah, yes, of course, I couldn't tell them apart, and the other one?

Anna.

He thought for a moment, then asked:

What's she doing now? Sofie?

She's with her grandma in Lofoten.

I see. But what's she doing?

Going to school.

Oh, what kind of school?

And so on, Anna and her drawings were forgotten. Sofie was still present in his class.

Ingrid remembered how hard for her it had been when the twins left Barrøy, her girls, who throughout their childhood had done more or less all she had asked of them, but then all of a sudden began to sabotage everything, from working in the cow barn to gathering eggs and carding the down. They wouldn't have anything to do with fish anymore. Not even Hanna was able to control them. Ingrid had attempted to make light of this, presumably because she realised that she herself would come unstuck if she intervened. But the girls had noticed this too and tried to exploit it.

They were overjoyed when they were eventually allowed to leave, their parents, Felix and Hanna, had realised they were so gifted they would have to go to school, they left on the fourth of January, on the *Salthammer*, which again was going to Lofoten, where Hanna's mother had been familiarised with the matter, thanks to extensive correspondence, and had promised to "keep the wenches under control". Hanna gave a wry smile when they failed to give her a farewell hug.

That Mamma of mine is a hard nut.

A joyful departure, but a tragedy in Ingrid's eyes, even though she was given all the hugs Hanna was denied. She was certain that this would be the last she would see of them, or else they would return in ten or fifteen years, on a sort of holiday, the type Suzanne and Bjørnar had spent here, as coquettes or as teachers or astute accountants, with husbands and children, to strut around the island of their childhood and point out how extremely small and forlorn everything was: just fancy, we actually grew up here.

*

Ingrid surveyed the wallpaper and curtains that had withstood the ravages of time, the same old chandelier, the tall, cylindrical stove, the teacher's dais, windows. But new desk lids, hinged to the frame so that they could be opened like coffins.

Lift your lids all at the same time when I give you permission, out with your pens and ink, paper, textbook, ruler, close them all at the same time, no banging them down at your own convenience.

The teacher had learned their dialect, but switched to his standard Norwegian when anything was important. "At your own convenience" meant he was in deadly earnest, as were terms like "satisfactory", "to mark", "to distract" and "you scamp".

Even Gabriel had withstood the ravages of time.

Now he came shuffling in, a silent and welcome character from the depths of history, not to light the lamps at this time of year but to wind the clock and signal that the day was over, should anyone not have worked it out.

What is the point of a bell when you have Gabriel?

Ingrid stood up, curtseyed, said thank you, goodbye, shook hands and the teacher said, don't mention it, and hadn't it been a strange experience sitting here?

Yes.

She added that was more or less what she had expected when she came over and he mumbled it was good she had, in a few years' time it will be too late, you see, the small schools were going to be closed down on the islands and a new central school would open on the main island.

This was the first time Ingrid had heard about plans for a new school.

On the way home Oskar and Mathias sat at the oars laughing and splashing and calling each other "you scamp" while Ingrid lay back on the sheepskin in the stern with Kaja, asking all those little questions that were necessary for her to gain a picture of the week's changes, questions about friends and events. She sniffed Kaja's hair and removed a speck of invisible soot from the back of her neck, while Kaja chattered away regardless as if she still didn't have a single secret in the world, she had learned some new words and a strange new mannerism with her left hand, those Russian eyes which looked more and more like her father's, the coarser scream when Mathias and Oskar splashed her, a joke that had to be explained to Ingrid, Mamma was so slow.

More important than Kaja, when mapping out these changes, was Mathias, Ingrid didn't need to ask him a single question, it was enough just to look at him, as always, and for him to look back at her, this pact they had, and for her to say that she would have to cut his hair when they got home, what a mess he was, he was beginning to look like Oskar.

A slight wind blew up, they set the sail, the changes in the children were becoming less marked and had disappeared entirely by the time the færing glided into the gully between the stone banks on Barrøy and the children could run and run while Ingrid moored the boat and walked up to the house with calm, measured steps, carrying their three rucksacks.

24

One thing was the changes from week to week, which were manageable, from week to week. But quite another matter was Svetlana's old newspapers, which she sent over with Daniel in small piles, usually marked with a cross or two where she thought there might be something of interest to Ingrid. And on the mainland the war still appeared to be in full swing because in Svetlana's highlighted columns Ingrid read reports about unfortunate children being called little krauts and languishing in orphanages and their own homes, sufferings which seemed to be almost a necessary part of peace.

Ingrid was shocked.

Next to one article Svetlana had drawn a big heart in blue ink, and, eyes agog, Ingrid read about a former German soldier who had returned to liberated Norway to fetch a daughter, to rescue an unhappy product of the war from a Norwegian family who had disowned her, and take her home to Germany.

The journalist clearly had well-disguised yet unmistakeable sympathy for the soldier and the girl, and Ingrid went around all day wondering what on earth Svetlana meant by this heart, a Russian who has endured the worst that life has to offer, was this supposed to be encouragement or a warning?

In the January gloom the warning seems to be the likelier of the two, January, with all the dark thoughts winter can throw at you, a phenomenon Ingrid knows she has to guard against, but against which she is just as defenceless every winter nonetheless, not least when the children are at school.

She wakes from dreams about the breathtaking whales in the crystal-clear ocean, and with the resultant awareness of transience, all things will pass, slip through her fingers, she stays in bed staring into the shadows, deaf to the lessons to be learned from Mathias, she doesn't light a candle and see the world as it is, the walls, the ceiling, the grey silhouette of a window, the bureau, and instead she hears a conversation down in peacetime Germany, where the lights are on all year, one evening when now-married Olavia and Ottmar Ehrlich are so close to each other that Olavia finds it natural to heave a sigh and say: Just fancy, we have a son in Norway too. His name's Mathias.

Ingrid can visualise such an evening all too clearly.

Or she can see Olavia in one agitated, angry moment feeling a need to blame Ottmar for something or other and bursting out with:

To think I abandoned my own son for you!

A son? You never said anything about that to me.

Olavia may then regret this outburst and try to trivialise

the importance of this son of hers, try to convince Ottmar that Mathias would want to stay with his father, he is happy there.

His father?

Yes, Mathias doesn't know any better. He loves Johannes.

Hmm, answers Ottmar, who has probably also heard about the wretched lives of German soldiers' children in peacetime Norway. And, from this moment on, he will have this son of his on his mind and try to imagine how he is faring, who he takes after and maybe ask himself whether *he*, the boy's biological father, bears a responsibility to pursue the matter, like the soldier in Svetlana's newspaper article.

Now there are enough men around who don't give a damn about the children they may have abandoned in some port or other. But such a callous frame of mind doesn't fit the image Ingrid has formed of Ottmar Ehrlich, a gentleman, as Pastor Samuel has called him, a staff officer, well liked by Olavia's family, a man with good manners, not to mention the dignified way he has expressed himself in the letters to the Storm family, and which Samuel has also told Ingrid about.

Ottmar Ehrlich is by all accounts a decent human being.

That, at least, is how he appears in Ingrid's battle with the winter darkness. She can vividly imagine Olavia telling him about Mathias as soon as the couple are reunited, perhaps accompanied by some motherly tears, and Ottmar nodding eagerly. Delighted? Concerned? And the couple agree this son of theirs obviously belongs here at home with us, with his siblings and parents. And from that moment – naturally enough – they are already making plans to unite their son with the family as soon as the war is at a suitable distance.

But then Olavia dies before this eternal war has reached the much yearned-for distance.

Will such a tragedy weaken or strengthen a decent man's potential need to bring home an unknown son?

But again: "home"?

Ottmar has never seen the boy, and he didn't know that Olavia was pregnant when he left the billet on the main island after the *Rigel* sank during the last winter of the war, Ingrid has this information from Samuel too, she has immersed herself in these details more than is good for her, but this is where her speculations run aground every time.

But in the January darkness, she is beginning to wonder why, and has to admit that she quite simply doesn't dare to pursue these thoughts any further, because in her wildest dreams she cannot imagine having a child in another country and not caring about it. In which case it is impossible for her to conceive of anyone else being able to do so, and definitely not the man who is Ottmar Ehrlich.

On one of her rare trips to the village with Daniel, Ingrid asks Svetlana to try to find Ottmar Ehrlich's address in Germany. Not because she has any plans to write a letter, but to have the option, should she ever work out what she might put in it to make it worth sending.

However, only a few days later she finds herself sitting at her bureau writing to this selfsame Ottmar Ehrlich in Fuchserde, she knows he can understand Norwegian.

First of all, a detailed description of Mathias, a good-looking boy with coppery hair and green eyes, who, as soon as he arrived on Barrøy, developed a close friendship with Ingrid's daughter, Kaja, bonds which over the years have become so tight and strong that not even our Lord would be able to break them, they are closer to each other than most true siblings.

Mathias listens to what people say, he is more than capable of expressing himself, he is full of original ideas and has a nice, dry sense of humour, eats whatever he is given, shows few signs of contrariness beyond what can be expected of a boy of his age, and is in fact far more easy-going than Kaja.

Generally, Mathias has a calming effect on his sister, he is like an anchor, he has the strength to bring Kaja down to earth when even Ingrid has given up, where does he get it from?

The children sleep in their own rooms, Ingrid is careful to emphasise, deftly omitting to mention that they usually sabotage this rule by sleeping wherever they like, sometimes together in the empty double bed in the South Chamber, this has nothing to do with Ottmar Ehrlich, it is just a stage they are going through after all and only happens when Ingrid can't be bothered to argue with them, they have become so strong-willed, they *are* growing up of course, and the bed issue is getting more and more problematic, Ingrid is well aware, but none of this has anything to do with Ottmar Ehrlich.

Instead, he is told that Mathias sits down calmly beside Kaja when she gets stuck with her schoolwork, he smiles at her and explains everything, it is the only method that works, Ingrid knows from bitter experience, her daughter with the Russian eyes has to be cajoled into learning, she has to play her way to adulthood, she is also gradually slipping away from her mother.

But this has nothing to do with Ottmar, either.

Ingrid is also writing for herself, some cautionary words, she knows she is. She is writing in order to get to grips with what can and should go on under her roof with two children who will soon be adolescents, all the things they are beginning to get up to behind her back, things she doesn't want to know about, she doesn't have the energy for it, if she did, it wouldn't be any comfort, what do I know, Ingrid thinks, and instead stresses once again how inseparable the two of them are, which she hopes Ottmar will finally understand.

And last but not least: Without Kaja and Mathias, Barrøy has no future.

That was another cat out of the bag.

This letter isn't going to be sent anyway.

However, on a separate sheet of paper, Ingrid has scribbled a significant afterthought, even in the winter darkness she of course knows that heaping so much praise on Mathias is ridiculous, although it is fully justified, the lad learns as quickly at school as he does at sea. But if her intention is to put an end to any longing or dreams the father might have, then she ought to say that the boy is unbearable, a pestilence and a plague, no good at anything and in poor health. Or at least put together some concoction of all this in such disheartening terms that it would kill off any desire to remove Mathias from Barrøy, even in a man like Ottmar Ehrlich.

But Ingrid can't do this. She has written one single sentence of this kind, Mathias is a difficult and at times obstinate boy whom she has difficulty understanding, but she will never write another, this piece of paper will be burned.

The letter itself, however, she keeps in the bureau. And then it is February.

But on a dark day the following winter, the whole issue comes to the fore again. Ingrid, in another equally troublesome bout of depression, thinks about the previous year's letter, takes it out and in disbelief she reads what she managed to put down on paper barely a year before, whereupon she realises this is in fact, strangely enough, a comprehensive account of all the self-torment she is once again subjecting herself to. With one notable difference: Yet another year has passed, the boy is another year older. Now he says Ingrid cannot decide over him. Kaja says the same. Ingrid can even laugh at this, or at least make a valiant attempt to do so, and feels a strange kind of relief, as though she has begun to believe the children are going to make it, they are going to be fine, this belief is a big risk for someone who knows that nothing weakens people more than hope, and she knows it.

25

In late spring it is not possible for anyone to walk across the yard or along the beach or through the potato fields without repeatedly casting impatient glances northward, in the hope that a speck will appear on the horizon, in the hope that it will gradually increase in size and turn out to be the Norwegian flag and the boat named the *Salthammer*, which is returning home after another indescribable winter, with a full crew, alive and well, four pairs of new shoes, dresses, board games, biscuits, chocolate, two canisters of sausages, last year Lars brought Ingrid an umbrella.

A blue umbrella decorated with flowers and half-moons, which hangs, open, above the bureau where letters are written.

In the last few years Ingrid has begun to long for letters, strangely enough, the absence of letters has become an ever-present murmur in her everyday life, she must be getting old, she thinks, or is this another sign of weakness? Which all means that little by little she has discovered the essential nature of letters, the freedom they allow the writer to talk to anyone they like, to whomsoever they like, on a sheet of paper, without having to look the person concerned in the eye, without allowing oneself to be influenced by grimaces and smiles and sceptical looks, there is a sincerity involved in writing letters that is not found in daily life. Until she recalls the curt and mendacious Lofoten variety, with all their fine weather and good-catch guff, the dutiful comfort provided for those at home knowing no better, and probably not wishing to know any better, if truth be told.

So, what about the letters she sends to Mariann Vollheim?

Well, yes, this is true of these too, to some degree. Ingrid well remembers Mariann's strong, forthright personality, which it was no easy matter dealing with face to face, all those things Ingrid had to shape and twist and hesitate over to express herself when they sat facing each other on the Vollheim farm, in a boat on Lake Tunnsjø, on a smallholding in Sweden, Mariann's lack of candour, secrets, mysterious past.

What about Mariann's letters to her? Easily digestible, everyday information about her daughter's life in Trondheim. Little Ingrid is well or has a cold and has learned four difficult words, abstract concepts, as Mariann calls them, or else she comments on things that annoy her at school or in town and sends regards from Herman, her father, who she thinks is going soft in the head, but who still remembers Ingrid's visit to his farm as if it were yesterday, he says, according to Mariann.

Ingrid likes to read all this, whether it is true or not, there is *something* here she has grown accustomed to, something from the outside world, both alien and alluring, which she looks forward to re-reading, she has to admit.

This also goes for the most diligent letter writer, Suzanne, who at least once a month in surprisingly beautiful handwriting informs her about double-glazed windows and bathtubs. In the spring she had persuaded Bjørnar to buy an ultraviolet lamp, a device that really makes Ingrid laugh when she eventually finds out what it's for. Suzanne has "refurnished" and "wallpapered" and been on a trip in a "cabin cruiser" with one of Bjørnar's friends and his wife, a childless couple who are irked by Hege being seasick and vomiting in the "cabin cruiser", and in calm waters too.

The last letter again contains a long account of her concerns about her son, Fredrik, who hasn't sent his mother so much as a peep over the winter, after scaring the wits out of her in previous seasons when he was a baiter and novice fisherman, Suzanne has come to the conclusion that she prefers signs of life to silence, however unsettling they may be. Would Ingrid be kind enough to give the lad a good talking-to when he comes home, nothing has happened to him, she supposed?

Ingrid herself has received two reassuring letters from Lofoten, from Fredrik himself, the best communicator among the uncommunicative men, and she assures Suzanne that everything is fine with her son and the rest of the crew, they go out from Fredvang, and yes, Fredrik will be given a real dressing-down, she can bet her life on that.

Ingrid has also noticed a gradual shift in Suzanne's letters, a growing interest in Barrøy, unless she is very much mistaken. Suzanne asks questions about whether the eider ducks have come ashore, how the potato crop is doing, what about the lambing, have they got three or four calves now, she even wonders how things stand with each individual islander, she refers to all of them by name, and Ingrid has to pass on her regards, otherwise they will forget me, and that won't do at all.

In her replies, Ingrid writes by and large one sentence per inhabitant: Hanna has been ill this winter, pneumonia after falling into the sea, for once they have had a doctor on the island, but she is well again now, and strong. Mathias and Kaja are growing and say thank you for the Donald Duck comics. And you wouldn't recognise Oskar, he is now as good as gold, a real worker and a budding fisherman, it won't be easy to keep a rein on him in his final year at school. Barbro's eyesight has got even worse, but she is looking forward to the summer and more daylight.

As for Selma, Ingrid writes that she has been out in a boat with her several times to pull in the nets, but to be honest Suzanne was better at it: She can't row backwards, that Selma. And they have got five calves.

Is Suzanne longing for home, down there in the capital?

After some thought, Ingrid chooses to take a more rational view of this: Suzanne is bored, she always has been, no matter where she is.

She rounds off by thanking Suzanne for the photograph of her daughter, Hege is lovely, so like Suzanne as a child, it is amazing, for the time being she is hanging from a nail above the bureau, but will be framed as soon as the menfolk come home with money.

But the *Salthammer* isn't the next boat to arrive, it is a modern sailing ship, with enormous tapering sails, as white as chalk, varnished mahogany on the foc's'le and in the bridge and all the fittings made of brass, a vessel no-one has ever seen the likes of in these parts. Pastor Samuel is on board, his wife, Anna Karina, and two members of the crew wearing white, double-breasted uniforms, and caps, they complain about how shallow the water is, the keel is so deep that they have to put the guests ashore from the bow and "swing at anchor" while they wait.

Samuel, as is well known, never arrives without an agenda, without some errand or other, a few words of praise to impart or an interesting piece of business to conduct, usually all at the same time, and today is no exception.

Ingrid doesn't know Anna Karina, but shakes her hand and welcomes her. Anna Karina smiles bashfully, but when she catches sight of Barbro standing by the house, she squints, strides up the hill and runs the last part and embraces her.

Well, blow me down, Ingrid thinks, and doesn't move, so Samuel is left to stand there and say why he has come.

However, for once Samuel doesn't, he just looks around, at

ease in Ingrid's presence, as if he were the spiritual proprietor of the island, on a flying visit to his dominion and chuckling in delight at the way it is being run.

Ingrid laughs and begins to walk up to the house, but hears Samuel clear his throat, he wants to have a few words with her after all, in private.

Maybe she has heard that Henriksen, the old lensmann, has died?

Yes, Ingrid saw that in the newspaper, which has begun to arrive again with the milk boat, renamed now as the packet boat, although it only seems to dock when it feels like it.

Samuel says Henriksen has to be buried.

And?

The next vacant spot in the churchyard is right next to the Barrøyers' resting place. And Nelvy's. It had occurred to Samuel that Ingrid might not want this?

Ingrid smiles.

Samuel mumbles shamefacedly, yes, there isn't much he has missed about what went on here during the war, this is after all his special field of interest, history, memories.

Ingrid merely stares at him.

I thought so, Samuel says, and explains that he has already made arrangements for the man to be interred in the opposite corner of the churchyard. Ingrid wonders where all this is leading.

But, for now, Samuel has no other business, it seems, and suggests they start walking, how are the children?

The children are at school.

They go inside. Barbro receives her kisses on both cheeks and Ingrid notices that Anna Karina rises when she enters and stands next to the chair with her arms hanging alongside her pleated tartan skirt, which reaches down to the middle of her calves, long, cream-coloured stockings, low, brown, laced shoes, her hair and skin and eyes shinier now that she is married than they have ever been before.

Ingrid pretends she doesn't realise that it is her job to tell people to sit down. Why actually does she do this? Has Ingrid got something against Anna Karina, Barbro's choir friend and the pastor's wife?

But then she sees that Anna Karina is expecting, smiles and tells her to sit down, over there by the window, that window where everyone has to sit on Barrøy, with a view of the new quay and the Swedes' boathouse and the sea to the west and north. If you press your face against the glass, you can even catch a glimpse of the islets, Oterholmen and Sandholmen, and the fairway to the Trading Post.

Ingrid and Barbro have done some baking in readiness for the arrival of the Lofoten folk. Ingrid makes coffee and slices a *kringle* cake while Samuel and Anna Karina are busy discussing Barbro's eyesight. They think she should go to see a doctor and get some glasses. Samuel adds that she should stop working in the dark in winter.

But we've got lamps, Barbro laughs.

Samuel explains that it is these fish-oil lamps that make people go blind, the light is so poor. Barbro laughs at that, but glances at Anna Karina, who nods and clearly agrees with her husband, so Barbro looks uncertainly at Ingrid, who is pouring coffee and says matter-of-factly that her aunt will be getting some glasses as soon as the men are home again.

A statement which in a way is about money, so Samuel is reminded of the next item on his agenda, Johannes Hartvigsen's farm, it isn't worth much as it is, lying abandoned for ten years now. But it is what it is, and the local council has decided to build a new central school on these very plots of land, Hartvigsen's, Gått's and Gudrun's. The latter two villagers have already agreed to sell, does Ingrid still have the deeds to the property, the ones she received together with the adoption papers?

Ingrid nods and remembers how wonderful it felt to receive these documents.

Just a minute, she says, they will be writing a letter, won't they?

A letter?

The council?

We-ell, yes, what does she mean?

Ingrid feels she needs someone other than Samuel either to advise her in this matter or to consult, but doesn't say so, and the pastor eyes her intently, almost disappointed, it seems, but Ingrid can't let herself be put off by this, which Samuel also appears to notice, so he mumbles it out of existence and changes the subject, to Anna Karina's relief, he praises the down that is produced on Barrøy.

Ingrid says it's a funny time of year to come for down, the eiders haven't even left the sea yet.

But she has a kilo in a sack left over from the previous year, which Kaja has cleaned and needs paying for, Kaja has a bank book too. And then Ingrid remembers a matter of her own.

She takes Samuel with her up to the barn and eases out the sack of down, unwinds the wire with the cardboard label for the pastor to stick his hand into the sack and feel the wonderful feathers and close his eyes. He wants to have an eiderdown made for Anna Karina, who is due to give birth this autumn.

Ingrid nods and asks him whether the Storm family ever receives any letters from Germany, a question she should have asked last winter, or indeed three years ago.

The pastor studies her closely. Ingrid closes the sack and hears him mutter something about that being a strange question, do you mean from the boy's father?

Yes.

Yes, Anna Karina does get letters, not often, but Ehrlich tells her about how the children are doing at school and in life generally, Anna Karina is of course these children's aunt. What is on Ingrid's mind?

Ingrid freezes: Anna Karina is Mathias' aunt.

The pastor heaves a weary sigh and says she is the legal adoptive mother, nothing can change that.

222

Ingrid is less interested in the workings of the law than in people, so she asks whether he has read these letters.

No.

Does Anna Karina tell the father about Mathias?

I would hardly think so.

Really?

Samuel sees that now he is the one who has been a bit stupid and tosses the sack into the air a few times while he thinks. They walk down the barn bridge and stop.

Well, that would be the natural thing to do, he says. Would you like me to ask her?

Ingrid decides that now there is no skirting the issue, she says:

That isn't so important. Does Samuel know anything about how these children are getting on in Germany?

Well, I think. Ehrlich's an economist. He has a good income.

Ingrid asks if he has remarried.

Not that I know of.

The pastor wonders whether he has been stupid again. But Ingrid lowers her gaze as if to signal the end of the conversation. And they go inside the house, where Anna Karina has a chance to stick her hands into the down and close her eyes. She straightens up, says thank you with a smile and adds she had hoped to see the children.

In a state of agitation, Ingrid manages to suggest that the pastor and his wife sail over to Havstein in that huge ship of theirs and fetch them, it is Saturday.

That's a good idea, Anna Karina says quickly.

Mm, why not? Samuel says.

Ingrid now endures the five longest hours of the spring. But then the sailing ship returns. With all the children. Oskar is the first to step ashore, then Kaja, again changed no more than Ingrid can accommodate. But Mathias stays down on the deck talking to Anna Karina about something Ingrid would have loved to hear.

And this conversation drags on. Both Mathias and Anna Karina find something new to say with every word the other utters, they stay down there for quite a while.

Ingrid stands on the quay holding her daughter's hand. Kaja asks her what the matter is. Ingrid has no answer.

When Mathias is back on dry land and the white-uniformed crew hoist the sail, she is still unable to ask what they were talking about, instead she patiently listens to a discourse about the impressive vessel's specifications, what its draft is, how many knots it can do at full sail with the engine running, the comprehensive "sail wardrobe", this miracle belongs to the pastor's eldest brother, who has come all the way from Bergen to spend his holiday here, he is the owner of a shipping company.

I see, Ingrid says.

26

The *Salthammer* returned home once again with a combination of money and necessities, and also the odd absurdity, such as the umbrella Ingrid has hanging from the ceiling, it was the tradition to surprise those at home with some ridiculous article from the world outside.

This year it was a bicycle.

A blue one, which the children took turns to sit on and push along the paths. A bike on an island. They might just as well have brought a top hat or an aquarium. Mathias was the first to master the art of riding, then Kaja, and last of all Oskar. His balance was poor; however, he achieved the highest speed and had the most spectacular falls. When evening came, they left the bike leaning against the wall of the house. And the following morning they wiped the dew off it. It came with a bell and a mudflap behind the front wheel. After they had moved away stones and clumps of grass and cleared a more or less straight path through the gardens and gates, Lars' son, Martin, mounted the bike and set a record down the stretch between the potato cellar and the huge tree trunk at the south of the island, the Bench, where a finishing line was solemnly drawn in the shell-strewn sand. A record that was beaten first by Kaja, then Mathias, timed on Ingrid's father's old pocket watch, which had a second hand, whereafter the path back to the house became the course. It was a lot more demanding because of the slope, and Hans won easily. Then they raced against one another there and back, Hans winning once more, and the bike was leaned against the house again, it was time to plant potatoes.

Lars was pleased with the interest shown in the bike.

Ingrid asked why he hadn't made sure that Fredrik wrote to his mother during the winter.

But he did.

No, he didn't, Ingrid said.

Are you sure?

Yes, Suzanne hasn't heard a word from him.

Fredrik passed by, pushing a wheelbarrow full of seed potatoes, was stopped and asked to explain.

No, I didn't, he said, trying to move on, but Lars held him back and said he had given a very different answer up in Lofoten.

No, Fredrik said again. Not a very satisfactory answer. Lars insisted Fredrik had been told to write to his mother several times and each time he said he *had* done.

All Fredrik could say was that he hadn't had time, so Lars asked if he was intending to continue not doing what he had been told to do.

Fredrik's face turned bright red, and he said no.

Good, Lars said.

The wheelbarrow was allowed to continue down to the potato plot. Ingrid felt she had achieved something at least and decided the time was ripe to tell Lars about his mother, about Barbro's poor eyesight, she needed to see a doctor.

Lars thought this over. Everyone's eyesight gets worse as they get older, doesn't it?

It could be something else, Ingrid protested.

Such as what?

Ingrid didn't know, an eye disease?

Lars said he would mull it over, they would have to keep a close watch on the weather, there was a salmon line he'd like to set.

Ingrid and Barbro were standing in the wheelhouse with Lars on the way to the Trading Post. In the wind and rain coming from the south-west. Lars asked his mother what seamarks, beacons and skerries she could see, and Barbro pointed, while Ingrid was wondering when it would be appropriate to mention the plans to build a new school, it seemed natural to her to do so as they passed Johannes Hartvigsen's old quay, the house on the hill had parts of the roof missing and the wall on the northern side was crumbling.

Ingrid suggested putting into the quay.

Lars asked what the point of that was.

Ingrid said she wanted to show him something, she needed some advice.

Barbro stayed on board while Ingrid and Lars walked up the hill that Lars had once carted an anvil down, and now he appeared to be uneasy at the scene of the crime. The front door was ajar. Ingrid pushed it open and heard bleating noises. A startled sheep and two lambs bolted out. In the hallway there was a thick layer of sheep droppings on the rotten floor, but the animals hadn't managed to push open the kitchen door. However, water had seeped in and formed black rivulets down the pipe and on the stove. On the floor there was a rusty-brown pool of water with a shimmering rainbow on the surface beneath decaying chair legs. In the sitting room there were two mouldy rag rugs lying cross-wise. Ingrid felt she should have come before, long ago, and asked if Lars had been upstairs. He said no, and again asked what they were doing here. Ingrid explained that the local council wanted to take over the farm and had already bought the neighbouring properties from Gått and Gudrun, and also wanted to move their houses to new sites in Stormyra.

Lars asked what Ingrid was thinking of doing.

She said she wasn't sure; she might not sell.

Oh?

Yes, she had no right to sell. All this belonged to Mathias.

He eyed her sceptically.

Ingrid went up the stairs to a corridor with three doors, two

228

of them water-damaged. In the children's room, the window was broken, a little bed had collapsed under the weight of water and leaves, the mattress was black, on the floor there were some toys on a grey pile of what turned out to be kids' clothing, above the bed hung a photograph of a faded face.

Ingrid grabbed the driest toy, a yellow wooden horse, and hurried out again, still feeling that she had come too late. She pressed down the handle of the undamaged door and entered a room with a four-poster bed that resembled a grid covered with earth, the canopy hung down at one corner. A wardrobe with four doors faced the partition wall. Ingrid opened them one by one and found mildewed clothes, dirty laundry, shoes, and at the back of the middle shelf, a box of old receipts, milk delivery slips and fish sale chits from Johannes Hartvigsen's time as a fisherman, beside a shoebox with a bulging lid that turned out to contain moisture-damaged letters.

Ingrid took a deep breath and went back downstairs, carrying the shoebox and the wooden horse.

Lars preferred to wait outside, getting drenched in the rain, staring across at Gått's house, which someone was in the process of demolishing. Gudrun Pedersen's house wasn't visible behind the trees, but between the two properties substantial roadworks were under way. Lars asked if Ingrid had found anything of interest. Ingrid showed him the toy and they walked back down to the *Salthammer*.

*

They moored the boat at the Trading Post. Lars accompanied Barbro up to the doctor's surgery. Ingrid said she had a few errands to run and went to see Svetlana in the post office. But Svetlana was busy with the telegraph, so she carried on to the former mayor, bank manager and librarian, Birger Sund, who was pouring himself a dram from a bottle he was unable to hide quickly enough in the cupboard under the left-hand drawer, an observation that she might be able to exploit, Ingrid thought.

She sat down and said she would like some clarity regarding the mystifying state of affairs whereby the local council had decided to use Mathias' property to build a new school, but hadn't even informed her in a letter. Sund still had a seat on the council committee, and she was sure he could explain. He said:

It's on its way.

Ingrid said once again it was strange that they hadn't already sent a letter, and told him she had seen in the conveyance deeds and on the surveyor's certificate that Johannes Hartvigsen's property was indexed under Cadastral Unit Number 11, Land Number 1, and that fifty years ago Johannes' father had sold off plots to Gått and Gudrun's deceased husband, these were now Land Numbers 2 and 3, they were merely small islands on Hartvigsen's property, Hartvigsen's land was immense.

Birger Sund studied his glass and had to think about this, perhaps not in order to find the truth, it seemed to Ingrid, but rather a few appropriate words, and what he eventually came out with prompted her to ask if they had forgotten that Johannes Hartvigsen had a son.

No, no, of course not.

He waffled on. Ingrid said she understood everything but needed time to make up her mind and asked what the council had paid for the properties belonging to Gått and Gudrun. Birger Sund again had to think, shuffle over to the filing cabinet and thumb through two different files, then came back, coughed and said: May I? And knocked back a dram without waiting for an answer.

Ingrid also wanted to know what it had cost to have the houses demolished and rebuilt on the new plots in Stormyra, and what they had paid for these.

She received an answer to this too, without Sund feeling any need to stand up.

Round about, he added.

Ingrid asked what that was supposed to mean.

No, no, that was the final sum, the exact sum.

Ingrid eyed him, and on he went again about the village's urgent need for a large school, people were moving from the smaller islands and gathering in droves on this, the main island, he talked about birth rates and electrification, and Ingrid interspersed a pensive yes whenever it seemed fitting, and he said she would just have to be patient, the matter would be dealt with, they would write to her, she got up and walked with a stronger sense than ever that she was invisible, feeling very uncertain that she had achieved anything at all.

Svetlana had finished in the telegraph office and was able to deal with the post Ingrid wanted to send. One letter. To Suzanne, from her son Fredrik, a letter that clearly had been dictated to him. After the incident in the potato fields Ingrid had taken Fredrik aside and asked him for an explanation as to why he hadn't written to his mother this winter, the *real* reason.

After a lot of difficulty, the answer she dragged out of Fredrik was that all his meagre free time was spent courting a girl in Fredvang, her name was Ragnhild.

Ingrid said this was exactly what he should be telling his mother. Suzanne would understand and be happy. Fredrik had then written to his mother saying he was sorry about not writing, but this was due to his work and . . . Ragnhild.

Ragnhild was eighteen, the daughter of a fish wholesaler in Fredvang, had brown eyes, long, dark hair and was incredibly pretty.

Fredrik had originally written "dishy", but Ingrid had made him change it. This was the third winter they had been seeing each other, during the first one Ragnhild had been splitting sole, but now she had been given the job of weighing fish and issuing sales chits as well as doing some accountancy admin for her father, she had no brothers and was to take over the business, she was competent enough too.

Ingrid said that Suzanne would be pleased to hear all this.

Svetlana stamped the letter and dropped it into the sack beside the chair where she was sitting and pushed a small parcel across the counter.

From Mariann Vollheim.

Ingrid asked if there had been any letters from Germany.

No.

The even more important question: Had a letter been sent *to* Germany recently?

Yes, the pastor's wife, Anna Karina, had sent one in spring.

When?

Erm . . . at the end of May . . .

So, after the boat trip with the children from Havstein, Ingrid noted. But as far as Svetlana knew, there hadn't been any contact by telegraph or telephone.

Ingrid wondered how she should interpret the fact that Svetlana wasn't interested in knowing why she was asking.

She walked back to the shop, bought a few items, packed them in a cardboard box and placed it on the bench Markus had constructed at the front, under a projecting roof to keep the rain off those sitting beneath, then she opened the parcel from Mariann.

It contained two books for the children, which looked impressive, but didn't mean much to Ingrid. And a letter. Ingrid still didn't quite understand Mariann's continuing interest in her and Barrøy, as though living in the wooded hills with apple trees, her husband and daughter and an interesting job, she hadn't managed to draw a line under what Ingrid too was still struggling with: Thoughts about Alexander.

A fate shared by two women who under normal circumstances would not have dreamed of writing a single word to each other, but who had now kept their two- to four-page correspondences going for years?

Alexander was never actually mentioned by name, but he was still there between the lines. If something was said about Little Ingrid playing in a Trondheim Park, it was almost as if this was a question about whether Ingrid had heard anything from Russia.

Ingrid wondered if this was only a figment of her imagination.

Mariann had learned all the names of the people who lived on Barrøy while she was here and asked how they were, politely, with interest. And Ingrid had no difficulty replying in the same vein, as though she didn't have Alexander in her thoughts either when she wrote that Mathias and Kaja were becoming more and more demanding, but she did.

27

They were well under way with the mowing before the packet boat arrived with the letter from the council that Ingrid had been waiting for. In a brown envelope without postage stamps. The letter described the progress of the school project in such complicated terms that Ingrid initially had to ask Lars and then Felix for some clarification. What annoyed Lars most was that he didn't understand what Felix understood, though he also found something to get irritated about when Felix eventually managed to explain that the rate the council had used for calculating the value of Cadastral Unit Number 11, Land Number 1, was based on the sum the council had already paid for Gått's and Gudrun's properties. However, Hartvigsen's, with its outlying fields, was far too large for the same high price per acre to be applied, the council argued.

In addition, the expenses for moving the two buildings had been subtracted from the price paid to Gått and Gudrun, the basis for the proposed figure, and Ingrid was in the picture.

We aren't going to move any buildings. Johannes' house is going to be demolished. We don't want a new plot, either.

Lars agreed.

Felix laughed and said: Yes, they're trying to pull more than one fast one now.

I'm not selling, Ingrid said ill-temperedly.

In that case, Felix said, they'll just expropriate it.

He explained what that meant, how they would have the legal authority to carry out such an action without her consent, and Ingrid said that at the very least she would have to think about it, and maybe they needed some expert advice.

Pastor Samuel again?

Nah, Felix wasn't so sure about that, but he could have a word with his friend Markus, the trader, who had learned a thing or two about many aspects of business at commercial college. Markus wasn't a council member any longer either, quite the reverse, Markus and his mother were involved in a fractious dispute with the local authorities, it was common knowledge. Markus wanted to extend the shop and call it a general store or even a retail business, but had had his application rejected for the moment, the executive committee did not sell off council property lightly.

They agreed that Felix should raise the matter with Markus.

There was no rush, Ingrid said, the council could wait as long as she had.

Meanwhile, a large proportion of the summer's mental activity was spent scrutinising the letters Ingrid had found in the shoebox in Johannes' decaying house, Olavia's shoebox, she had deduced.

Ingrid didn't open it until it had been on the bureau for several days, an unconscious deferral, or timidity, what did these letters have to do with her?

She had to extricate them carefully from the damp envelopes bearing washed-out postmarks and stamps, and then carefully unfold and separate the sheets of paper and leave them to dry on the windowsill, where they became as stiff as flatbread, before it was possible to decipher them.

All nine letters came from the Storm family, Olavia's mother and three sisters, and were written when she lived with Johannes in Hartvika.

First of all, Ingrid had difficulty reading the handwriting, and then understanding the content, not least because Olavia's reply was missing, here was only half of what at times was an extremely complex conversation. And something quite odd: the Storm family had sent one another letters over a distance it wouldn't have taken a horse and cart a couple of hours to travel, not to mention how fast the journey would have been on a bus, which had transported the letters anyway.

The contents were of the ordinary, run-of-the-mill kind, but livened up towards the end of one letter from Amalie, who was clearly replying to a plea from Olavia: Stick it out. Twice. Her mother emphasised that she only had herself to blame for the mess she had got herself into, since she absolutely wanted to keep this "love child" instead of getting rid of "it", "no family wants that kind of thing".

Ingrid re-read these lines several times, in the hope that she had misread them, but the message only became all the clearer. And again she had the feeling she shouldn't be reading this, it had nothing to do with her, she didn't need to know, they would have to be burned.

But then she was struck by the completely opposite notion, that Olavia might have deliberately left the letters hoping that one day somebody would find them and read them and understand.

But who? Johannes? Her sisters? Mathias?

To what end?

So they would take pity on her? Or get angry and wreak revenge? So they would feel remorse?

One thing at least was certain: The letters were not meant for Ingrid's eyes. She herself had letters in the drawer that weren't kept for other people to read, no-one, on no account. But if she was planning to run away, she would hardly leave a shoebox containing letters of this kind.

Ingrid began to feel unsure again.

How secure was a letter in a drawer?

Why keep letters at all?

The purpose varies from year to year, from occasion to occasion, from one pair of eyes to another. Ingrid had no well-thought-out system for what she kept and what she got rid of, it was all a matter of a gut feeling, and perhaps that had been the case with Olavia too.

Two of the letters had been penned by her younger sister, Elisabeth, and at least contained a few words of consolation: Mattis was so sweet and well behaved when Elisabeth visited them in Hartvika in October, everything would work out fine, Elisabeth prayed for Olavia every night.

Similar sentiments were expressed in the letters from Gyda and Anna Karina, who had written two each, although one of Gyda's was illegible, in the other though she said life was no longer worth living in the Storm household now that Olavia had moved out, so Gyda had applied for a place at the nursing college, against her parents' wishes. After all, she should be able to put up with a bit of a rumpus when Olavia had endured so much more.

Anna Karina rounded off both her letters by saying that unfortunately she felt unable to comply with some wish Olavia must have expressed. You know Father, she said. Olavia should stop pleading, it just made matters worse. And one piece of information that made Ingrid's eyes pop out: Olavia was the apple of her father's eye. None of the other daughters could have broken his heart the way *she* had.

The pages of the last letter from Amalie, her mother, were the most difficult to separate intact and Ingrid had to hold each one of them to the light to make out the old lady's handwriting: Again, some introductory banalities, then a sharp rebuke for her daughter not having shown sufficient gratitude for the 112 kroner her mother had apparently sent her for the "journey", it was everything Amalie owned. And if Olavia believed anyone would take care of "that German kid of yours" she had another think coming, "think of your father" she said, "who is now doing everything he can to get back on his feet again after the war".

Ingrid spent many hours mulling over these letters, both in the North Chamber and on the Bench. So Olavia really had abandoned a son for a man she couldn't live without, a gift for Olavia from the war.

This unbearable truth was, herewith, unambiguously confirmed in writing, in a letter, so Ingrid got up from the Bench searching for something else to think about, a triviality, a way out.

Now the haymaking was over, the hay racks were swaying gently and reassuringly in all the beautiful gardens and on Gjesøya, out there across the sound where they had once dug ditches and converted ten acres of marsh into arable land only to use it for grazing in later years. Ingrid wanted to plough it again, while Lars flatly refused every time she brought up the matter, they had enough land, even though his own mother in her prime had contributed a superhuman amount of work in this eternal struggle between woman and man, land and sea.

Ingrid left the Bench and strode up to the house, spotted Lars in Bosom Acre at the whetstone beneath the cow barn's lean-to, and made a beeline for his back. Lars was sharpening scythe blades, Oskar was turning the grindstone, neither of them was saying anything, they were working, concentrated, silent, all words superfluous, men who never make a wrong move, who know exactly where the other is at any moment, Lars, who this summer had devoted himself heart and soul to the land while he no doubt had only salmon lines and whaling in his thoughts, was this the right time to bring up the matter of the land on Gjesøya, right now?

Maybe not.

Ingrid went into the house and cast an eye over the food Barbro had prepared, as if that were necessary, Barbro who hastened to put on her new spectacles, which she only wore for the sake of peace in the house, Barbro didn't like walking around with a frame in front of her face.

Ingrid went out again, still feeling ill at ease, and stood motionless in the yard until she could see all those dear to her, three young men on board the *Salthammer* with paintbrushes and buckets under the silent supervision of Felix, while Mathias and Kaja were in the rowing boat, Mathias at the oars and Kaja lying back in the stern like a complete loafer, laughing at something or other, and now Ingrid had her feet back on the ground, hadn't she?

She went up to the North Chamber and opened the right-hand drawer in the bureau. A glance at the stiff sheets of paper from the Storm estate was all it took for her to realise that she would never show these festering boils to anyone. Neither would the yellow wooden horse she had found in the children's room in Hartvika ever meet anyone's eye, even though its size meant that it had to be kept in the cupboard beneath the drawers, which had no lock. But that didn't matter, Ingrid had decided to send the letter she wrote in January to Ottmar Ehrlich and tell him what a fantastic son he had up here in the north.

Or maybe she should wait a while?

This was quite a decision, wasn't it? In short, it was impossible to make.

Grub's up, Barbro shouted from down in the kitchen. Shortly afterwards, her aunt was in the yard with her glasses on, bellowing the same words across land and sea.

And Ingrid went downstairs.

28

The property affair with the local council dragged on and the number of letters increased. Ingrid's written refusal to sell Hartvigsen's property on the grounds of the unsatisfactory sum offered was responded to by the executive committee with a revised offer, upwards. To show their goodwill, they said. The new school was a matter of urgency, the construction of the access road had already begun, two houses had been taken down and moved and one had been demolished.

Ingrid was still writing with the help of Felix, who by now had really been spurred into action.

The committee hasn't mentioned a word about expropriation, he said with glee, that is a good sign.

This piece of wisdom wasn't his own, he had acquired it from Markus, an expropriation case will take time, first it would have to go through the court on the mainland, then an appeal.

Felix also knew what an appeal involved, the local council had itself to thank that they didn't have the time.

Ingrid wrote back that she didn't want to "oppose" the

"progress" mentioned, formulating her response – still with Felix's help – as officially as possible, expected a "reasonable offer" and used "a fair estimate" twice, to Felix's delight. In passing, she stated how much it had cost them to get Gudrun and Gått to move house, information she had coaxed out of former mayor Sund. And, as a last point: Hadn't the council acted unilaterally by commencing the building works and demolishing Hartvigsen's house before making a property transfer agreement with the rightful owner?

That's a work of art, that is, Lars declared. But shouldn't they also consult the actual owner, thirteen-year-old Mathias?

He doesn't know anything about it, Ingrid said curtly.

Why not?

Because then she would have to tell him about Johannes, and she didn't want to, she also said curtly.

Lars and Felix looked at her askance.

Now he'll be getting this money when he comes of age, Ingrid felt she had to say. And they looked at her askance again. She said that Mathias hadn't spoken about his "father" since he came to the island, that had to mean something.

They pondered this.

He doesn't call you Mamma, Lars said hesitantly.

No, he never had done, unlike Kaja. Mathias called her Ingrid. Didn't that mean something too, Lars wondered.

Ingrid didn't think so.

He knows more than you imagine, Lars said.

Ingrid had shared the same suspicions for almost as long as the boy had been there, but she was also glad he hadn't asked about all the painful things, these were not only forgotten, they had ceased to exist. Now she was glad too that Johannes' dilapidated dwelling had gone, it had been a nagging cause of unease for all these years, there is so much in a house, and now there was nothing.

Lars and Felix exchanged looks.

They only had to wait a week for the council to reply, and their offer was even higher, it was now double the original amount.

But Ingrid had had another idea, which she acted upon without Felix's help, he was at sea with the rest of the menfolk. She sat down in the North Chamber, as if it were a kind of office, picked up her pen and wrote about the old lighthouse that had stood in the south of the island, which she and Barbro had blown up during the war and not rebuilt, partly because of the Barrøyers' own dilly-dallying. But the council would have to work that out for itself. Once again, she referred to the bit about goodwill, wrote that they had missed the light-house, adding she had seen a picture in a newspaper of one on an island further south, equipped with a signal system that the islanders could utilise, should the need arise.

That same afternoon she despatched the letter with the packet boat.

An answer came surprisingly promptly, and it was a flat

rejection. Again, the school was a matter of urgency, more than ever before. Ingrid had heard from Daniel that they had already started marking out the foundations. And, of course, the council had nothing to do with lighthouses and seamarks, Ingrid would have to take up the matter with the lighthouse authorities.

Kind regards, the executive committee.

Ingrid immediately replied that of course she knew the lighthouse authorities dealt with lighthouses, but couldn't the council help her to put some pressure on these people and try to improve safety measures in island waters?

Before the next reply arrived, Felix was back, standing on the quay waiting for the packet boat. He opened the letter and read it before Ingrid could even come out of the house and angrily asked what the hell she was up to now.

We don't want a bloody lighthouse, there are enough beacons and buoys, the ships will only be confused by yet another light. And didn't Ingrid realise that she had strengthened the council's hand?

Look at this!

Ingrid wasn't sure.

She read the letter, in which the council said they were willing to contact the lighthouse authorities, she would be notified. And point two: their previous offer was still open.

Ingrid asked Felix how he thought the lighthouse authorities would answer. Felix said, of course, they would say no.

Besides, we have a radio on the boat. Soon we'll have one on the island as well.

Ingrid still wasn't sure, she had sensed her way forward to this strategy rather than thought it through. And it still felt right, so she said that then it would be the council's turn to make the next move once the lighthouse authorities' rejection had arrived, wouldn't it?

Felix was about to throw his hands in the air in despair, but instead stood looking at her, suddenly beamed and called her a crafty devil.

The next letter came the following week, it was November now, and the herring nets were out. The *Salthammer* had just unloaded nine hectolitres of shark-liver oil on the new quay, Ingrid, Barbro and the children were busy gutting and salting, while Felix and Lars were having a meal in Karvika, recovering.

So Ingrid got her hands on the letter first, and with trembling fingers, and nails covered in herring scales, read that the lighthouse authorities could not, of course, erect a new lighthouse on Barrøy, even if there had been one there before the war.

An accompanying telegram explained that the rejection was due to technical and financial concerns, broadly speaking the same objections that Felix had put forward.

But in their letter, the council first emphasised that now the urgency of the matter was greater than ever, so the offer with regard to Hartvigsen's Land Number 1 had been increased by a further six thousand kroner.

Ingrid almost jumped in the sea with joy, tore off her apron and ran like the young girl she was again, up past the house and over Oskar Hummock. And this time she didn't knock on the door, she burst into the kitchen, where Felix and Lars, with their wives, were sitting over their food and laughing at something or other. Lars looked up and asked if war had broken out.

Ingrid sat down and placed the letter on the table. Felix met her eyes, put down his knife and fork, took it and read aloud that the council's offer for Johannes Hartvigsen's property had been increased threefold since the summer.

Well, I'll be . . . Lars mumbled, and carried on eating. Felix called Ingrid a genius. Ingrid was radiant.

But, Felix said pensively, picking up his knife and fork again, maybe we should wait a while before replying?

What?

Mmm. Felix had heard that the school site had already been marked out, the access road had been bad enough, now it looked as though they were breaking the law. So, wait.

For what?

We'll see.

More herring arrived. Barrøy salted and spiced around thirty tonnes a month and they were well ahead with preparations for the Lofoten season before anything new happened.

*

What happened was that Daniel Malvik brought over both the present and the former mayor to Barrøy one morning when the menfolk were out fishing again. The gentlemen stepped ashore in heavy snowfall, unnoticed, and had to find their own way through the swirling snow up to the house, not because Ingrid wished to put their excellences in their place, these weeks of waiting had never been longer, she almost jumped for joy when she heard the clatter in the porch and realised who it was.

Goodness me, fancy coming over here in such weather.

Daniel said it wasn't so bad, tore off his oilskins and boots and made himself at home on the peat bin like the regular guest he was.

The two mayors stood while Barbro took their wet clothes and Ingrid told them to take a seat, there by the window, she said to the new mayor, a tall, gaunt figure in his mid-fifties, stooped, with short, thick, black hair and bushy brows above eyes that almost seemed shy, it struck her.

Ingrid gave a welcoming smile and put the pot on for coffee, carried out the spinning wheel and the loom, then set the table in the time it took the former mayor to complain about the weather and tell them he had never been here before.

The new mayor introduced himself as Bonsak Sandvær, he originally came from a small island like Barrøy, but as a child he had moved with his family to the main island and had lived there ever since. Now it was nice to be back, he mused. He even seemed to mean it. His parents had, furthermore, heard all about Ingrid's mother and father. They exchanged a few names, remembered various faces and events, made some comments about the doomed school in Havstein, people were leaving the islands in droves. Bonsak Sandvær thought the only thing that could save the coast from complete depopulation was electricity, he called it "light".

Oh, yes? Ingrid said.

Yes, people need to have light.

Mhm?

Yes, the electricity company's working on it now.

Mhm? Ingrid said again.

But, of course, they had come to talk about a completely different matter, the mayor said, turning down the offer of sugar for himself and his predecessor, and staring at Ingrid with eyes that were no longer shy, but not unfriendly either, he almost had a smile on his lips as he commented that Ingrid really was a tough customer.

This directness took her by surprise, but she sat down on the other side of the table and simply asked him what he meant.

Nothing.

And she was at ease again, talking calmly and dispassionately about how the disagreement could be resolved, in her opinion. Bonsak Sandvær had been extremely open during his introduction, revealing too much about himself, and now he had nothing up his sleeve, no secret weapons.

Ingrid said that if it had been up to her, there wouldn't be an issue.

Bonsak Sandvær nodded thoughtfully and said that, whether Ingrid believed him or not, personally he hadn't been aware of the property situation in Hartvika until Ingrid began to inundate him with letters.

Ingrid nodded.

But now he'd looked into the case, had read all the property's title deeds going back almost two hundred years, the surveyor's certificate, he was well aware of the size of the farm, and if Ingrid remembers the original letter . . . ?

No.

There the executive committee wrote that the council was only interested in the land around the house. Now they'd reached a point where they were able to make use of all of it. For that reason, they'd like to double the last offer.

Ingrid narrowed her eyes.

Of course she remembered the first letter, she knew it off by heart, and there was nothing in it about them wishing to divide up the property. It was almost as if they wanted the meadowland into the bargain, that had been her impression, or else they weren't interested in it or believed *she* wasn't.

But now?

Then it occurred to her that Bonsak Sandvær perhaps wasn't here to try to cheat her once again, but might well have come to pull a few chestnuts out of the fire and save the council's face.

It took her time to come to this conclusion. Time the mayor used to place a wet leather briefcase on the table and remove some papers, which looked trustworthy enough, a contract and a copy of the deeds as well as a notebook and a fountain pen, placing everything between his own and the former mayor's coffee cup.

He asked Ingrid if there was anyone she wanted to consult.

Yes, Ingrid said, playing for time again, as the *Salthammer* was at sea with all the men, including Mathias, and even Felix was perhaps not a high enough authority at such a crucial time.

Ingrid looked Bonsak Sandvær in the eye and said she could go over to the main island with them at once and speak to a friend of hers, then meet the mayor at the bank and settle the matter today.

No holding you back, is there, Sandvær said drily.

Ingrid asked what he meant.

Nothing.

Ingrid asked if they had a deal.

He saw from his wristwatch that it was five minutes past eleven in the morning and asked Ingrid how she was going to get back.

Ingrid said that Daniel would take her. If not, she could stay with Svetlana until the *Salthammer* returned.

Ingrid is standing next to Daniel in the wheelhouse on their way over while the two gentlemen stand with their legs apart leaning against the rear bulkhead. The former mayor repeats that he hasn't been here before and produces a hip flask. The new mayor turns down the offer of a dram and repeats that if there is something he really misses, then it is this.

What?

Sandvær moves across the floor and stares at the sea and the islets through the hailstones hammering against the grimy wheelhouse windows.

Ingrid brings up the matter of the electricity, which she has seen mentioned in the newspapers for months and has regarded more as a surreptitious invasion than a blessing, maybe they are one and the same, something is happening to the coast which she doesn't fully understand, once again, and now it isn't even wartime, it is this unpredictable peace.

Sandvær explains that the electricity board is forcing local councils to buy shares in the new "light" to have any chance of getting it, and also every household has to pay approximately a hundred kroner, as far as he can remember.

Ingrid asks if you can pay more to improve your chances. Bonsak Sandvær turns away and smiles. Ingrid waits for an answer. Sandvær looks at the former mayor, who shrugs and says he doesn't know.

They walk together from the Trading Post. Ingrid knows the mayors think she is going to visit the pastor, and that is fine. But as soon as they part company, she turns and goes back to the shop and in the back door, where Markus the shopkeeper is bent over piles of accounts in the tiny office he likes to curse, there is no future in this office, where his mother and father and grandmother and grandfather had spent their days in very different times, it was a squeeze then, now it is unbearable.

Markus asks Ingrid what she wants.

As she knows he is aware of the case, through Felix, she only informs him about the latest development, lays her documents on the table and asks him to check if there is any more trickery going on.

Markus throws up his hands in frustration, but starts reading and slowly warms to it, smiles from ear to ear and at length shakes his head in admiration. He furrows his brow, an expression which Ingrid cannot fail to understand, then swears and says that from now on it is not going to be cheap to acquire council property, no it certainly isn't. Congratulations.

However, on Barrøy there were no great celebrations. Ingrid arrived home as if after an uneventful shopping trip, intending to bury her success in the depths of oblivion, the way she had managed to do when she sold the milk boat.

But Lars and Felix were no longer as amenable as they had been, this was perhaps a way out for the heavily debt-burdened *Salthammer*, Barrøy's driving force, which was kept afloat from day to day by the Herculean efforts of six men.

The evening after their return, fortified with Dutch courage, they walked in shirtsleeves in the snowy winter darkness up over Oskar Hummock to Ingrid's to ask if they could borrow some of Mathias' money to create some breathing space for the island and reduce their debts.

In the kitchen, Ingrid was sitting alone, for which she thanked her lucky stars, then asked what they meant.

Lars declared, in a rather solemn tone, that now they have someone living on the island with more money in his bank account than any of the rest of us has ever had, a young boy we've taken in who has no idea how much he does or doesn't own.

Ingrid was momentarily non-plussed, was Mathias supposed to pay for the years he'd lived here, without his knowledge and against his wishes? Or could this money have some other significance, in which case what?

Couldn't they make ends meet, she asked, so far they always had.

Yes, yes, but you know ... the instalments.

Ingrid repeated they had always managed in the past.

Lars asked angrily what difference it would make to Mathias.

And Ingrid said, it isn't right.

What isn't right?

This was the most unpleasant conversation she had ever had with her menfolk. But after the sale of the milk boat the only possible answer was no, it's Mathias' money.

We only want to borrow it.

Ingrid couldn't bring herself to say that she didn't believe a word of it, so she pretended that she had other things to do, she cleared away a plate, wrung a dish cloth, stoked the fire and waited for them to go, without saying a word.

Lars said: Shall we go?

Felix said: Ingrid, look at me. Don't you trust us?

Ingrid had to think about this. Lars got up. But Felix sat waiting for a reply.

Ingrid said: Yes, I do.

Well, what's the problem then?

I don't know. I can't do it.

Then Felix got up too and said he had never seen her like this. Ingrid was indignant and said she was like he had always seen her, since he came to the island as a boy, without a krone in his pocket. Well, no, with a box of Polish porcelain, she corrected herself, she could hear she was being far too unreasonable and added that in less than six months school would be over, they could talk again then.

They left without questioning what the children's schooling had to do with anything and made no further mention of the matter before their departure for Lofoten. Ingrid didn't notice any changes in Selma and Hanna either, not the slightest hint of a grudge, it was Christmas, a calm Christmas, even the sea was calm.

29

January is not only a month for reflection, something which should be avoided if at all possible. This is also when the most violent storms rage, which darkens one's thoughts even further. Ingrid had just whacked her aunt with her spade and broken her glasses: she was attempting to dig down into the snow-covered potato cellar when a gust of wind tore the spade out of her hands.

They went into the house and examined her injuries. Barbro's forehead was grazed, her nose swollen and her glasses were done for, both lenses smashed and the frame bent and buckled.

Ingrid lit the lamps, sat her aunt down in a chair and picked the splinters of glass out of her skin.

You should have seen that coming, Barbro shouted, to make herself heard above the creaking in the house.

But it is an ill wind that blows nobody any good.

Bugger the potatoes. We can eat the cinnamon biscuits.

The last remains of the Christmas baking, dry, hard and perfect dunked in coffee. Ingrid got two stoves going full blast and they felt the house shaking, they had now been holed up in the parlour for two days, as were two other women in Karvika, waiting to be able to drag themselves over Oskar Hummock again.

What about setting up the loom?

Barbro would rather do some spinning, then she didn't need to see. Ingrid went upstairs and fetched Suzanne's Christmas letter, sat down to read it again, aloud, while Barbro worked the spinning wheel with the yarn.

Suzanne had run into trouble with the housing association, since she had been out working again, after Hege started school, and sat on the production line in a chocolate factory, as a result she wanted to do her washing in the common laundry room in the cellar when it was convenient for her.

But they were not having that, she wrote.

Barbro laughed.

Suzanne had swapped days with a neighbour, who was still pacing her flat and therefore "flexible", she said. But that wasn't allowed either, for a variety of interesting reasons. And nor were you allowed to wash clothes in the bathtub and especially not to dry them on the balcony, where Suzanne had set up six clothes lines and had been told that the place looked like an Italian slum now, there had to be some rules, Suzanne could be fined for this.

Barbro laughed.

Bjørnar was teaching Suzanne to ski, she would soon be as good as Hege, but she fell a lot and had just sprained her ankle, how was it going on Barrøy, poor things, I am thinking about you all the time, and count myself lucky not to be there in all that pitch-black darkness. Have you heard anything from Lofoten? Say hello to Barbro and the other old biddies, ha ha.

PS: Now the housing association chairman has come and complained about us adjusting the radiators ourselves, but he was sorry about the laundry problems, from now on I am allowed to do my washing on Saturdays between eleven and one, in the daytime.

Poor Suzanne, Barbro said.

Ingrid fetched her pen and paper and insisted in her reply that things had never been better on Barrøy, more birchwood than ever before, thanks to some good advice and Daniel Malvik. They washed their clothes whenever they pleased, by the way, and stayed inside or went out as the mood took them, or the weather, tonight we will probably have to sleep in the kitchen, it is pretty rough at the moment.

Kaja and Mathias go to school, but in spring they will have finished, they are growing so fast that you wouldn't recognise them, but I've already told you that. Oskar also had six months left, but it was impossible to hold him back when the *Salthammer* headed north, you wouldn't recognise him either, as tall as Fredrik, looking more and more like his father, except for the blond curls, but at last Hanna has cut them off, you can't be in the bait shed with long hair, she did the cutting with a heavy heart, the locks, that is, and has saved them in a scrapbook.

Barbro squinted at a knot in the woollen yarn.

Ya, it's goen t' bi borin' when th' young'uns gang.

By contrast February can bring short breathing spaces when a turquoise sea laps against white rocks and islands beneath a green sky, which turns bluer and bluer, and even the sun appears. On one such exceptional day Daniel Malvik puts in at the new quay.

But on the wrong day of the week.

Ingrid has finished milking the cows and is struggling with some bread dough in the kitchen, unaware of his arrival until it is a fact. So unlike her. Barbro is knitting without her glasses on. Through the island's most important window they watch as Samuel Malmberget clambers onto the quay, but there is something odd about Samuel today, in his long reefer jacket, wearing a strange hat on his head. And he stands there with his back turned to them, reaches down a hand to help up another visitor, who turns out to be his wife, Anna Karina, who is wearing a long, black skirt and a bonnet on her head, also black. In her wake comes another woman, her youngest sister, Elisabeth, as far as Ingrid can make out through the salt-smeared pane, Elisabeth is similarly dressed in a black skirt and bonnet. And, indeed, there is yet another figure climbing up the ladder, it is Markus the shopkeeper, who hasn't been here since he delivered some goods when he was a young lad. But it is only when stocky Svetlana is helped ashore that Ingrid realises what is going on.

Realises that something is terribly amiss. She knows what too. But she doesn't hear her own screams.

Something brings her back up to her knees, she manages to struggle to her feet and out into the cold, with Barbro in tow, and they have managed to stand upright in the yard as Samuel, at the head of an indescribably slow-moving procession, makes his way up the snow-covered slope, all these people with their tenuous links to Barrøy, and he stops in front of them and doffs his stupid hat and announces that the *Salthammer* has gone down, disappeared, in the sea between Myken and Røst.

In the storm ten days ago.

Some wreckage has been found. Near Værøy and Røst. But no men.

What were they doing in Myken? Ingrid whispers.

Picking up a seine net.

Ingrid looks at Samuel Malmberget's face and doesn't recognise him, but knows that she has been expecting this ever since she was born, that this has been hanging over her from the first moment she saw the light of day, she has just never articulated the thought, nobody has talked about it, but everyone has known, always.

She collapses into the snow. Barbro sinks down beside her, and Anna Karina crouches and wraps an arm around Ingrid's shoulder, she doesn't feel it. Through the shadows she sees Svetlana in all her Russian misery, Elisabeth at her side, who has never suffered any real hardship but is sobbing more loudly than anyone, there is Pastor Samuel, who is struggling to write a book about things he cannot see, and Daniel Malvik, who is doing his best to be what he always has been, Barrøy's most reliable anchorage in the world, while Markus the shopkeeper doesn't know where to look.

Ingrid has a daughter and a son.

Now she whispers to Markus that he, he of all people, the most distant and unscathed of those in the group, should go to Karvika and bring the news to Hanna and Selma, and don't forget, Ingrid says, that Selma has lost everything, Selma who is so happy that she has no daughters, so be sure to keep an eye on her when they cross the Hummock. Hanna has twin girls and can walk on her own. Markus nods and disappears from her field of vision.

30

Had Samuel been a wiser man, he would have known that no-one lives longer than those who are lost at sea. Even Johannes Hartvigsen had left a deeper wound than Olavia, who is now a closed chapter, resting in the family grave on dry land.

When someone goes missing at sea, the bereaved search for explanations, in their imagination, in the newspapers, in plausible and implausible witness statements and accounts. Was it a mælstrøm, a Russian submarine, an unmarked skerry, a freak wave, a collision, cargo slippage, drifting trawl nets, an open hold hatch? But, in their hearts, they know that all of this is putting plasters on wounds that cannot heal, plasters that will inevitably disintegrate, and the wounds persist, for they have only one hope: that the crew perished in seconds and were spared any length of time in the icy waters, suffering. Furthermore, they can hope all six succumbed at one and the same time.

It isn't Ingrid but Hanna who sets Samuel's mind thinking along these lines, several months later, when all hope and hypotheses have been exhausted, when everyone who believed they had seen something or understood what had happened has had their say, and all that remains is one single question:

How long did it take?

Long, extensive searches were made, there was a Shipwreck Commission, several bits of wreckage appeared over the spring, floats and flotsam bearing the *Salthammer*'s number in black, line tubs and planks all found near Røst and Værøy, witness testimonies in Fredvang and Myken, one hushed voice after the other, but no concrete observations, no cries for help heard, only incredulous mumbling about how a whole crew could be lost without trace, how such a robust ship as the *Salthammer* could break up.

Was it human error?

Wrong question.

The right one: How long did it take?

Hanna has two daughters who won't let this question go, no more than she will. Ingrid has two children. Barbro has Ingrid and Ingrid's children. Suzanne has Bjørnar and Hege. Selma has no-one.

So Hanna and Ingrid take turns to sleep with Selma through the spring. Not that Selma sleeps, she is out of her mind and gets up when they doze off and wanders half-naked around the island and wants to throw herself into the sea. They have to keep her away from knives and glass, and sit on her. But Selma is strong, she falls into comas, comes back to life and stares with clear eyes, and they think the worst is past, but then she breaks down again. And when they finally have to accept that something has gone for good, Daniel Malvik comes with a doctor who gives her an injection and takes her away with him.

Ingrid has packed her suitcase. It contains the clothes Selma thought were too fine to wear on Barrøy. They give her food for the journey, shoes and a photograph of her two sons holding a lively five-year-old Oskar in the air above their heads. Ingrid wonders who took the snap. Oh, yes, Samuel did. And they don't see Selma again until the commemoration service two months later, the last Sunday in May, sitting, apathetic and heavily medicated, between her aged parents, who will take her back home to Lofoten after the ceremony.

Ingrid is on the Barrøy Bench, with a child on either side. Hanna is sitting in an introspective and holy silence between her twins. Suzanne is more or less recumbent on Barbro's lap. Bjørnar is comforting Hege, who refuses to accept that her mother has changed for ever. Barbro isn't singing in the choir today, she is singing on the Bench, loud and clear.

31

On the Bench too, strangely enough, sits Mariann Vollheim from Trondheim. Mariann is holding Kaja's hand. Mathias is seated to the right of Ingrid holding Little Ingrid's hand. Mariann Vollheim has already been on Barrøy for three weeks and is planning to stay for four more, to talk some sense into Ingrid, this has been announced, loud and clear, in all the letters she has sent up north since she read about the disaster in the papers, letters that were never answered.

When Mariann Vollheim arrived on Barrøy one rainy afternoon at the beginning of May, she didn't at first recognise Ingrid, which Ingrid noticed, but tried not to let herself be affected by. The other islanders lined up around her, dirty, wet and exhausted after the day's exertions, erecting a fence around the meadow on Gjesøya, so that the sheep had to graze on the crags. Daniel will do the mowing when the time is ripe. On the trip over, he had prepared Mariann, telling her she would recognise neither Barrøy nor those who lived there.

So, *you've* come, have you? asked Ingrid, who had no difficulty recognising Mariann. She appeared to have spent a lot of money, and used a good deal of imagination, on looking the same as she always had done.

She said reproachfully that she had written four times, four letters, without receiving a single reply.

Ingrid said she had better things to do than write letters.

Mariann looked as if she was weighing up whether to call her an idiot or not, but caught sight of Kaja, and that well-preserved face of hers completely fell apart. Mariann Vollheim was speechless and dropped to her knees. The situation wasn't improved when she burst into tears.

Kaja cast anxious glances at her mother.

Ingrid shrugged and reached down a hand to an eight- or nine-year-old girl Daniel was helping ashore, and asked how old she was.

Little Ingrid curtseyed, said hello and announced in a Trondheim dialect that her name was Ingrid, the same as you, I know who you are, Mamma talks about you all the time.

Ingrid smiled, complimented her on her dress and asked if she wasn't cold.

Yes, a bit.

Little Ingrid had blonde curls, big, blue eyes, a mole on her left cheek and bare, slender arms covered in goose pimples. She now turned to Kaja, who had backed away from Mariann's open display of distress, and told her too what her name was and how old she was, without any trace of shyness.

Kaja was taken aback by her dialect but immediately replied and glanced at her mother again for an explanation.

Mariann managed to pull herself together, but could do no more than look on as Daniel winched up the eight bundles of fence-posts – Mathias rolled them along the quay – as well as three sacks of grass seed and two sacks of what might have been onions, then came her suitcases.

Ingrid realised that she would have to explain to Kaja what was happening and said soberly that this is Mariann, she has seen you before, she recognises you.

Kaja asked when.

Tha war little then.

Hvur ald?

Ten month mayhap. Tha war still crawlen.

Mariann seemed to understand what Ingrid had told Kaja and what she hadn't, bent down and opened the smaller suitcase – the other one looked as if it was bound for America – took out a cardigan and wrapped it around her daughter while Mariann asked, without looking at Ingrid, what she was planning to do with all these posts, they are for sheep, aren't they?

Ingrid didn't answer, she could see that this visit was going to be long and all-pervasive. She might not have answered Mariann's letters, but she had read them, carefully, and knew that she was the object of a mission, of some reasoned argument that she should turn her back on Barrøy and live a normal life in a normal place amongst normal people, as it was phrased, after a calamity like this no-one can live on an island.

She told Mariann it was good you came, here we need all the help we can get, not even the potatoes are in the ground.

Mariann appeared to give up, at least temporarily, and also abandoned her attempt to give Ingrid a hug.

This is Mathias, Ingrid said, my son.

Mariann smiled and said, what a lovely boy. Mathias smiled back, he too perplexed by the visitor's reaction to Kaja.

Ingrid said that Mariann was amazed to see how much Kaja had grown, nearly fourteen now.

The children's schooling was also a main theme in Mariann's letters, based on reports Ingrid had sent her over the years, about what Kaja and Mathias were good at and what their interests were, proud and hope-induced exaggerations from the time when hope and white lies still existed, all of which had sown ideas in Mariann's head about them getting a proper education. As if he were a mind reader, Mathias asked if she was a teacher.

She said yes. Mathias asked where. Mariann said in Trondheim. And he told Kaja where Trondheim was. Kaja rolled her eyes, which Mathias deftly ignored, he wanted to know whether Mariann had a car.

Yes.

What type of car?

A Ford.

Which model?

Mariann laughed. She had no idea.

Kaja put up with Mathias pointing out to her the differences between two models, after which he again addressed Mariann and said it was strange to have a car and not know what model it was.

My husband drives the car, I don't, Mariann said. I just sit in it.

Mathias wondered what kind of answer that was, but Kaja sent him a glance seemingly to tell him to keep his mouth shut. And he did, convinced that Kaja would explain what was going on, as soon as they could be on their own, an exchange of glances between the youngsters that Ingrid noted with unease.

After the disaster, Kaja had returned to her mother, as it were, and throughout the spring had watched Ingrid's comings and goings like a hawk, scared out of her wits by Selma's breakdown, and also by the changes in her aunt, Hanna, who had not only immersed herself in the Bible, but who now had streaks of grey in her hair and worked like a Trojan from the moment she got up until she went to bed, and only broke down when she thought no-one was looking. But Ingrid didn't like to be watched over, especially not by her daughter, and told Kaja to leave her alone, I am a strong woman. Kaja had tried to laugh it off, or rather yell it off, obstinate and resentful, she wanted Ingrid to say something.

What should Ingrid say?

Preferably something that would blot out the tragedy, show that it wasn't true. Kaja cried and was a small girl again and sat on Ingrid's lap in every conceivable context, in the fields, at the dining table, and never took no for an answer.

Mathias, however, was able to ask Ingrid directly whether she was depressed when he saw that she was, and to accept the lie: No. And Ingrid had asked him the same, one afternoon when the two of them were sitting on the slope by the smoke oven. He hung his head for a moment, straightened up and said: They aren't dead.

Ingrid was startled, was this madness taking hold of him too? But Mathias said calmly: I remember them.

Ingrid promptly asked which one of them he remembered best. He said Oskar, but changed his mind and said: All of them. Looking at her at the same time as if to gauge her reaction.

Ingrid had to lower her gaze. She had known from the moment the pastor stood before them that day in February with news of their men's demise that from now on, and for the rest of her life, she had only one straw to cling to, which was to hide what was going on inside her, from everyone, otherwise they too would go to pieces. And Mathias, not Kaja, was more difficult, perhaps because Ingrid suspected he could see what she was battling, and even more frightening: He was glad.

Now Barbro too comes down the slope towards them, a snowy white Barbro, who has to walk all the way to the edge of the quay to see that visitors have arrived, and up to Mariann's face before she can recognise her, and fortunately she does.

Barbro remembers that Mariann likes saithe and says that they have started frying them with onions, which they are going to grow themselves this year, the sacks are over there, has Mariann ever heard about fried onions with saithe, it is such an unusual welcome that the visitor has to look around in embarrassment at this island she remembers all too well after being here only once.

Ingrid walks to the edge of the quay, thanks Daniel and arranges the next call. Ever since Barrøy was overrun by strangers the previous winter, by the Shipwreck Commission, who examined the boat sheds and the wharf houses and buildings, and by insurance agents, journalists and photographers, Ingrid has banned all unannounced visits, especially those visitors who think they have spotted something in the north and love to go around spreading hope because they don't know that as long as there is hope, there is suffering, a ban that is enforced ruthlessly by both Daniel and the skipper of the packet boat.

People will have to write letters.

Not that they will get a reply. Ingrid only maintains a restrained and polite tone with the insurance company, Lars and Felix's papers are in order. No sign of human error or negligence, any of the things the imagination still struggles with in this battle with the eternal question: How long did it take?

32

Mariann Vollheim made her presence felt, but gently and indirectly, so as not to embarrass her host, Ingrid suspected. Only two days after her arrival, Daniel appeared with two light-green plastic bathing tubs, ordered by the visitor. Before that, Mariann had also managed to hold some disheartening lectures about the water quality on the island. Ingrid asked if she thought it didn't rain enough.

No, but there should also be a rainwater tank under the roof of the new quay house.

Hm, well, that was something to bear in mind.

But what was the point of having water if they weren't going to live here?

Mariann didn't let this discourage her. Her America trunk contained enough clothes and shoes for two city people to spend two months in this most uncivilised wasteland, plus eight bottles of apple juice, two bottles of brandy, some books for Kaja and Mathias, an impressive pile of towels, cloths and soap and detergent for bodies, hair, floors, windows and cutlery, as well as lime for the lav, there was no way of misunderstanding this.

Ingrid decided to go along with her wishes, so when Daniel arrived the following week, there were two pallets of bricks on the deck, a cement mixer and ten sacks of cement, twenty-four metres of guttering and sixteen metres of downpipe. Daniel had also organised a three-man gang of bricklayers to come the following week.

Mariann asked whether this was not a touch radical, a word she first had to explain, and whether it wasn't expensive, in line with what she had on a couple of occasions called "Ingrid's bizarre use of money".

Ingrid had told her in confidence about half of her financial assets: the insurance payout and the sale of the property in Hartvika. She didn't mention that a large proportion of the former had been used to pay off the debts on the *Salthammer* and that during the winter she had been forced to "borrow" from Mathias, though this money had been put back into his account. Or that she had also bought shares in the light company, to bring electricity to the island, light, this was nothing to do with Mariann either, it was all Ingrid's mysterious and highly personal form of atonement, after her refusal to let the men borrow some of Mathias' money, the only way to atone, to modernise the island, to close her eyes and wait for another day to pass.

The weather was grey and miserable, but Ingrid insisted on finishing the fencing on Gjesøya, a particularly depressing affair in her visitor's eyes. Mariann wore the brand-new, far-too-big boots she had brought over with her to this barren land amid the bare crags, and couldn't hold back from saying what she felt.

Hanna and Ingrid, Kaja and Little Ingrid, as they had begun to call her, were there, with a basket for collecting gulls' eggs. Together with Mathias, the man on Barrøy. When the *Salthammer* had sailed north with Oskar on board, Ingrid had asked him if it wouldn't be lonely on the island with only women. Mathias had answered no, and this was probably because of Kaja, he took his schooling as casually as Oskar had done, despite being the school's best pupil, it wasn't easy to know what was going on inside Mathias Barrøy's head.

Now he asked her why Mariann was there.

Mariann looked at him.

Didn't she want to lend a hand with the fence?

Mariann laughed wryly.

Mathias worked the iron bar while Mariann held the sledgehammer. When the hole was ready and she didn't react, he grabbed the sledgehammer and drove the fence post that Kaja was holding upright down into the ground and cut off the superfluous bit at the top. Ingrid and Hanna followed in their wake with a roll of fencing wire wrapped around a hay rack pole and rolled it out on the ground between them. Mathias gave the sledgehammer back to Mariann, grabbed the iron bar and told her to pace out three metres and keep the line. She did as he instructed. Mathias made another hole, grabbed the sledgehammer and banged in another fence post, gave her back

275

the sledgehammer and told her to measure out another three metres. But this wouldn't do at all. Mariann was a landowner and didn't take kindly to being ordered around by a young boy.

Ingrid overheard what she said and shouted that at her father's farm in Vollheim the women had to stay in the kitchen, didn't they?

Mariann hurled the sledgehammer away and strode back down the line, told Ingrid to give her the hammer and the bag of fencing cramps. They all stood in a circle around the visitor and watched her hammer three staples into a post. Kaja clapped. Mariann didn't say a word, she kept the hammer and bag, and from then on only looked up to keep an eye on Little Ingrid, who was running around beneath the flocks of gulls, under strict instructions not to touch the nests containing only one egg. Now that Mariann had calmed down, Kaja could walk beside her, brandishing a pole to keep the aggressive gulls away from the egg collector, Little Ingrid.

Two days later Ingrid confronted Mariann with Mathias' question again, what was she doing on Barrøy, they were sitting at the dining table with a bottle of brandy between them, the sun was low in the west-facing window, the rest of the household was asleep.

Mariann answered that there were some things you can't forget, no matter what.

Ingrid realised it was hardly likely to be *her* that Mariann couldn't forget. And, unprompted, Mariann explained that the children she had lost during the war, and Alexander, could never be forgotten.

Ingrid looked at her.

What about your Olav?

Mariann said Olav was a fine man.

But? Ingrid said.

You understand, Mariann said.

Ingrid drained her glass, pulled a grimace and said she might have understood before the disaster, now she understood nothing.

Mariann told her she knew a researcher at the university in Trondheim who was writing a thesis about the Russian prisoners of war who returned to the Soviet Union, it was called repatriation, he hadn't found a single piece of information on Alexander Nizhnikov, he had vanished without trace.

Ingrid said she knew.

Mariann asked how she could know.

Ingrid just knew.

Since when? Mariann asked. And Ingrid had to think about this, she had begun to realise the previous summer, when Kaja suddenly wanted to know who her father was.

At first, whenever Kaja brought up the question, Ingrid had allowed only the most impersonal information she could think of to be coaxed out of herself, a tiny, innocuous fragment of a memory. A Russian prisoner of war, yes, he had been injured on the *Rigel*, yes, one hand, but it healed, staying on the island for both him and Ingrid was very dangerous, the death penalty, he had to try and return home, since then she hadn't heard from him, no, no photographs.

What did he look like?

Ingrid was getting into difficult territory. Kaja looked at her but didn't repeat the question. Instead, she asked if Ingrid had tried to find him after the war.

More problems.

But now Kaja wouldn't give up and was told that Ingrid had taken her to the south of the country, the year after she was born, and visited the last internment camp, but didn't find anything. Nothing.

But this wasn't good enough, Ingrid heard herself say, and from then on there was no stopping Kaja.

Yes, on foot, by bus, train, boat, the town of Trondheim, a farm somewhere inland, they had also been to Sweden, barren mountain landscapes, rain, trees, sun, midges, silence.

Gradually, Ingrid learned to prepare herself, to steer around any signs of danger, no, not that way, this way, managing bit by bit to rein Kaja in, with explanations Kaja could accept, credible enough for her, as far as Ingrid could judge, what she considered Kaja could take, perhaps also what she thought her daughter wanted to hear, so that when these bouts of interrogation slowly decreased in number and Kaja began to repeat herself, Ingrid, on the few occasions the subject still cropped up, could answer that she simply didn't remember, or she might even say "maybe" when she judged that yet another minor detail might be permissible, for Kaja to be able to come to terms with her origins.

But after the *Salthammer* went down, their roles changed. And after the doctor had taken Selma away, Ingrid took her devastated daughter aside – Kaja, who was unable to reconcile her anguish at Selma's sufferings with the relief at not having to hear her screams anymore – and said she wanted to show her something.

Kaja eyed her suspiciously.

Ingrid said she hadn't been entirely truthful about her father, she did have some photographs, did she want to see them?

No, Kaja said, and walked out.

Ingrid could see her through the window, sitting on a snow-free spot on the south side of the potato cellar. Mathias was standing in front of her with something in his hands, a float, which he threw in the air and caught like a ball as they talked. Kaja stood up and came back in, sat on Ingrid's lap and said that only the *Salthammer* and Selma were in her thoughts, her father was not important.

Ingrid nodded.

Had Mathias told her to say this?

Kaja shook her head, hugged her mother and went outside again.

But when they returned from school next time, Kaja wanted to see the photographs of her father after all, and sat staring at them, wide-eyed, Alexander in an unfamiliar sitting room, in the snowdrifts on a farm somewhere, pictures taken by the man who had saved his life, unless it was the other way around. Kaja said he was good-looking.

Yes, Ingrid said. Kaja didn't ask any more questions.

But, after another week in Havstein, she asked if she could hang one of the pictures on the wall in her room.

Ingrid nodded. Kaja perused the photographs again, but couldn't make up her mind, gave them back and said it could wait.

So, the only thing to do was wait.

It took Kaja two more weeks to formulate the next question: Is there anything else?

What would you like to know?

Kaja shrugged.

Ingrid said she could show her a letter from her father.

A letter?

Yes.

Well, maybe, Kaja said. Ingrid waited. Kaja repeated herself, well, maybe. And Ingrid led her to the North Chamber and took out the letter Alexander had given her the night he left the island. Kaja recognised the Cyrillic symbols from Svetlana's children's book, smiled and said that it looked like a poem.

Yes, it is a poem.

What does it say?

It's to me.

Kaja smiled charily. Why did her mother want to show her this?

Don't you think it's nice? Ingrid said.

The writing?

Yes.

Mm, it's nice.

Another week passed. It was April now. Two members of the Shipwreck Commission had spent the whole day on Barrøy. Ingrid had guided them round like sheep, as she put it, showing them all of the *Salthammer*'s equipment that had been left in wharf houses and boat sheds, had watched them taking notes on a form that they shielded from her, so she couldn't see, and they whispered when she was nearby.

She asked them if what they were doing was a secret.

They looked at her in surprise. She asked whether they had ever done any fishing themselves. One answered yes and the other nothing. They finished taking notes and were collected by Daniel at the appointed time.

Mother and daughter stood on the quay seeing them off, while Ingrid, her eyes focused on the boat's foaming wake, told Kaja what the words in the letter meant. It cost her nothing.

Now you know everything, she said.

I know, Kaja said.

Ingrid asked if she had told Mathias everything.

Of course.

She looked at her daughter. Kaja asked what was wrong.

Ingrid continued to look at her. Kaja was ill at ease and had to avert her eyes. Ingrid left her and walked up the slope. Kaja ran after her and jumped on her back for Ingrid to carry her into their house like a child.

There was only one piece of information Kaja was not allowed to hear, that she had a half-brother in Russia. And that this half-brother was presumably the reason she had grown up without a father. But Kaja had had enough fathers, Lars, Felix, all the men on the island.

Now Ingrid told Mariann this, what she thought Mariann needed to hear of what she had thought Kaja had needed to hear. Mariann nodded and said this was more or less what she herself would have thought a daughter needed to hear.

They drank.

Did Ingrid still have the photographs?

Ingrid fixed her with a stern gaze. Mariann had seen them before and it hadn't gone well.

Are you up to it?

Mariann looked as though she was saying both yes and no. Ingrid sat waiting. And Mariann said that strangely enough she envied her.

Yes, strangely enough, Ingrid answered. Mariann had done her hair. Ingrid had started braiding her own again, into one thick plait which flapped between her shoulder blades when she walked too fast, or a pigtail on each side, which Kaja said made her look like a Red Indian. The visitor's other standards of hygiene had also been implemented, but so gradually that no-one had noticed.

33

Then Suzanne arrived, with Bjørnar and little Hege, and at first she was of no help at all, smashed two chairs and threw food at the wall, as though she had a right to do so after the loss of a brother and a son, unlike Ingrid, who hadn't lost anyone at all.

Ingrid controlled her fury. Bjørnar called his wife a hard woman and bitter, worn down as he was, this was not the first furniture Suzanne had taken out her temper on, Bjørnar was beginning to wonder what kind of person he had married, Bjørnar was at his wits' end.

So was his daughter, Hege, who one day in February suddenly had a new mother to grapple with. Ingrid regarded Bjørnar with contempt and he felt it, but without saying anything he could use in his defence. But he had plenty of alcohol.

Ingrid put the couple in the Swedes' boathouse and let Hege stay with her in the North Chamber, where so many disorientated souls had slept before her. And it came as a relief to everyone when one morning Suzanne donned some old rags from the chest in the bedroom and went into the cow barn with Ingrid, pulled at the teats and rested her forehead against the cows' bellies, mucked out and carried in dry hay from last year, wiping away the tears that had fallen over the winter.

And Hege learned how to milk too.

Little Ingrid already knew her way around the island and could now take Hege along with her from eider house to eider house, from beach to crag, and explain all about them. Hege also planted potatoes: There, there, there. Wherever her mother pointed. Suzanne herself couldn't see the point of growing potatoes, this wasn't heaven on earth, it was just shit and damnation, a living hell, what was Ingrid thinking of?

Mariann had begun to take an interest in Suzanne, and these outbursts didn't go unnoticed. And Mariann's mood was further improved by seeing how Suzanne ignored Ingrid whenever she, Ingrid, told her to shut her mouth and pull herself together.

They fished around the closest skerries using a hand line, Mathias and Kaja with the little girls, Ingrid, Mathias and Suzanne in the færing on the far side of Gjesøya, cod, saithe. Mariann could neither bleed nor gut fish, to Suzanne's great delight.

I can do everything, she screamed, tossing entrails around into the flock of seagulls. The lot!

Is that so? Mariann said.

Yes, and there's nothing even *you* can't learn.

Ingrid had seen her sneak off with one of Bjørnar's bottles and said the only thing Suzanne hadn't been able to do was walk, she didn't learn to do that until she was three, and since then she had run, cut and run, like her mother.

Suzanne called Ingrid a "fathole", broke off and said: Do you remember that word?

Yes, it was one Felix had used, sometime in his childhood, or was it Lars, and the dreaded question reared its ugly head again. Suzanne screamed and pulled out the bottle, drank greedily and hurled it into the sea.

But it didn't sink, it bobbed about, the corkless neck above the surface of the water. Suzanne leaned over the side, splashed water over her face and screeched that Ingrid should row over and grab the bottle. Ingrid laughed and rowed. Mariann was first over the side, snatched the bottle and drank, pushed Suzanne away and passed it to Ingrid, who also had a swig, grimaced and slung it into the sea again, and this time it sank.

Suzanne seized the bailer, intending to hit her with it. But it was heavy, it was made of wood, and made by a man who had carved his initials on the handle. Suzanne stared in confusion and slumped back down on the thwart, carefully put down the irreplaceable treasure and said: Oh, shit.

Then the twins returned, after passing their school-leaving exams and receiving praise from their teachers and grandparents for enduring the suffering and keeping their concentration. Sofie and Anna had lost their father and brother and, what was more, arrived on Barrøy with a bad conscience for having left their mother alone, even though Hanna herself had instructed her own mother in a letter to keep them at school, in the name of God, even if you have to tie them up. But the girls didn't know that, so they stepped ashore in tears, heavily burdened with guilt, two well-dressed young ladies with groomed hair and make-up on their faces, identical dresses and cardigans, but with differently coloured stockings. Sofie in low, white canvas shoes, and Anna in Daniel's gumboots, after a slight accident, as she called it, at the Trading Post, holding a pair of shoes by way of explanation, another pair of low, white canvas shoes, wet and stained with fish blood.

Ingrid, Mariann and Hanna were there to welcome them. God bless you, children. And there wasn't a lot to say to the incoherent remarks they had to give vent to as they were led, exceedingly slowly, up towards the house, where they suddenly insisted on sleeping, in the old parlour with "our Ingrid", and not in their horrid childhood home in Karvika.

This wasn't a problem, Hanna was already under the same roof, in the South Chamber, so the school-leavers also installed themselves there, piled a load of unusable clothes and shoes on their respective shelves in the cupboard, as if they were planning to stay for good, and perhaps they were, for now. Anna had also brought a large, brown envelope, which she handed to Ingrid, telling her not to open it, ever.

Ingrid assumed it contained the drawings Anna had once made of the people on the island. Ingrid said she could bet her life on it she wouldn't, but it was good to know that the pictures were here now, in a drawer, in the North Chamber.

Down in the kitchen, the girls didn't know what to say – everything had been said – or what to do, our Mamma is so quiet.

Ingrid told them to go out and walk south through the gardens and see if they could find two little girls. Then they should ask them their names. If they answered Hege and Ingrid, then they should introduce themselves as strangers here and ask them to show them all the island's secrets.

That was an odd idea, wasn't it?

Yes.

They looked at Hanna, their mother, they could see she was at breaking point and that the only thing to do was to comply with Ingrid's orders, for that was what they were.

As soon as they were out of the house, Mariann said Ingrid and Hanna should go and rest, she was going to cook some food. Where's Barbro? She's in the rocking chair in the parlour. Let her sleep.

34

Pastor Samuel had failed monumentally when he kept delaying the trip to Barrøy – because he wanted to be sure of the facts, which is what he told himself and others, to have the catastrophe irrevocably confirmed before he delivered such devastating news – but this was made much worse by the people out there on the island not having a radio – until his wife and the stout Russian woman knocked some sense into him.

Now he was also going to speak at the commemoration ceremony, not on his own though, but with Mayor Bonsak Sandvær, and an M.P. and the Fisheries Minister. And something did have to be said, a prayer for forgiveness, perhaps, for his inconceivable dereliction of duty, the result no doubt of a flaw in his character.

He had rejected the idea of throwing earth on yet another empty grave to commemorate the six lost souls by means of a specific burial place, where strictly speaking they had no reason to be, Samuel concluded. It would have to be a monument, positioned in that beautiful part of the churchyard which for four hundred years had been reserved for the islands' great men (and two women), among them many of Storm's ancestors, a patch of grass that at the moment looked somewhat run-down with its rusty iron crosses all askew, its metal plaques and half-sunken gravestones whose inscriptions you would need a degree in linguistics to decipher. Yes, indeed, erecting a monument here to commemorate the lost men of the *Salthammer* was an idea that Samuel could still espouse, even though, to be honest, there was very little of Barrøy's history that fell within the bounds of tradition. On the other hand, tradition was all he had.

But what should he say? He discussed the question with Anna Karina, it had taken her a month and more to forgive him. It was even worse with the Russian. But he had made no progress writing the speech until it occurred to him that perhaps on this occasion he should not make such a big thing of Our Lord, maybe even God would be seen as both powerless and pointless, yes, out of place even, in a situation like this.

And then there was Hanna's question: How long did it take?

This was simply too much, too massive and moreover Barrøy's private affair.

There wasn't much help to be had from Paderborn's two schools of thought on how to officiate at funerals either. Nor was this really a funeral, more a memorial service for believers and non-believers, grieving relatives and a sympathetic and inquisitive public, so what about saying bluntly that he wasn't up to the task, just as he wasn't up to finishing the book he was writing, it began to dawn on him, a book about hard-working people living through thick and thin on a ravaged coast. And the clouds began to clear:

"I stand here powerless" were his opening words, on paper.

But then the Fisheries Minister stole a march on him, a growling giant of a man from Finnmark – and in the wrong party, for Samuel's taste – who had seen his share of tragedy, and stood at a good distance from the pulpit, with tears in his eyes he acknowledged that once in a while life is hell and that once in a while is now. For example. And it always will be. I know what I'm talking about.

Besides, he reminded the congregation, the *Salthammer* wasn't just any old whaler or fishing boat, the *Salthammer* had transported refugees from Finnmark after the Germans' scorched earth policy, the *Salthammer* was an inalienable symbol of humanitarianism . . . for the most part.

Bonsak Sandvær was generous enough to talk of Barrøy in the same warm and sober terms his parents had used about the island, a vital element in the nation's life, out there in the sea, and mentioned the names of both the deceased and their ancestors in a voice that resonated through the church, and got in a political dig at the Fisheries Minister, saying it was time the government set up a committee with a mandate to investigate the safety of the coastal population, conditions were dreadful, this wasn't the first disaster at sea.

The M.P. – also in the wrong party – went even further and declared that at the first opportunity the opposition would demand that the so-called Gabrielsen Commission – which no-one present had heard of – should be reinstituted, it had been shelved by the current government under the pretext that it was financially indefensible. Now it should be taken up again and forced through parliament, whatever the cost.

Only after this did the temporarily Godforsaken priest drag himself up onto his own podium. He too eschewed the pulpit today and took up a position in front of the font, where the Finnmark speaker had stood. His eyes scanning the crowded church, known and unknown faces in the jam-packed congregation, black-clad figures bunched up against walls and the organ, journalists and photographers, he declared he quite simply wasn't equal to this task, which he deeply regretted.

As it happens, he had been looking through his father's papers and found many an oddity, I have to confess, quite a number of you will doubtless recall my father, at times a pompous and emotional man, perhaps not always overly succinct, but once, in a sermon, just after the war, I believe, he had asked the rhetorical question: Is man great or small? And he concluded that man is great. As I mentioned, this was shortly after the war, or in the last year of it, now I've forgotten that too, not that it matters, what does matter is that until this morning, well, until a moment ago, while I was listening to the previous speakers, I had been intending to contradict my father on this point, by saying that in these modern times we have learned to acknowledge our limitations, we have become less great over the years, more vulnerable. But now as I stand here surveying this gathering of familiar and unfamiliar faces, many of you have travelled from afar, a huge number of you, in fact, and God bless you all for that, but now I believe that my father was correct: Man is indeed great.

Yes.

He also said a lot more, which neither he nor his audience committed to memory, while he constantly did his best to avoid looking at the Barrøy pew, yes, also at his wife and the Russian bear. But all these distracting concerns about his own performance slowly but surely ate away at something in his innermost soul and set in motion such a pervasive sense of wretchedness that it was all too much for him. Samuel Malmberget went to pieces. His life as a pastor lay in ruins. And since he didn't feel a scrap of self-pity as he made this shocking realisation, he experienced the truest moment of his career. His despair was absolute. Before him he saw the six faces that had been swallowed up by the foaming waves and forgot both himself and those sat staring at him, dumbstruck. He didn't even come across as pitiful, only as utterly honest, weak like all mankind, because he wasn't aware of any of this, while everyone around him was.

After this battle was over, he even needed help from Anna

Karina to walk down the aisle, realising through a hazy mist of insidiously recurring egotism that throughout spring he had taken this task far too casually, during those months he had certainly known it was going to be tough, nevertheless he had allowed his self-confidence to rule his head, he had fallen victim to his own arrogance.

Then, after he had more or less managed to compose himself, outside the church in the meaninglessly wonderful May weather, still with Anna Karina at his side, he became equally flustered when Ingrid Barrøy, with the family behind her, came towards him without a tear in her eye and shook his hand at length, thanking him from her heart with trembling lips. Then Hanna came too and said he had given a wonderful speech, thank the Lord. Kaja and Mathias didn't have much to say, but there was no doubt in the pastor's soul that their gratitude was sincere rather than merely polite. Even the burly construction machine operator from the capital seemed moved. His wife, Suzanne, was on the verge of a nervous breakdown, but there was no doubt there, either. And the pretty twins. The pastor almost broke down again as he realised that God was returning to him after this formidable, vicarious suffering, even though he hadn't suffered any personal loss.

The only person that didn't seem to have observed this miracle was the introspective and heavily medicated Selma Barrøy, who was supported by her two aged parents, although they had enough difficulty standing upright themselves. Now she stood in front of Pastor Samuel, and, unable to recognise him, said:

Who are you?

35

Herons are not like other birds, eagles, gulls, eiders; herons are signs in the sky that make one stop in mid stride. On her walk home from yet another private breakdown on the Bench, she had seen two birds, and soon afterwards a third, three herons landed like gigantic snowflakes on the Lundeskjære skerries, and she had to sit down.

Thinking about that last conversation with Lars and Felix. Ingrid's "no".

It had turned out to be quite a "no".

Kaja saw her from the window up in the house. And Mathias realised that Kaja had spotted something unusual, put down his knife and fork, got to his feet and walked around the table and stood behind her – and watched with her, staring at Ingrid's back, down there in the meadow where no-one had sat before.

Mariann, too, could see that something was amiss, got up and stood behind the youngsters. Then Suzanne came and began to stare in the same direction.

Had Ingrid fallen?

No, she has only sat down.

Something is wrong, Mariann said, we have to help her.

Wait, Mathias said.

Now Barbro and Bjørnar and the twins were also standing with them, and Mariann repeated that something was wrong, she could feel it in her bones, she knew, she was sure. And Mathias repeated that they should wait.

The Barrøyers stood and sat around the dining table, staring southward through the window, and looked on as Ingrid got to her feet, holding a rock in one hand, placed it on a stone wall and walked up towards them. When she was close enough for them to be able to make out her face, they sat down again and continued eating in a silence broken only by Ingrid, who came in and eyed them in puzzlement, thought for a moment and asked where the dessert was, one of Suzanne's creations from a housing cooperative in the capital.

36

Bjørnar had taken time off work, but he said it was skiving and he would soon have to leave to make up for lost time, during what was called a company's annual general holiday. But first of all, there was a job he had to do for Ingrid. The meadow on Gjesøya hadn't been ploughed up again, as Ingrid had wanted, but at least grass had been sown, and it needed to be mowed using a horse, and it would be very difficult to get the animal to the island alive, not to mention the mowing machine. The old nag could easily have swum across the sound, but it was too far and too cold, thought Daniel, its owner, so all they could do was run an eye over the old raft.

It had been washed ashore in a storm and had lain rotting in the southernmost field for fifteen years.

But parts of the wooden frame were oiled and solid, and more beams could be bought, just like the ten empty oil drums that Bjørnar had got for a song after haggling with Vig, the Trading Post owner. Vig didn't have much time for the pushy brute of a man from Oslo, but he did have some sympathy for the rest of the Barrøyers, so he offered them the drums for ten kroner apiece.

One krone, Bjørnar said, that's all they're worth.

He immediately rolled the first drum onto the quay, where Daniel and Mathias loaded it on board the *Malin*. When the fifth was home and dry and the sixth on the way, Vig shrugged, said, OK, what the hell, and walked off.

Over the next few days Bjørnar, stripped to the waist, a cigarette in his mouth and with Mathias as a helper, knocked together a new raft. In the evening he sat in the parlour drinking and playing bridge with Kaja, Sofie and Mathias, a full team on a haunted island. While Anna clung on to Ingrid's skirts asking why it wasn't possible to take her mother back with them to Lofoten.

Ingrid told her to leave Hanna in peace: she'll go when she goes.

Yes, but she doesn't want to.

Well, there you are. Was Anna trying to kidnap her?

No.

Perhaps she prefers it here.

Anna found that hard to believe, but didn't feel she could say so, instead she said her grandparents needed her, they were old and this daughter was all they had.

They've got three others, Ingrid said.

Yes, but they're in Oslo.

Aren't there any trains?

Ha ha, no, they want to stay there.

Where?

In Oslo.

I see. Hanna's also got brothers.

Yes, but they're in Tromsø. Or in . . . Anna didn't remember, she had only seen one of these uncles, once, the one in Tromsø.

Ingrid could feel there was something in the air and asked Anna what she thought, would *she* prefer to live here with Ingrid or at home with her grandmother?

Anna looked as if she would prefer not to answer. She said her grandparents lived alone in a big house in Leknes.

Ingrid asked how many people lived in Leknes. Anna lost her train of thought again.

Ingrid asked her if she still drew.

Yes. But she had applied to study languages, English and French, Sofie was going to read law.

Where?

In Oslo.

Ingrid looked her in the eye and asked if there was anything she would like to tell her.

No, Anna said.

The following morning stormy weather set in from the south-west, but Bjørnar carried on with work, head down, still stripped to the waist, it was as though he had been mentally afflicted by his stay here, still with Mathias at his side, wearing oilskins – but this had no effect on his work rate. Mathias asked:

Why are you half-naked?

To be as miserable as possible.

Mathias laughed and asked what that was supposed to mean. Aren't you cold?

Bloody frozen, Bjørnar said, and announced that if Suzanne should ever insist on coming north again, he would remember a day like this and say not on your nelly.

Mathias laughed out loud.

Is it so terrible here? he enquired.

It's as terrible as it can be. What do you think? You seem to be quite a bright spark.

I think it's alright here.

You've no idea what you're talking about, young man.

Mathias laughed again, and Bjørnar added that it didn't really matter, you're probably going to stay here anyway, aren't you?

Oh, I don't know about that.

They carried on working.

You lot don't say much, either.

You what?

See what I mean. Chuck me that box of nails and I'll show you how to hammer in two of the buggers at once.

Mathias watched Bjørnar bang in two four-inch nails with three blows of the hammer, but it just looked stupid, two nail heads close together.

What's the point?

No point, Bjørnar said. Don't you ever do anything for the fun of it?

No.

Don't you remember how we tricked that idiot at the Trading Post to get the oil drums?

Yes, Mathias had noticed.

Bjørnar straightened up and surveyed his work, three times three drums, three in each section, symmetrically distributed beneath an almost complete deck. The raft was getting heavier, so they had moored it with two ropes. The tide raised it gently twice a day, a perfect dock, according to Bjørnar, a floating dock. But it needed a gangway for the horse and the mowing machine.

We'll do that tomorrow, Bjørnar said. I'm freezing to death here.

The gang of bricklayers had finished the rainwater tank back in May, against the southern wall of the new wharf house, it had taken them three days, and on the fourth they added gutters and drainpipes, but they didn't make a lid. Ingrid said, we'll see to that ourselves, paid them and thanked them for their work.

The wind turned east and abated, there was sun and warmth, a breathing space, everything green, between spring chores and the first round of mowing, a few idle days, which used to be spent catching salmon, cleaning the boat with the cooing of the eider ducks in their ears, some tines on the rakes needed forging, scythe blades sharpening. And when the gangway to the raft was finished, they lay in the sun on the gently bobbing deck for an hour, and Bjørnar took a nap. He woke with a start, sat up, lit a cigarette and squinted across the sleeping ocean and almost seemed to be mumbling that it would be strange to leave this place.

In fact, he'd had an idea.

They walked up the hill to the rainwater tank, which was full and resembled a swimming pool. The water was cold, but much warmer than the sea, and Bjørnar suggested that Mathias should go up to the house and pinch a bar of soap. Mathias looked at him and said it was drinking water, reserves for when the other tank was empty.

Bjørnar lit another cigarette and just looked at him.

Mathias went up to the house, where Barbro was having a midday doze on the kitchen bench, grabbed a bar of soap and by the time he was back Bjørnar was already in the tank. Mathias undressed and jumped in. There was a lot of splashing. Little Ingrid and Hege were the first to arrive, then the twins came and Kaja, and all of them stood around admiring the bathers. Suzanne had been having a snooze in the Swedes' boathouse, was woken by the noise, came out and leaned against the sun-drenched wall with her arms crossed, but she didn't say anything. Ingrid heard the clamour while she was busy labelling the egg barrels in the Lofoten boat shed. The girls were in the tank now too, fully clothed, while Suzanne seemed to be considering whether to join them.

Ingrid said nothing.

Bjørnar had soap in his hair, ducked down, came back up and shouted to Ingrid: Could she count?

Ingrid didn't understand.

We've got one oil drum left over. The herring barrel over the smoke oven is too small, and moreover rotting away, Bjørnar could knock out the top and bottom of the remaining drum and put it there instead?

Ingrid slowly shook her head.

What do you think? Bjørnar said.

Ingrid smiled wanly and before her she saw her father and grandfather, who had built this wharf house in the worst autumn weather, her mother and Barbro standing on the quay in their oilskins passing up the roof beams to the carpenters. Battens were nailed onto the beams and slate tiles laid, the only building on the island that was covered with something as precious as a tiled roof. And leaning against the wall was a bicycle.

37

The next to leave was Mariann, and this was a more complicated business than Bjørnar's liberating departure:

Take care of yourselves, you poor devils, he shouted from
Daniel's foredeck. I'm never coming back.

That's what you think, shouted Suzanne, who was standing
in the morning sun with Ingrid and Hege saying goodbye,
and told him not to forget to water the flowers in the balcony
box.

Little Ingrid started having a tantrum, as Mariann called
it, whenever there was any talk of leaving. Mariann was being
forced into doing overtime. They had agreed that she should
enrol Kaja and Mathias at a secondary school in Trondheim
and find a place for them in a student hostel. If they arrived
earlier, they could stay with her.

They won't be coming earlier, Ingrid said.

Mariann had been over to Svetlana's twice, and rung her
husband, Olav, who said he missed them, according to both
Svetlana and Mariann. But there were still eider ducks nesting,
which would perish if Little Ingrid didn't look after them until

the chicks had crept out of the nests and safely made their way down to the sea.

Ingrid wondered whether Mariann was losing her grip and wanted her opinion of a boat she had seen for sale in the newspaper.

Had she completely lost her mind? Mariann said.

Ingrid asked Mariann if she thought it strange that they talked so little about those who had died.

Mariann looked at her with tears in her eyes.

No.

The next day Mathias and Kaja went over with Daniel and had a look at the boat, with the help of Markus, the shopkeeper, who knew more about money than boats, but the flywheel, oil pump, rudder, controls and compass were in full working order, they checked for algae and mould and thumped the hull and stuck knives in the keelson. In due course Daniel gave a thumbs up, tired as he was of his own toing and froing to Barrøy, and Markus haggled the price down a few more kroner.

Mathias steered the new acquisition homeward, with Kaja standing on the deck in front of the wheelhouse like a galleon figurehead, in light drizzle. The old tub was only a twenty-five-footer, the engine was a simple Bolinder, with long intervals between the excessively high-pitched pulse beats that sounded out of place among the islands. Furthermore, Mathias thought the boat was too slow.

Ingrid watched them put in below the new quay. But here the vessel looked even more like an eggshell compared with the ship that belonged there, so Mathias put out again on his own initiative and steered between the iron rails leading up to the Swedes' boat shed, from which Kaja was able to step elegantly down onto the slipway.

Ingrid asked if he was planning to tie it to an anchor buoy.

No, they would be able to fix up a mooring with an ordinary buoy and get on board using a dory.

By breakfast the next morning, Mariann had collected herself. But there were still ducks in the nests, among them a mallard which thought it was an eider and which Little Ingrid had named Anton.

Ingrid pointed out that it was a female.

Little Ingrid said that didn't matter.

Across the table Hanna asked what the point of all this talk of leaving was, and the others around the table said: They should just stay here. Barrøy's mantra. Even Mariann laughed.

Ingrid imagined Mariann had come here out of some kind of pity, but that now she had realised that perhaps there was no need. And for this she would have liked to thank her, but couldn't bring herself to do so, any attempt would have ruined everything. She told Little Ingrid that this was Anton's third summer as an eider duck, he would be here again next year too, she could come back then.

Little Ingrid got up and ran out screaming. But no-one followed her. They glanced enquiringly at Mariann. Mariann calmly finished eating, said thank you for breakfast, rose to her feet and said that now she was going to do her packing.

38

After the Trondheimers had departed, Ingrid went to the North Chamber and read through the letter she had once written to Ottmar Ehrlich, the January letter, to see whether it should now be burned so that the chapter about Mathias' childhood could finally be laid to rest.

Instead, she discovered that the letter had stood the test of time remarkably well, all through the usual, annual winter travails and the catastrophe that had changed everything.

She amended a few details, crossed out two lines she thought might be interpreted as crowing, with regard to Mathias, took it to the village and showed it to Svetlana, who had closed for the day and read it slowly over a cup of coffee in her private quarters. Svetlana reflected, re-read it and asked if Ingrid really intended to send it.

Ingrid wasn't sure, that was why she was here.

Svetlana said she shouldn't, the man has nothing to do with Mathias.

Why hasn't he? Ingrid asked.

Why has he? Svetlana said, and Ingrid couldn't come up with an answer.

Does Mathias know about the letter?

No.

Does he ask after his father?

No. Kaja does, and gets an answer. Mathias doesn't say a word, and Ingrid had no intention of telling him anything, Ingrid couldn't weigh him up.

Svetlana said, you're just a mother, and sons are unfathomable.

Ingrid wasn't so sure of that. She told her about the yellow wooden horse Kaja had found in her bureau and then shown to Mathias, it was a toy from Hartvika. Mathias hadn't recognised it. Perhaps he doesn't recognise anything from the time before he came to Barrøy?

Svetlana stood in front of the window looking out at a summer that had turned yellow and mumbled that Johannes had once told her that Olavia had brought some toys with her from the Storm household, but that the boy wasn't even allowed to see them. Johannes didn't understand this. Mathias didn't have any other toys.

Ingrid asked if they had beaten him.

Svetlana didn't think so, there was no evil in Johannes, he was stupid, that's the worst that could be said about him, but this isn't a sin.

And Olavia?

Svetlana didn't think so either and repeated that Ingrid shouldn't send the letter, maybe in a year's time, or ten.

Ingrid was still unsure. What she had added to the letter concerned the school in Trondheim, she considered the rest of the story should be left to father and son, in other words, the father.

Svetlana asked whether she wanted a word with the pastor.

No.

Why not, Anna Karina must know something. She received a letter from Germany only last month.

Has she answered? Ingrid asked quickly.

Svetlana smiled at her: Not yet.

She nodded towards the wall, where four framed photographs of her grandchildren hung, a boy and a girl of different ages, and said she had never seen them, except in these pictures.

Ingrid said, don't they visit you?

No.

And you don't visit them?

Svetlana shook her head, took down one photograph, wiped invisible dust off it and kissed it as though it were an icon, held it up and said to Ingrid, aren't they lovely, the children?

Yes.

Svetlana hung it back on the wall, made sure it was straight and asked Ingrid if she wanted any more coffee, she also had some *lefse*, I'd forgotten about them, Nordland *lefse*.

Ingrid said no, got up and left, with the letter in her

hand. She made a few purchases at Markus' shop and carried on down to the fishing boat moored by the Trading Post, where Mathias was waiting.

They stood together in the cramped wheelhouse on the return journey. Mathias showed Ingrid the starter and the clutch and didn't forget to explain how the compass worked either. Ingrid asked what they should call the boat, it had to have a name after all, and at that same moment she felt something vanish, a dark shadow.

Yes, Mathias said, still in this world, he had thought about calling it Kaja, but maybe it should be Tatjana.

Tatjana?

It's a nice name.

Romantic?

He blushed for once and said he had found it in one of Mariann's books.

But, Ingrid said.

Well, this really isn't much of a boat, so Kaja would be upset, and Tatjana was too fine a name, the boat would ruin it. So he had wondered if they could call it the *Skogsholmen*, which didn't mean much.

They laughed at that, the thought of Ingrid chugging around in the *Skogsholmen*.

What about the *Bjørnar*? Ingrid suggested.

They laughed even louder at that.

After mooring the boat, Mathias showed her where to fill the fuel and told her how much the tank could hold. And Ingrid felt even more shadows leaving her, and as she walked up to the house the feeling that had kept her afloat so many times before returned, the feeling of having achieved something.

They cut the grass and hung it on the drying racks. They carded the down and stuffed it into sacks. Ingrid slaughtered a lamb that had broken a leg. They brought in the hay from Gjesøya on the raft and wheeled it on a cart through the gardens up to the barn. They rowed from island to island and made sure the cattle had fresh water in their troughs. Suzanne didn't leave Ingrid's side for a second.

When the dog days were coming to an end, everyone packed their bags without any fuss, with the slight exception of Kaja, who had to have a dress Mariann had given her taken in and shortened. Ingrid did this while Kaja was standing on a kitchen chair, fiddling with her hair, and she wasn't satisfied with anything. She asked what life would be like in a town.

Ingrid didn't have much to say, other than that it would be strange.

Strange?

Yes, Kaja had been there before, twice, without being aware of it, it would be different now.

Kaja asked in what way.

Sofie, who sat watching, said Ingrid should take another inch off the dress and Kaja didn't need to worry.

Kaja said she wasn't afraid.

Ingrid said that was good.

It wasn't necessary to make any alterations to Mathias' clothes, all sizes were available in Barrøy's large stock of clothing. But Ingrid had bought him a jacket, so he looked like a cross between a ship's pilot and a dandy. He was given a new suitcase too, by Svetlana. Not that it was actually new, it had been in Russia before the revolution and during the war it had been used by refugees escaping from Finnmark, but it still appeared suspiciously unused, brass fittings, click locks and leather straps, much swankier than the suitcase Kaja was given, Ingrid's old one.

The last six travellers departed in the same boat, just as everything comes together when there is no alternative. Suzanne's job was to guide the children over, first to the town, then on the ferry and finally on the train. Mariann was to pick up Kaja and Mathias at Trondheim station. And in Oslo, Sofie and Anna would live with Aunty Suzanne at first, in Hege's room, behind the left-hand blue cross on a photograph of a housing cooperative that Ingrid had shown them.

It's much nicer now, Suzanne said, there's a lawn, trees, tarmac, garages.

Which all meant that Hanna was not going anywhere. So, the three of them were left on the quay waving as Daniel sailed away with the party of six, Barbro wearing her new glasses, Hanna and Ingrid. Ingrid had never felt so relieved to see the end of a summer. In the light drizzle on the way up to the house she told Hanna that Anna was expecting.

Yes, I saw, Hanna said.

Didn't she say anything?

No. We'll no doubt hear when she's ready, Hanna said. She's grown up.

Then came the autumn.

GLOSSARY

Ingrid Marie Barrøy	Owner of Barrøy, daughter of Hans and Maria. Ingrid inherited the island as a young woman.
Barbro	Ingrid's aunt, sister to her father Hans.
Alexander	A Russian P.O.W. rescued from the wreck of the *Rigel*. Father of Ingrid's child and the love of Ingrid's life.
Kaja	Daughter of Alexander and Ingrid.
Lars	Son of Barbro, named after a Swedish worker on the island who may be his father.
Selma	Lars' wife.
Martin and Hans	Lars and Selma's sons.
Suzanne	Daughter of Zezenia and Oskar Tommesen. Brought up by Ingrid after the death of her parents.

Bjørnar	Suzanne's husband, whom she meets in Oslo after leaving Barrøy. They have a daughter called Hege.
Fredrik	Suzanne's son, fathered by a German soldier during the war.
Felix	Suzanne's elder brother. Also brought up by Ingrid after the death of his parents.
Hanna	Felix's wife.
Oskar	Felix and Hannah's son.
Anna and Sofie	Felix and Hanna's daughters.
Mariann Vollheim	A lover of Alexander, after Ingrid. Married to Olav, she lives in Trondheim and has a daughter called Little Ingrid.
Olavia Storm	Mother of Mathias and wife of Johannes Hartvigsen.
Johannes Hartvigsen	Husband of Olavia Storm and stepfather of Mathias. Skipper of the milk boat before his demise.
Mattis/Mathias	Son of Olavia Storm and a German officer, Ottmar Ehrlich. Brought up by Ingrid after his father's death.

Alfred Storm	Father of Olavia Storm. He lives on the main island.
Amalie Storm	Alfred's wife and Olavia's mother.
Anna Karina and Elisabeth	Daughters of Alfred and Amalie Storm and sisters of Olavia.
Daniel Malvik	Boat-owner and friend of Barrøy.
Svetlana	Russian refugee who lives on the main island and works in the post office.
Samuel Malmberget	Pastor, son of Pastor Johannes Malmberget.
Henriksen	Lensmann or local police chief who became a German collaborator during the war.
Nelvy	A girl Ingrid took in and who died young.
Markus	Shopkeeper on the main island.
Karvika	A cove on Barrøy where Lars and Felix built a new house.
The Bench	A log from an enormous Russian larch that washed ashore many years ago (as told in *The Unseen*).